Love Me Softly

ELLIE HARPER SMITH

First paperback edition May 2025

Cover Design by Lyssa at Booked Forever Shop

ISBN 979-8-9928013-2-3(paperback)

ISBN 979-8-9928013-0-9 (ebook)

Contents

For anyone that's ever felt like you only know how to love in the wrong way. You are worthy.

To my younger self, sorry I took so long to make our dreams come true.

Author's Note

THANK YOU FOR PICKING up my book. Before you dive in there a few content notes I'd like to discuss.

Riley is demisexual and bisexual. Her identity as both was inspired by my own identity, but her story is entirely her own. Throughout the book Riley discusses her definition of demisexuality and her journey to discovering the label, but it is important to note that like all sexualities demisexuality is a spectrum. Her story does not represent everyone that identities this way.

Riley also has a chronic condition called Polycystic Ovary Syndrome – referred to as PCOS throughout the book. Again, her struggles with this condition are inspired by my own as well as that of people around me. Like all health conditions, symptoms and severity vary from person to person. Due to her condition there are mentions of possible infertility, experienced infertility of a side character, body insecurities, weight loss and gain, diet culture, and specialty diets. While all of these play a role in Riley's life they are not focuses of the story and all mentions of diet culture are condemned by the narrative. Any mentions of steps Riley has taken to manage her PCOS are not meant to be taken as advice. If you have or think you may have PCOS please do your own research and consult a medical professional.

Chapter 1

Riley

June

"**G**IVE ME YOUR PHONE," my sister said from behind me.

I zipped up my empty suitcase, pushed it under my bed, and turned around to where she lay spread out on the bed on her side of the room we would be sharing for the next week. Even with us both in our mid-twenties and living together, there was something about being forced to share a room again that took me straight back to being kids. It felt different from just sharing the small house we rented. Being on a family vacation where we all shared this cabin in the mountains added to that. The older we got the more the annual family vacation to Copper Ridge made me feel like a child.

"Why do you need my phone?" I crossed my arms over my chest.

"Because I said so." She rolled her eyes and shoved her hand out toward me. She pushed her jaw length highlighted hair behind her ears as she sat up. "God, I just sounded like Mom. Please just give me your phone."

I rolled my eyes and lightly slapped my phone into her hand. "But Moommmm." I tried to say with my best preteen attitude, but it came out with a laugh.

She swiped away at the screen for a couple minutes and then handed it back. There were three new app icons on my home screen. "Open them and use them. You have five minutes before I start using them for you."

I squinted at the screen. "These are dating apps." I pressed on one until the option to delete popped up. "I told you I'm done with relationships forever." After she picked me up from the apartment I shared with my best friend on that disaster of a night six months ago I decided that being alone forever would feel better than ever having to live through another breakup again. The feeling of loneliness was nothing compared to that pain.

"Please don't make me say it. I never wanted to hurt you. I never wanted to be one of-"

"One of those people that falls out of love with me while I'm falling in love?"

"Plus, we're on vacation," I added as I dropped my phone onto my bed.

"I'm not saying you need a relationship. I think you need something casual. Something fresh and fun with someone you haven't known your entire life. It doesn't have to go anywhere past this week. Hell, it doesn't even have to be the same person all week." Emery delivered her reasoning like it was a speech she had been practicing.

"Everyone I've dated hasn't been someone I've known my entire life." I rolled my eyes again. Only my sister could have me rolling my eyes like I'm thirteen again.

"Let's see," She held up her hand and started counting them off on her fingers. "Our brother's best friend. Your former high school enemy turned college roommate. Your best friend's brother. Your best friend. Riley, your dating history sounds like a bunch of failed romance tropes and you've known every one of them since you were a kid."

I threw a pillow at her. She was right. My dating history sounded like I'd been chasing every romance trope hoping one would finally stick. The important detail she forgot was that none of it was my fault. They all started it. It always started with them confessing their love for me and asking me to give them a chance. They all said they would wait for me to fall for them as long as I would give them a chance. I fell for those words every damn time. Every time I told myself that it would be the last time I did.

"I know what I said. But it's been months of waiting for you to figure out what you want. I need someone that knows they want me, that doesn't need to figure out what they want."

It always turned out the same. I would finally tear down my walls and fall in love only for them to change their mind. While I was busy falling in love, they were always busy falling out.

I sat on the edge of her bed with my eyes still glued to my phone screen. "There's one fatal flaw in your plan, I don't even know how to use these or what to say on them. What am I supposed to put on my profile? Doesn't do casual or serious? I'll make you fall for me but never love you back? Guaranteed to give you a bad time?" I've never understood the appeal of dating apps, I already struggle enough with dating people I met in person. How could I just look at a profile and decide that this person was the one? Immediate attraction wasn't a thing that happened to me. It took me a lot of thinking things over to even decide to date someone, don't even get me started on how long it took me to commit to a relationship. I threw myself back into the mattress and tossed the phone onto her stomach. "If you want me to do this you might as well man the controls."

I didn't want to do this, but maybe I could appease Emery by letting her create everything and leave her under the impression that I would give things a try. I could delete the apps later.

"Christ, Riley, stop throwing yourself such a pity party. You're young, pretty, and on vacation. Have some fun."

Emery sat up against the pillows and started typing something on my phone. I looked over at her studying her features. We practically looked identical. We shared the same ash brown hair, light brown eyes, roman nose, and down turned lips. My own hair was long and wild despite all the effort I put into trying to style my curls while hers always looked flawless. Somehow the features all just fit together better on her than they did me. We even shared the same plus size body type and slightly above average height. Her curves read as feminine and a little sexy while mine just make me look like I let myself go. The biggest difference between us were the tattoos that covered almost every inch of her skin below the neck. Our whole lives I always felt like I was the prototype while she was the perfect mix of our parents' genes. It always caught me off guard when she called me pretty.

I covered my face with my hands and shook the thoughts out of my head. Emery could always read my mind, and I was not in the mood to hear a self-love speech on top of her sudden need to force me to date.

"Fine, find me someone to have some fun with, little sister."

"Please tell me you two aren't in here fighting like old times," a deep voice that was hard to distinguish if it belonged to our dad or brother said from the doorway.

I uncovered my face to see our older brother, Milo, standing there with his arms crossed over his chest. He looked nothing like Emery and I. Somehow, he came out as a clone of our dad with his tall thin build and warm brown hair. The only thing he inherited from our mom was her snub nose, the only feature Emery and I didn't get from her.

I shot a glare at Emery warning her not to say a word to him about her plan. "We've made it six months sharing a house. I think we can make it one week sharing a bedroom. We're mature adults now," she said while still focused on my phone. Sharing a house was stretching the truth. Our situation was more like I was a long term guest in her house.

I jumped up and slapped my hands against my thighs. "Please tell me my favorite nephew is here," I said. I needed out of this room and this conversation with Emery.

He pointed over his shoulder as he said, "In the kitchen with Mom and Jenna. I think he's already trying to talk Mom into letting him have smores for dinner."

I bounced out of the room ready for a hug from our nephew Aaron. He was five and the sweetest kid I had ever met. A hug from him was always the best medicine for anything. I left my phone in Emery's meddling hands, telling myself I would deal with it later.

"Hurry back. Don't think you're using Aaron to get out of this that easily," Emery called after me.

Chapter 2

Riley

I STRETCHED OUT IN my bed after a long evening spent reconnecting with my family. My skin felt warm and sticky from most of our time being spent outside on the large porch in the humid Tennessee mountain air. Even with it being only early June the high for the day hit ninety.

My phone had been vibrating with notifications from the apps Emery had signed me up for through the evening. While she was setting everything up, she had also taken the liberty to swipe - or whatever it was one did on there - to give me a few matches. Most of them were men with fishing or hunting pictures on their profiles. I had matched with a couple women as well, but they were both locals. Risking meeting someone on vacation was already more than I was willing. Risking meeting a local I may run into during future vacations sounded even worse. Aside from those two everyone mentioned in their profile that they were on vacation making me suspect Emery had used that as her criteria for matching with them. I scrolled to the about me section on all three and changed them to say "my sister is making me do this."

There were a handful of messages from the fishing/hunting guys. They were all a variation of asking "what's up babe," or "how long are you in town?"

"Anything good?" Emery asked from across the room.

I jumped and dropped my phone on my face. Pain shot through my nose making me grimace as I rubbed my nose. "I thought you were asleep."

"You know I need at least an hour for the melatonin to start kicking in and another hour of my sleep music to actually get to sleep."

"Well, nothing good. Congrats you made a bunch of randos with thrill for killing fish and deer message me calling me babe and asking me what's up." I moved my phone to my nightstand and plugged in the charging cord.

"Give them a chance. It could be a lot worse." I knew she frequented the apps back home to some extent since she would often share information with me about who she was meeting with in case anything happened. She had been using me for made up emergencies a lot lately. I tried not to think about all the things that could be worse. I knew what kind of horrors could be waiting on these apps.

"I wish you would let this go so we can just enjoy this time together as a family," I told her.

"Tell you what, give it until this time tomorrow night. If you still don't think it's worth it, you can delete everything." I heard her rustling around and then the room was lit up by the flashlight on her phone. Her noise canceling headphones were around her neck and a pink sleep mask was pushed up to her forehead. "Please, do this for me and actually try."

I put my hand up trying to block out some of the light burning my eyes. "Why are you so desperate for me to find someone?" I bit back a retort about how if she needed me out of her house that bad all she had to do was tell me.

"Because maybe if you find someone, I'll finally get my chance. I'm sick of all the toxic losers I keep attracting." She tugged the sleep mask down to hide the tears welling up in her eyes. "Break your curse so I can break mine," she said before slamming her headphones back on top of her head.

I bit my tongue and rubbed my eyes. Emery never shared a lot about her dating life with me. I always thought she was happy with the casual dating life. She never seemed to see the same person for longer than a month or two after her engagement ended nearly three years ago. I had no idea there may be more to it. We were best friends, and while we had both kept secrets from each other in the past, I thought we were to the point of sharing things like that.

I opened the nightstand and pulled out the notepad branded with the cabin rental company. I tossed it onto her bed to get her attention knowing she wouldn't be able to hear me over the headphones. The notepad bounced off the edge of her mattress and landed on the floor with the pages fanned out.

"What!" She snapped.

"I'm here whenever you're ready to talk about it. What else are big sisters for?"

Emery stayed quiet long enough to make me wonder if she was ignoring me or just hadn't heard me over her headphones. "Maybe another time," she said a few minutes later.

Chapter 3

Riley

"RILEY, WAKE UP."

I pulled the covers over my head only to have them yanked away. I opened one eye to see Emery standing over me. Her toothbrush hung from the corner of her mouth and she shoved a mug of coffee in my face with one hand.

I sat up to take it and reached toward the nightstand for my phone. It felt too early to be awake on vacation. My hand met only the empty wood surface. *What the...?*

I opened my other eye and looked back to my increasingly more annoying little sister. She held my phone in one hand and brushed her teeth with the other.

"I think you've been on my phone more the past twenty-four hours than I have," I grumbled into the coffee. It felt like I hadn't had any time for scrolling since we got here because she had been hogging my phone so much.

She walked toward the small bathroom to finish brushing her teeth.

"Phone!" I yelled after her.

"Hold on," she said. I waited while she rinsed her mouth and then returned. She sat down on the edge of the bed and turned the phone toward me. "I think I found someone."

I raised my eyebrows. "Someone?" I closed my eyes and took a sip of coffee. I guess we were still doing this. I really needed to delete those apps.

"He looks like your type. No dead animals in his pictures. He looks sweet. Looks strong but not in the spends all his free time in the gym way. More so in the can lift you but still will be comfy when you lay on him way."

The coffee shot out of my nose coating my sinuses and hands in burns on its way out. "Em, what are you talking about?"

"Just look at him."

She forced the phone into my face. A picture of man with dark blonde hair short on the sides but longer on the top and styled pushed back out of his oval shaped face filled the screen. His smile showed all his teeth, the two in the front a little too big. His downturned eyes squinted from smiling but I could just barely see a peek of ice blue. There was a light dusting of stubble on his face.

I swiped to the next picture. In this one he wore an ugly Christmas sweater and Santa hat, his face turned slightly like he was talking to someone out of frame. He wore thick framed glasses, and his hair was falling down onto the sides of his forehead. Even while talking he smiled.

"So, is he for me or you?" I asked. I moved the mug of coffee to the nightstand.

"You. He's way too sunshiney for me. You know I like them tall, dark, and grumpy."

I swallowed the retort on the tip of my tongue regarding her type and what she shared last night, instead choosing to motion for her to hand me the phone so I could look over the details of his profile.

Matt F.

29
5'9"
Looking for: Not really sure
About me: Passionate about teaching and music. Going through some life changes and am not sure what I want. Not good at casual but willing to try. I'm pretty good at making people laugh. My favorite hobby is learning new things.

"He doesn't seem like the type that spends a lot of time on these apps," Emery said as I read.

I shrugged. I didn't spend enough time on these apps to know how to tell if he was or not. If either of us was going to know if that was the case it would be her. "Yeah, I guess he seems different from the ones last night." I couldn't place my finger on why I thought that.

"You already matched. You should message him."

I shook my head and pushed the phone back toward her. "It just feels weird. Plus, he said he's not good at casual."

"He could just be saying that." She pressed one hand against the edge of the phone to push it back to me.

I look at the picture again. "He just looks so genuine. I don't think he's the type to just say that."

She took the phone away and swiped at the screen. "And that is exactly why he's perfect." She scrunched her face up in concentration for a moment before she started typing.

My skin prickled with nervous sweat as I watched her type. It felt like an eternity before she finally tossed the phone in my lap.

"Get up and take a shower," she wrinkled her nose up to emphasize the shower. "Mom is making French toast."

I stared at the back of the phone until she left the room. My palms tingled with desire to check what exactly she had gotten me into. I tapped my nails against it a few times before I flipped it over and swiped to unlock the screen.

> Good morning!

> So, teaching and music? Does that mean you're a music teacher?

That wasn't that bad. In the grand scheme of things she could have chosen to say, that didn't even make the list of so mortifying I'll never be able to vacation here again. The exclamation point was a little cringey even if I was the type to overuse exclamation points.

Three little dots appeared to show he had started typing. My heart jumped into my throat, and I threw the phone at the end of my bed.

It buzzed once. Then twice. Then a third time.

I swallowed and patted my chest where my heart should be. I should look. He was nice enough to message back promptly. I thought about that smile in his photo. He really did look so sweet.

I took a deep breath and opened the messages.

Matt F.

> Good morning, Riley.

> Band teacher, actually.

> So, your sister is making you do this?

I bit my thumb nail and smiled. He used my name instead of just calling me babe. It shouldn't have felt like a green flag, but after last night it did.

> Band teacher/ music teacher…Aren't those same thing?

> Yes, she says I need to meet people and have some fun.

I laid my phone face down on the nightstand and counted to three before I stood from the bed. I walked toward the bathroom. When I reached the doorway, I stopped and drummed my fingers against the frame.

What if he messaged while I was in there? I couldn't just leave him hanging.

It was a dumb thought. Of course I could leave him hanging, he was a stranger on a dating app. I didn't owe him an immediate response or to even continue the conversation. I sprinted back to the bed to grab my phone, opening the message thread again. I should just put a stop to this, let him know that I didn't have any intention of following through with anything on here. A new message from him popped up.

Matt F.

> No, not the same thing. That sounds like something my sisters would say about me if they were making me do this.

There it was, the perfect opportunity to apologize and end the conversation. I tapped my thumb nails against the screen trying to think of the best way to let him down. Or maybe I could keep messaging him a little longer? It wouldn't hurt to just try to talk to him. He knew Emery was making me do this so surely he took that as a sign that I wasn't actually interested in anything. A little conversation to distract me couldn't hurt.

Riley H

> Hmm, if you say so. Maybe you'll have to explain the difference to me sometime. Happy to hear no one is making you talk to me. Tell me more about your sisters.

Why did I say that? I shook my head and tried to delete what I had typed. My thumb slipped and hit the button to send the message instead.

Shit. Shit. Shit.

> I do say so. I might take you up on that one day but until then you'll just have to trust me that they're different. Is it weird that I'm happy your sister is making you talk to me?

> I have three sisters – two older and one younger.

> I've never been very good at trusting people…. It must be rough being the only boy in the middle of that many sisters. I have an older brother that my sister and I used to torture growing up. I don't know how he survived.

That was too honest. What was wrong with me? I closed the app and pressed on the icon to delete it. No, I couldn't just ghost him like that, that was mean. I had to tell him and then I could delete the app.

> Maybe we can work on the trust thing. It wasn't too bad. There was some torture for sure growing up but for the most part it was nice. I think I grew up to be a much better man than I would have without them.

There's no working on the trust thing. I'm permanently broken. Don't try to act like you don't have trust issues, everyone does. Funny enough, my sister-in-law says the same thing about my brother.

My only trust issue is that I trust too much.

I smiled at my phone as I walked down the cabin stairs into the sitting room. This was stupid, reckless even. There was too much honesty happening in the conversation.

A conversation with a stranger.

Why couldn't I bring myself to put a stop to it?

Emery grabbed my shoulders before I could make it to the kitchen.

"That smile looks promising," she whispered as she used her full body to block me from the view of everyone else. "May want to get rid of it before anyone starts asking questions."

I schooled my face into a neutral expression. "It's nothing."

"Riley, I know you and I know your face. That smile isn't 'nothing'."

I shrugged her hands off and pushed past her, tucking my phone against my chest to hide it from her. I promised her I would give things a try until tonight, so that's what I would do, distract myself with some harmless messaging for the day and then I would let him down tonight.

Chapter 4

Matt

M Y FINGER HOVERED OVER the delete profile button on my phone screen. I rested my head against the back of the rocking chair and scrubbed a hand over my jaw. Last night my youngest sister called to apologize for the hundredth time this weekend for the way things had worked out with our family vacation this year. As in, it wasn't happening.

Madison and Grace's kids all had summer activities they couldn't get away from. Shelby was working two jobs trying to pay off the student loans for the degree she didn't finish. Mom and dad said it just didn't feel right if everyone else couldn't come. I didn't have the heart to tell any of them how much I needed this vacation more than ever. Just a couple more weeks and then I would be back home with all of them. Was it really that important that we all be together for vacation this year? It's not like this was our only opportunity to spend time together before we went our separate ways until the holidays.

Last night the emptiness of the cabin got to me. I had watched the clock hit midnight only to realize that it was the first birthday I'd ever spent alone. Happy birthday to me. Another year older and no closer to where I thought I would be by now.

I thought I would be married by now, maybe even have a couple of kids. My wife and I would have moved back to Georgia, back to our hometown so our kids could grow up surrounded by our families. I would be established in my dream job, would be the teacher all the kids loved.

This week marked a change in my life, a new step in the direction I wanted it to go after feeling stalled for so long. I may not be married, may not have kids, but things were finally falling into place with my career. The house I had bought with my ex was sold and packed up, ready for me to move out when I got back at the end of the week. At least I would be back to being surrounded by my family soon. Lost in the thoughts of all the things I wanted, all the changes happening, I downloaded a dating app last night. I don't know what I was thinking. I hadn't been on a first date since high school and everyone around here was on vacation. It was midnight and I was sad, of course I hadn't been thinking at all.

The thought that anyone I met here would be a one time thing didn't hit me until now, hence the sudden reconsideration. I don't do one time things. My ex had been my high school sweetheart, my first everything, my only everything.

Maybe that's what I needed, someone to get past the daunting first step of getting back out there that I had been putting off. I would never have to worry about running into them again after I embarrassed myself. Because I would embarrass myself. My winning moves involved passing a note in class that said "do you like me? Check yes or no."

Okay, so no, that wasn't what I actually did, but it might as well have been.

I blew out a breath and looked back at the delete button on my screen. A notification popped up alerting me to a new message. I opened it. I would let her down gently and then delete my profile.

Riley H

> **Good morning!**

> **So, teaching and music? Does that mean you're a music teacher?**

The message was simple. I opened her profile. I remembered seeing her while swiping last night. She was pretty in a gentle girl next door kind of way. She looked like someone that would be easy to talk to. In all her pictures her curly brown hair was pulled back from her face, a gentle smile on her full lips, and soft kind brown eyes. Her face was angled in each like she was trying to hide her nose.

I scrolled down to the about me section.

Riley H.

27

5'7"

Looking for: casual

About me: I'm a teacher. Spend most of my free time with my sister, who is also my best friend. My sister is making me do this.

I didn't remember that last part being there last night. I chuckled lightly as I imagined Shelby making me create a dating profile. She would probably put something in my bio about her being my best friend.

> Good morning, Riley

I sent the response before I could think about it. There was something about the woman in the pictures that made me think maybe this could be just what I needed. She was a teacher and close to her sister, two things we had in common already. If her sister was making her do this did that mean she also wasn't very good at this sort of thing? I remembered the question in her message and typed out another response.

Band teacher, actually.

I drummed my fingers against my leg. I should ask a question about her. My brain went back to the part about her sister. I could relate to that.

So, your sister is making you do this?

Her answers came through quickly.

Band teacher/ music teacher...Aren't those the same thing?

Yes, she says I need to meet people and have some fun.

I chuckled. Music teacher was a general term, someone who taught kids about music and how to read it. As a band teacher I taught kids how to play instruments. Since graduating college, I had been working as an assistant band director at a high school. This year I would finally get to live my dream of teaching middle school back in my hometown. It seemed like such a small dream to have, but it had been mine since I was a kid. I would get to be the person to teach kids how to play for the first time, giving them the skills they would need if they chose to continue on with band in high school and college. I would get to be the person that helped them fall in love with making music.

I opted not to tell her. I didn't need to scare her off with how much of a nerd I am when we had barely even started a conversation.

Just like that we slipped into easy conversation, chatting all day about small things. Our messages were flying back and forth so quickly most of the time I didn't have time to lock my phone before a new one appeared. Before I knew it the day had slipped into late afternoon, and I hadn't left the cabin. My stomach rumbled letting me know that the only thing I'd had to eat today was a cup of coffee and birthday cake.

I should go get something to eat.

> I'm being told that I've been on my phone too much today, my brother and sister are putting me in time out. Sorry if I don't respond for a little while.

As much as I was enjoying talking to her, I was glad for the forced break.

> I guess we have been talking a lot today. It's been nice. Be good and maybe they'll let you out early? Talk to you later.

> Following instructions has never been one of my strengths.

I resisted the urge to respond, knowing that if I did we both might not take the break we needed to. *This isn't going anywhere*; I had to remind myself.

***

> I have officially eaten my weight in smores and hot dogs. My sister made me clean up after everyone before she let me have my phone back.

I have an important question.

How roasted do you make your marshmallows?

On what scale?

1 being just starting to turn brown and 10 being burnt to a crisp.

10 all the way. The only right way is to stick it in there until it catches on fire. It gets perfectly burnt on the outside and gooey in the middle.

Hmm…I'm starting to doubt that this might work out.

THE ONLY RIGHT WAY

The right way is to hover it over the flames until it's a caramel color.

You're right, this isn't going to work out. I can't have fun with someone that likes their marshmallows rare.

Says the person that insists on turning them into ash.

I'm right. You're just going to have to trust me.

Until I can prove you wrong. I'll teach the right way to roast a marshmallow someday.

I don't think you can, but you can try.

Does your cabin have a porch?

I'm sitting on it right now. How about you?

Me too. The stars here are beautiful. I wish I could bring this view home with me.

I have a confession to make.

I'm not good at casual.

Or not casual.

My fingers fumbled my phone, sending it bouncing across the deck until it landed face down a few feet away. I leaned forward in the rocking chair, resting my elbows on my knees and dropping my head into my hands. There it was. She was going to try to let me down easily. I should have done it this morning before I spent all day talking to her.

I tapped my fingertips against my forehead. My heart thudded against my chest and my mouth went dry while I stared at my silent phone where it lay. Today may not have been the day I had expected or hoped for. I couldn't deny that I kept catching myself checking outside to see if my family had decided to surprise me today. I hadn't even let myself plan anything to get out of the cabin just in case. Talking to Riley had been a nice distraction.

No, not a distraction. Things may have started out that way but somewhere along the way today I started looking forward to a new message from her, opening those notifications faster than the ones from my friends and families. Less than a day and here I was already getting attached to her.

That's me. The guy that always gets attached too fast. I couldn't do casual because I didn't have a casual bone in my body.

I stared at my phone, willing another notification to come through. Nothing happened.

That was fine. I should just get ahead of this now. I didn't have to wait on her to do it, it was obvious where she was going with those messages. I blew out a long breath and forced myself to pick up my phone. A thin crack stretched diagonally across the screen. Just great, this screen protector had only been on for a week.

> I understand. Thank you for talking to me today.

Three dots danced across the screen stopping me from sending anything else. I watched them appear, disappear, and reappear a few times. I held my breath and sent a silent plea that her next message didn't say what I was expecting.

> This is going to sound stupid, but maybe we can keep messaging while we're here? I did enjoying talking to you today

> ...and it'll keep my sister off my back.

Oh.

Okay.

It wasn't exactly great, but I would take it. She had added the part about keeping her sister off her back almost as an afterthought. She enjoyed talking to me. I couldn't decide if it was mixed signals or her not being willing to admit that there was something here.

***

I woke up the next morning to my phone on my pillow, the battery dead from me falling asleep messaging Riley. I reached for the glasses on my nightstand after plugging my phone up, rubbing the sleep from my eyes and focused on the time glowing on the digital clock. 5 o'clock. I had only been asleep for four hours. I pulled off my glasses and rolled over. I tossed and turned for an hour trying to get myself back to sleep before giving up. The faint light of dawn glowed around the curtains when I pushed myself out of bed.

I walked to the kitchen, popping a coffee pod into the machine to brew while I warmed a breakfast sandwich in the microwave. I booted up my phone as I waited for my breakfast. There was one more message from Riley.

> Thank you for talking to me today. It was nice.

She just wanted to keep talking because it would keep her sister off her back, I reminded myself. That's all this was.

I pictured that soft smile and kind eyes as I read her simple words. She had no idea that I was the one who had needed yesterday, had needed someone that was so easy to talk to. I had been so upset at the thought of spending my birthday not surrounded by family for the first time in my life and needed the distraction to make me forget about that.

I typed out a quick good morning message to her, sending it even though she was probably still sleeping. She had told me last night that she was a night owl and not a morning person. I was an awake at all times type of person, there was never enough time in the day to do everything I wanted. I stayed awake until I crashed and woke up with the sun every day. It wasn't healthy to run on how little sleep I did, I knew that but nothing I tried ever fixed it. If I stopped taking my ADHD medication I could sometimes get in little more sleep, but the amount wasn't worth giving up because of how much the medication helped me focus. With the medication at least I could focus enough to finish things instead of skipping around leaving behind a trail of unfinished projects.

On the back porch I settled into a rocking chair with my breakfast, snapping a quick photo for Riley of the sunrise. My mind wandered to what she would look like next to me taking in the beauty of the mountain sunrise. One day of texting and I was already picturing her as part of my life.

Don't take this seriously, I told myself. It didn't matter if she was easy to talk to, she was just temporary. She had told me that she wasn't looking for a relationship right now several times yesterday. I lied to both of us saying that I wasn't either.

I Googled hiking trails nearby as the pinks and oranges of the sunrise faded away. Photos of a rocky overlook at the top of the mountain filled my screen. The trail looked easy enough and was one of the highest rated for the area. I saved the trail map to my phone.

> Good morning. You weren't kidding about waking up early.

> I'm being forced to go ziplining with my family today. They have all informed me that

there will be no phone service. I promise I'm not ignoring you if you don't hear from me for a while.

***

Ziplining was as much fun as I remember it being. I think the best part was getting to watch my nephew experiencing it for the first time.

Sounds like something I need to try while I'm here.

What did you do this morning?

I found a trail to hike that looked like it would be beginner friendly. I think I took a wrong turn somewhere because I ended up on a trail that was straight up a rocky hill for a mile.

Ouch

The view from the top was nice. I'm still un-decided if it was worth it.

I sent her the photo I had snapped of the view at the top of the mountain, followed by the selfie of me collapsed on the ground. My hair was soaked from sweat and I had pushed it back with one hand so it wouldn't be plastered to my forehead. My eyes were closed as I tried not to focus on how my legs were shaking even laying down, a smile taking up my whole face. There had been three trails that all led up to the top and I had lost confidence in myself after a few wrong turns, choosing instead to follow another group that I crossed paths with. I had almost given up several times during the climb.

> You look like you had a great time.

> Don't let the pictures fool you. It was miserable. I don't even want to talk about the climb back down. I think I slid most of the way down.

A photo came through of Riley squatted down next to a kid, her arm around his shoulders. She wore a helmet and harness. Her hair was in two braids hanging down her shoulders, frizzy pieces escaping in a million directions. The kid had both his arms around her smiling in a cheesy little kid way, Riley mimicked his smile.

> You look like you had a much better time than I did. Is that your nephew?

> It is. He's the best kid I've ever met. I hope I get lucky enough to have a kid like him someday.

***

> We're headed out hiking today. Any chance we may run into you while we're out there?

> As much as I would like that, I don't think it's going to happen. I can't move. I think I need to take it easy today.

> I hope you feel better!

> I'll try my best. You enjoy the hike. Avoid the one with red markers.

I spent Tuesday morning spread out on the couch of the cabin. My whole body ached from the hike the day before. As the day passed by the thought of tomorrow being my last day here before returning to reality loomed over me. Riley and I hadn't discussed yet what would happen when it was time for us to go back home.

> How much longer are you and your family staying?

> We're leaving Saturday morning. You?

> Tomorrow is my last day. I need to head back home Thursday morning to start taking care of some of those life changes.

> I really want to meet you before I leave.

> I don't know. It's been a lot of fun talking to you, but I don't know if I'm ready to date anyone.

> I kind of have a complicated past.

Me too. I was with my ex for a long time. It's been a while since I've been on a first date.

It's been a while for me too.

Most of my past relationships were with people I was already close to. I don't think I've ever been on a real first date.

I wish I hadn't told you that.

We're both on vacation. Chances are we'll never see each other again after this. What do you say to just one date to help us both get past our pasts?

Like a practice date for future first dates?

Sure, if that's what you want.

It just doesn't feel right leaving and never getting the chance to meet you.

Okay. But I'll have to find a way to get away from my family.

Make your sister cover for you? She is the one that made you do this after all.

I like the way you think. I think everyone was planning to go downtown tomorrow for a shopping day. Meet me for a late lunch somewhere?

Have you ever been to Blackberry Café? It's my favorite place to go when I'm here. I could eat my weight in their pastries. Meet me there at 1?

It's a date.

Chapter 5

Riley

I TOOK A DEEP breath and rested my forehead on the steering wheel. "You can do this," I told myself as my fingertips fiddled with the edge of the steering wheel cover.

Twenty-seven years old and this was my first real first date. Everyone else before this had all been people I knew for a while. Already knowing them so well before the first date always made it feel more like something we were just getting around to checking off a to-do list rather than like a true first.

He was a stranger.

Not really a stranger. "You've been texting him for three days," I muttered to myself. I tapped my forehead against the steering wheel and exhaled. Three days of constant butterflies that only increase with every message. Before this week I didn't know it was possible to get butterflies from a stranger I only knew through text messages. Could you really know someone just from texting and only texting for three days? Surely that doesn't count.

Even if no one else has ever made me feel this way with just a few messages. Butterflies weren't an early in the relationship sort of thing for me.

I took another deep breath and glanced at my phone. Ten more minutes until we said we would meet. How early was too early to get out to look for him? Do I go in and just wait? Wait outside?

Another deep breath. He was a stranger. I had no reason to be nervous. This could all go horribly wrong, and I would never have to see him again. We would both go back to our regular lives, and this could just become a funny story I would tell about a stupid thing Emery talked me into doing.

My phone vibrated in my hand. Could that be him?

I took another deep breath.

A car door somewhere close by opened and closed. I glanced up and saw a man with dark blond hair and a casual navy button down with the sleeves rolled up to his elbows paired with a pair of dark wash jeans walk toward the café. Even without seeing his face to confirm it was Matt, my heart jumped and the fluttering in my stomach multiplied.

I flipped down the visor for a final check in the mirror. I had Emery help me tame my curls to not be as wild as normal, not that all the work made a difference since the humidity was already making my hair puff and frizz. I grabbed a small claw clip and pinned the top half back and left a few loose pieces out to frame my face. I went with simple makeup knowing that anything heavy would be too much in this heat, but I did a quick touch up of my lip gloss.

I smoothed my hands over the fabric of my light coral summer dress. It was one of my favorites and always gave me a boost of confidence when I wore it. The bodice was structured enough to push my chest up allowing the low-cut square neckline to show just the right amount of cleavage. The skirt flared out at the top of my stomach hiding the part of my body I was the most self-conscious of. I pulled a perfume rollerball from my purse and added a little more to my wrist, inhaling the peach and sandalwood scent.

My phone vibrated again. This time I looked down to see I had two messages.

Matt F

I'm here.

The second was a photo of Matt sitting at a metal outdoor table smiling with all his teeth showing and giving a thumbs up.

A nervous laugh escaped from my lips. It was now or never. If I was being honest with myself, I knew that this was the best chance I would ever have at a no pressure something casual with someone new.

"Just have some fun. It's practice for him as much as it is for me," I told myself remembering his words from last night.

Before I could change my mind, I opened my car door. The table he sat at was only a few feet away so I knew he could see me. I glance in my rearview mirror for one more peek before I turn to face him. He stared down at his phone and tapping his foot.

He almost looked as nervous as I felt.

I closed my car door as quietly as I could.

Don't overthink this, I reminded myself. On the count of three I walked toward him.

He looked up and his whole face lit up. His smile in person felt even more magical than it did in photos. He stood up and stepped toward me with his hands in his pockets. My stomach and heart jumped in unison. It felt like my whole body was nothing but butterflies and electricity.

"Riley?" Matt asked. His voice was timid as his eyes met mine.

My heart flipped in my chest and skipped a beat. *Finally*, I heard it say. A sudden calm washed over me. I smiled shyly at him. I am in over my head. This man is meant to be someone important to me. I don't know what that means but I'm not scared.

I've never not been scared.

"Hi, yes, that's me." I let out a little giggle. *A giggle.* "You must be Matt."

He rubbed his hands on his jeans. "I can't believe I'm doing this. I'm so glad you came."

Is this what people mean when they talk about love at first sight? I'm not in love but it feels like my whole body is saying I could be. Maybe not now but some time I will be. Sometime sooner than I would ever think possible.

Love at first sight didn't exist. Right? That was a myth. Right? It was an idea created by people looking back with rose colored glasses once they already knew the ending. A romanticization after the fact.

"Me too," I say. "Can I be completely honest with you?" I cringed a little.

"Yeah, please. I want to be completely honest with you too. I'm really nervous."

Just like that the little bit of my walls that were remaining crumbled into dust. My shy smile morphed into a wide grin followed by a laugh. My whole face hurt from smiling so hard. Was I wrinkling my nose? I think I was. My eyes were scrunched up to the point of being almost closed. "Me too. I know I already told you I don't really know how to do this whole first date thing. Or meeting strangers. I feel like a teenager again." I chewed on my lip for a moment and thought back to all my past relationships. Back to all the times that they left me thinking they weren't being up front with me about what they were thinking. "Can we make it a rule to be honest with each other this whole time? I want to know everything you're thinking."

"Yes!" He rubbed a hand through his hair. It puffed up after his fingers passed through it. "I mean, yes, I think that would be good for both of us." He held his hand out to me, "how about we go inside?"

I took it, wrapping my hand around his in a loose hold. Electricity shot up my arm and I was surprised to not see sparks flying from our hands. What was that?

At the counter his face lit up as he pointed out things on the menu. My brain buzzed so much trying to make any choices about food felt too overwhelming. "It all looks good. Why don't you order for both of us?" I suggested.

He held my hand the whole time and kept his eyes on me like he was checking for my approval with everything he picked.

We picked a table tucked into a corner. There was a small vase with wildflowers in the center, I let my eyes linger on them for a moment before focusing on Matt again. I wanted to look around and take in the place, but I couldn't take my eyes off the man in front of me. "So, um, I've been thinking about it all morning," I said, rubbing my hands together. "I think we should set some ground rules."

"Whatever makes you comfortable," he answered. His hands were clasped in front of him on the table. I wanted to reach out and brush my fingers against his to see if that same electric zap would happen again. The hand he had held felt cold without his wrapped around it. I rested my hands on top of the table instead.

"Since this is practice for both of us, a chance to test the first date waters, I think rule number one should be we tell each other everything we're thinking – the good and the bad."

"I think we've already been over that one." He unfolded his hands and laid one out on the table a little closer to mine.

I took a deep breath and tried not to focus on that hand. I shifted my eyes back up to his face. "It's an important one." I waited for him to nod before I moved on. "Rule number two: no last names or details about where we're from. We can talk about our lives but nothing identifying enough that we could find each other again."

I let him think about the second rule for a minute. He opened his mouth to speak but closed it back without a word.

I drummed my fingers on the table. "This is a no risk situation. We just have today. No worries about if it will lead to anything else because we know it won't," I elaborated.

He nodded his head but worked his mouth like he was working hard to choose his next words.

"Rule number one," I reminded him.

He nodded again. "I'm not going to lie and tell you I'm okay with a one-time thing, but I'll take today only over nothing."

"I just really need this to be a no risk thing," I looked down at my hands. Looking at his face suddenly felt like too much. "I don't really do one-time things either but it's all I can handle right now."

His fingers brushed mine. There it was again, an electric zap followed by a tingling warmth. "Riley, it's okay. We're only going to do what you're comfortable with." I looked up to see his blue eyes wide with concern.

"Th-those are the only rules I have so far," I stammered. "Additional rules may be added if either of us deems them necessary."

He lifted his hand out to me as if asking for a handshake. "I agree to your terms."

We shook on it.

Our order number was called, and Matt went up to grab it. He came back to the table with enough food for a full family. I had no idea how much he had ordered. There were sandwiches, pastries, salads, some kind of dip with crackers, two iced coffees, and two pink colored drinks. He moved the vase of flowers over to another table and moved everything from the tray onto the table.

"Did you order the whole menu?" I asked as I took everything in.

"Their signature watermelon mint limeade and whatever experiment the barista wanted to make today," he explained as he moved one coffee and pink drink over to my side of the table. "I thought we could just sample a few of my favorites," he motioned to the food and then placed an empty plate in front of me. "Take your pick."

I picked up half of what looked like a chicken salad sandwich. Then I served a portion of the salad topped with strawberries, nuts, and cheese crumbles onto my plate.

"Good choices." He pointed to the sandwich, "that is their lemon dill chicken salad. One of my personal favorites. The salad is their strawberry balsamic and it is a summer staple."

"You come here a lot?" I asked before taking a bite from the sandwich. "Ohmygod, I think that's the best chicken salad I've ever had." My sister loved to cook and frequently experimented with new recipes meaning I didn't say things like that lightly. The chicken salad was made with grilled chicken giving it an extra burst of flavor. I had to tell Emery about this later. It seemed like something she would love to try out.

He beamed as he watched me sample the food. "My family rents a cabin up here every summer. We eat at this café almost every day."

"But you're here by yourself this summer?" I took a sip of the watermelon limeade and closed my eyes as I took in the fresh flavors. It paired so well with the chicken salad.

"Yeah, there's a lot going on for all of us right now so we couldn't find a time that worked for everyone. I almost didn't come but it didn't feel right to miss out on the trip." He tilted his chin toward the coffee. "Try that."

I swirled the cup around a few times and took a sip. At first all I could taste was the coffee but then the raspberry and coconut started to come through. I knitted my brows together in confusion.

"Don't like it?"

I shook my head and took another taste. "It's good but different. I've never had fruity coffee before. I usually just stick to the basics."

"Fruity coffee?" He took a sip of the coffee. He lifted the lid of the one he kept for himself and sniffed. "Here, this one may be better." He placed the second coffee in front of me.

A blend of mocha and hazelnut filled my mouth. "Much better. We could share this one if you want."

"Nah, every time I come here, my sister and I tell them to surprise us with different flavor combinations. We've been in competition to find the weirdest." He took another sip. "This one is high on the list. Actually, Shelby might like this one."

He kept his eyes on me as he started to move some of the food onto his plate. "I have a question I've been dying to ask you since last night."

I stabbed my salad with a fork trying to get a little of everything on it for the perfect bite. "Ask away."

"You said you had a complicated past. Will you tell me about it?"

I focused on the forkful of salad. "It's a long story. Are you sure you really want to hear it?"

His foot tapped mine under the table. "I've got all day. I'll tell you mine if you tell me yours?"

I gave him a soft smile and took a bite of the salad. I chewed slowly while I tried to decide where to start. "So, the first time was my brother's best friend. It was just after their graduation. He kept waiting for the best time to tell me that he was in love with me and since he was going out of state for college he didn't want to risk not getting to spend the summer together. We dated all summer and then he left for school. I thought everything was great. Until October when I felt ready to say I loved him. He broke up with me two weeks later saying that the long distance wasn't working."

I stabbed the fork back into the salad and kept my eyes focused on building another perfect bite. "Freshman year of college I was assigned to a dorm with this girl from school that I thought hated me. I was always confused by her since normally I'm the kind of person that gets along with everyone. I knew a lot of people from my class had all picked the same school, but I never thought that I would end up rooming with one of them. We spent the first semester constantly bickering and competing again. One day in the middle of an argument she told me she was in love with me. We lasted four months. A week after I told her I loved her she ended things. According to her I wasn't very good at showing my love."

I laid the fork down and reached for the sandwich again, still making sure I avoided looking at him. I could feel his gaze bearing down on me. I waited on him to say something while I chewed my food.

When he didn't, I continued, "after college I moved in with my best friend. One day her brother showed up while she wasn't home. Told me that he had been in love with me forever and he always regretted never saying anything. We lasted an entire year before he realized I never would say I loved him. When we first started dating, he told me that he understood my history and knew it might take me a little longer to come around. When he asked me about it on our anniversary, I told him I did love him, but I had been too scared to say it. A month later I got a speech about how bad I am at showing love."

I took a long sip of the watermelon limeade before I could continue to the worst one. "I came back to the apartment crying and of course my best friend was there to pick up the pieces like she always was. Except this time, she tells me that she can't handle watching me get my heart broken over and over like this. That they were wrong, and I was one of the most loving people she'd ever met. Gave me the best kiss of my life and asked me to give her a chance. Told me she knew it may take me a while to figure out my shit, but she'd be there waiting. She gave me six months. The night I was finally ready to confess my feelings she told me I took too long to choose her."

I looked up to him to let him know I was done.

"Damn, Riley, that's all terrible." He tapped his foot against mine again. One hand lifted like he might reach for mine, but the table was too crowded with food.

"Well, that's my curse. Destined to take too long to fall and be bad at showing it once I get there." I reached for my limeade to find relief for my mouth suddenly feeling desert dry. My face heated as the realization that I just told a stranger all that caught up with me. "Your turn now. Think you can top my tragedy?"

"It's not a competition, sweetheart." His eyes dropped to his food, uncertainty washing over his face. "Promise you won't think I'm an idiot after this."

"Sweetheart, huh? I bet you use that one on all the women."

"Only you. It just felt right. Do you hate it? I won't do it again."

I didn't hate it. Despite all my romantic struggles I always enjoyed being called terms of endearment. Sure, it was odd to hear a stranger calling me sweetheart with such ease. Like everything else about this date, about our time talking, the ease felt natural. "No," I said as a blush started to creep up my face. "I don't hate it."

He reached out and brushed my heated cheek with his thumb. Warmth flooded my body. He kept touching me in all these little ways that felt so familiar despite having just met. "Keep blushing like that and I'll never stop calling you sweetheart." His hand dropped away and he leaned back in his chair. "Now, about that promise" He raised an eyebrow.

I held my hand over the spread of food, poked out my pinky, and smiled. "I pinky promise. You better not be over there thinking pitiful thoughts about me either."

He locked a pinky with mine. "No pitiful thoughts. Only thinking about giving all your exes a piece of my mind."

I expected him to follow up with a chuckle, but his face was stern.

He reached for his limeade and fidgeted with the straw. "We were high school sweethearts. I thought I was going to spend the rest of my life with her. Had it all planned out. Every time I tried to talk to her about the future, she would tell me it was too soon. She wanted to wait until after college. After college she always had an excuse. Our ten year anniversary was coming up and I decided to just go for it. The day before the big romantic proposal I got this weird feeling. Something told me I needed to try to talk to her one more time. I sat her down and told her that I needed to know if she was really in this with me. She told me that she didn't see a future with me and hadn't for a while. She was just too comfortable with what we had going to end things."

I bit my tongue to try to keep quiet like he did for me. It didn't work. "I can't believe she just strung you along like that. I mean, I know I'm bad about taking my time to figure things out, but I always came around in the end."

"Ten years," he exhaled hard. "Don't get me wrong. It wasn't bad and I really loved her. It's just.... That's ten years I could have had with someone that I had a future with. Not to mention that I felt like I missed out on learning how to navigate the adult dating world."

"Never fear, that's why I'm here," I said to try to lighten the mood. "Not that I have much more experience in the real dating world." I picked up my fork again and proceeded to stab at the salad. "So how long has it been since you broke up?"

"Two years since we broke up. It took me a little while to get over her and feel like I was ready to move on. We had moved to another state together for her work. It wasn't my dream place to work but it was good. I was an assistant high school band director. Last year I found out the band director at the middle school I went to was going to be retiring at the end of the school year. That was my dream job, getting to follow in his footsteps. I managed to keep it a secret from her that I would be moving back home. She found out a couple weeks ago."

My eyes widened as I realized where this was probably going. "No, please tell me she didn't." My fork stabbed into the salad a few more times.

"Showed up on my doorstep saying she had made a mistake in leaving me. She had just needed time to figure things out. Now she had and she realized that we were meant to be together."

"Do you still love her?"

"Having her there begging for me to give her another chance was when it finally hit me that I didn't anymore. I had already planned this vacation. The timing worked out perfectly to get me away from her until it was moving time."

I took a bite of my sandwich trying to process everything he just told me. There are so many questions I want to ask but none of them feel appropriate. The rule we set about no identifying details flashed across my mind. Most of my questions would break that rule.

"You promised no pitying thoughts," he said, breaking the silence that had settled over us.

"Just trying to figure out how I can get a few minutes with this woman and give her a piece of my mind."

"She's not worth it."

"Well, none of my exes are worth it either but you said the same thing about them."

He drummed his fingers on the table. "How about we change the subject? Tell me a little about your job."

"You already know I'm a teacher too. Well, I have a degree, but I'm waiting for a position to open up. I want to teach kindergarten but it's one of those school districts where I have to wait for someone to retire or not come back from maternity leave. I've been working as a sub in the meantime." I left out how I had also been working closing shifts at a local hardware store, tutoring, and doing delivery services on the side to make up for not working full time. Even with my sister as a roommate, rent was expensive despite living in a small town. Then there were also all the medical bills that had piled up while I worked through my diagnosis.

"I get that. Where I'm moving back to is one of those districts where everyone loves their job so much, they don't want to leave. I was starting to think I would never get the chance."

"Yeah, same kind of district. I'm starting a long-term sub position in the fall. There's a teacher there that's due to have her baby at the beginning of August. I'll be covering her maternity leave."

"And secretly hoping she doesn't come back?" He asked with a raised eyebrow.

"Of course. It's a first-grade position. Not my dream grade level but it's pretty close."

***

"Excuse me," an employee said from beside our table.

Matt and I broke eye contact to look over at the teenage girl.

"We're getting ready to close. Is there anything we can get y'all to go before we shut down?"

Matt and I looked back at each other. Close? How long had we been here? The silent question floated between us.

"Um, no, I'm good. Do you want anything else?" He asked me.

"No, I think I'm good too," I said.

"Okay. Well, we're closing in fifteen minutes. You're welcome to sit at the patio table if you want. Just need you to, um, not be in here anymore," her hands twisted in her apron. She smiled, showing a mouth full of braces.

"Yeah, yeah, we can do that," I stammered and started to push back my chair.

Matt's eyes widened as he looked at his watch. "It's almost five o'clock," he said. "We've been here for almost four hours."

I looked at my phone for the first time since we sat down. "We just sat here talking for four hours," I said in disbelief. "So much for being bad at this."

We each scooped up our trash from the table and headed toward the trash can next to the door.

"I don't think I've ever just sat and talked to anyone for four hours," he said as he pushed the door open with his shoulder. "Best first date ever," he added as he motioned for me to go ahead of him.

I looked back over my shoulder as I walked through the door. "We didn't even really do anything special though."

"Being comfortable enough to talk to a stranger for four hours isn't special for you? Wow, and I thought we were on the same page here." He clutched at his heart in fake hurt.

I laugh. "No, that's a first and special for me. It just doesn't feel like something most people would call the best first date ever. I thought that was a description that had to be saved for grand romantic dates."

"We can make this a grand romantic date. Turn it into a marathon of a first date. What do you say? Where to next, my lady?" He swept out his arm. "The night hasn't even started yet."

I laughed for what had to be the thousandth time today. My face was going to be so sore tomorrow from the workout all the smiling and laughing had given it. "You don't have anywhere else to be?" I asked.

"Do you?"

I thought about my family for a moment. Emery covered for me for lunch, but we never expected me to be gone this long. It was shocking that she hadn't already started blowing up my phone.

This is her fault, I remind myself. She could cover for me a little longer.

"Nothing my sister can't get me out of. This whole thing was her idea after all. Just let me call her real quick."

"If you need to get back to your family it's okay. I won't hold it against you. You are on vacation with them."

I chewed my bottom lip. "This is going to sound crazy but I'm really not ready for this to be over." I stepped toward my car as I pulled up her contact.

It didn't even ring before she answered. "Well, if it isn't my long-lost sister. I was starting to think you had abandoned me for some stranger after all."

"Well, about that," I said.

"Wait," she yells. "Are you abandoning me for some stranger? Who are you and what have you done with my sister?"

"It's just... you were right," I whispered. I looked back to make sure Matt couldn't hear me. He still stood in front of the door scrolling through his phone.

"Shit. Are you okay? Tell me where you are, and I'll be right there. Did he hurt you? That has to be code for something being wrong, right?" She yelled so loud I was sure he could hear her. I turned my volume down a little.

"Nothing is wrong. I'm actually having a really great time. We've been at the café so long that they kicked us out so they could close. I think we're going to go somewhere else."

"OHMYGOD" she squealed. "You're head over heels already for him. Okay, yeah, I'll cover for you with everyone. But remember I get to give a speech about how I'm the reason you met at your wedding."

"It's not that serious. It's just, this feels different and I'm having a lot of fun. I'm never going to see him again after this. I'm just not ready for the fun to end yet." I rubbed a palm over my face. My cheeks were burning up.

"Whatever you say, big sis. Just drive yourself wherever you go. Can't have you getting murdered or anything. I couldn't live with that on my conscience."

"You were just saying you're so sure he's the one and now you think he might be a murderer?"

"Can never be too safe. Love you!" She hung up without giving me the chance to say anything else.

I looked up to where Matt stood next to the door with his hands in his pockets watching me. "All good," I said, giving him a thumbs up.

Chapter 6

Riley

I followed Matt in my car as he led the way to a festival he found while I checked in with Emery. When he suggested it to me I pictured something much smaller than we pulled up to. This looked like a hybrid of a farmer's market and fair. There were tents everywhere with tables set up full of vegetables, fruits, and handmade items. Behind those a collection of food trucks lined up along a small street with blockades on either side. There was a field with an assortment of inflatable slides and bounce houses. Another field was set up with carnival rides including a Ferris wheel. It was all finished off with a few tents with fair games.

I parked my car next to his and did a quick refresh of my hair by swapping my small claw clip for a bigger one so I could pull my hair up off my neck. Matt came around and opened my car door for me as I struggled to untangle my fingers from the knots that had formed in my hair. He rested an arm on the top of the car and leaned in a little. A combination of citrus and spice with a hint of mint filled my nose. "I don't really know what we're getting into here. I just saw the word festival and thought it could be fun," he said.

Anything with you would be fun, I wanted to say. "It looks interesting," I said instead.

He laughed and lifted his head to look over the scene in front of us. "It looks like someone couldn't decide what event they wanted to have and just slapped the name festival on it."

"It's a lot, for sure." I took in his shoulders and chest as his shirt pulled tight over them, remembering what Emery had said when she first showed me his pictures. She was right, he looked broad and strong, but there was a softness to him.

He dipped his head back down to look at me. His smile had dropped, and his eyes pierced mine. "We can go somewhere else if you want."

My fingers prickled with an urge to brush against the stubble along his jawline. "Let's give it a try first." I motioned toward the games with my chin. "I bet I could beat you at some of those."

He held out a hand for me to take. "Winner picks the next stop," he said. He wrapped a hand around mine, sending another flood of warmth through me and pulled me out of my car. "Where to first, my lady?"

We stood there a moment, bodies pressed together, lost in each other's eyes as the sounds of the crowd buzzed around us. The slam of car doors around us and kids yelling over each other pulled me from the spell. I stepped from between him and my car, then tugged him toward the games. Once we were standing in the middle of the tents, I stretched an arm out in front of me pointing. "Close your eyes and spin me," I told him with my eyes closed.

His hands hovered over my shoulders, touching just enough to urge me to spin. After a few turns his hands closed over my shoulders bringing me to a stop. I opened my eyes and found that my hand pointed at a giant claw machine.

A wicked grin spread over my face. "Not exactly something we can compete at, but I am really good at those."

"Are you going to win me something good?" Matt asked as I took my place in front of the machine. His hand appeared in front of my face and pointed to a treasure chest. "What about that?"

"I'll let you in on a little secret to winning these things. It's not about getting what you want, it's about going for what is sticking up the most." My eyes scanned over the assortment of stuffed animals and treasure chests. I spotted a bear in the corner that looked like it had been picked up and dropped a few times leaving it in a clear position to reach. If whoever had been trying for it had tried one more time they would have gotten it. "I hope you like bears," I said as I slid quarters into the slot.

"That's cheating," he said as the bear dropped into the retrieval slot.

"The claw machine chooses for you, that's not cheating," I said.

He shook his head and pulled quarters from his pocket. "Let's see what's in those treasure chests," he said.

He gave up after ten rounds of various chests slipping from the grasp of the claw. I passed him the bear and looped my arm through his. "What do you say we find something more your speed?" I asked.

He looked around as he tapped a finger against his top lip. "I've never been good at any of these," he said.

"Don't give up already," I said, poking out my bottom lip. My eyes stayed fixed on where his finger rested against his mouth. I wonder how it would feel to place my own finger there, to press my lips there. Every touch today made my body buzz but also felt so familiar, like his touch was made for me. *Would kissing him feel the same?*

What a strange thought.

I forced my eyes away and leaned my head against his shoulder. He was only three inches taller than me so I ended up leaning more against the side of his head and neck than his shoulder. His hand moved to cup my cheek holding me against him.

"I can't think with you touching me," he said.

Same, I said to myself. "Then don't think," I said to him. I pulled back so I could see his face. His smile was wide but there was a small glint of sadness in his eyes. "Let's play some skeeball," I said, "maybe I'll let you win this time."

"Maybe I'll let you win," he shot back.

***

We worked our way through most of the game tents over the course of the next hour. Neither one of us were able to win anything. That may have been partly due to our distracting each other with constant little touches every chance we got. A brush of legs here, and caress of hands there. I lost all ability to make eye contact with him because each time sent a fresh wave of butterflies to my stomach.

"Want to take a ride on the Ferris wheel?" he asked me.

I looked up at it and grimaced. "Have you ever seen how they put those things together? I don't know if I want to test my luck tonight."

"I'll keep you safe," he stepped behind me and wrapped his arms around me. My face and neck heated as my whole body tingled.

I relaxed back against him and ran a hand along his forearm. "I think I'm going to need the details of your plan to keep me safe. We're going to be stuck in a dangling bucket all the way up there."

His lips brushed my ear and made my knees weaken. "I'm making this up as I go along, sweetheart. If you want to find out, you'll just have to trust me."

I closed my eyes and licked my lips. "I feel like now might be a good time for a new rule, but I can't think right now," I whispered.

His arms loosened around me. I clamped my hand down on his forearm holding him in place. "If you want me to stop touching you, you can tell me," he said. He kept his arms loose but didn't pull them away.

I shook my head and moved my hand to hold his. I turned around to face him. The muscles in his face tensed.

"Rule number one, what are you thinking?" he asked.

I smiled hoping that it would make him relax. I squeezed his hand a couple of times and shook my head. "I don't think I want you to ever stop touching me."

His face tensed more as his eyes studied mine. I knew he was thinking the same thing I was.

If we keep saying things like that, rule number two is going out the window.

Chapter 7

Matt

RILEY TOLD ME SHE didn't want me to stop touching her, the words made it harder for me to remind myself that today was just a one-time thing. I switched to telling myself that if I was only getting one day with her I would make the most of it. I was already attached so there was no use in fighting it. Our hands stayed locked together as we walked around the festival, letting go only long enough to take a bathroom break.

My hand was sweaty in hers from the early June heat and from nerves. I kept sneaking glances at her fingers intertwined with mine to check if she was giving any sign of disgust from it.

After a while of walking around she asked for a break. We sat on a bench close to the entrance of this hodgepodge of a festival. She pulled my arm around her shoulders and leaned against me, her hand holding mine against her shoulder.

She grinned as she pointed to a group of kids fighting with foam swords. Her small purse trapped between us started to vibrate against my leg. I tried to focus on the words she was saying, her voice soft with a Georgia accent that became more prominent as the day went on. The vibrating stopped and then started again.

"Riley," I said, giving her hand a long squeeze.

"Hmm?" She asked.

"I think your phone is ringing," I tapped her purse with my free hand.

She pulled out her phone, holding it up in a way that I could easily see the screen from the way she leaned against me. She had two missed calls from someone named Emery and a text message. She opened the message and a photo of the two of us filled the screen. In it her face was tilted up to me, her body relaxed against mine as we spoke. We looked good together. If someone showed me that photo I would have guessed that those two people had been together for years.

I was so fucked.

I should ask her to send that to me.

"Shit," she said under her breath as she pressed the call button on her phone. I pulled away so I could see her face, the corners of her mouth pulling down as she chewed her bottom lip. I could hear the phone ringing between us.

"You two look cozy," someone said in a whispered voice. I leaned closer worried about what was happening.

"Please, please tell me you're the only one here," Riley said, panic filling her voice.

There was rustling that sounded like a hand covering the phone and I heard a muffled, "I'll be right back."

"Em, seriously."

"We're all here," the voice on the phone finally said. "Jenna heard someone in town talking about this festival today. Apparently, they do fireworks every night and you know how much Aaron loves those."

"We have to go," Riley said, tilting her face to me.

I squeezed her hand and stood up, pulling her up with me. "What's wrong? Is your family okay?"

"Ooh, he-"

"Not now, Emery," Riley snapped. "My family is here," she said, shifting her focus back to me. "We need to leave before they see us." She shifted so the phone was pressed between our heads allowing me to hear.

"It's not that big of a deal, Riley. I told everyone that you ran into a friend while we were in town and wanted to catch up. Just get a little less cozy and they won't know the difference."

I looked down at our fused hands. Even if we were to "get a little less cozy" I knew that they would figure it out. Based on the photo this Emery person had sent I would say it would be obvious to anyone that saw how we looked at each other what was going on.

"No, just get them as far back from the entrance as you can. We're going to leave." She shoved her phone back into her purse and sprinted toward the parking lot, pulling me behind her.

We were both wheezing when we made it to her car.

"My legs are still too sore from that hike for running," I said leaning against the side of her car, holding my side with my free hand as I fought back a smile.

She burst out laughing. She had a sing-song laugh that was louder than I expected from her speaking voice. "I can't believe I'm hiding from my family like this."

"What was that you said about feeling like a teenager again?" I brought our still joined hands up to my mouth, planting a kiss on the back of hers. A blush crept over her chest and cheeks as I did, her eyes turning heavy. "Your laugh sounds like-"

"You better not be able to feed me some cheesy line about my laugh sounding like music or some shit like that," She cut me off in a stern tone.

"Do you always interrupt people this much?" I asked with a laugh. I brushed my lips against the back of her hand again, the way her blush deepened sending a wave of joy through me. I dropped my eyes to her mouth where she bit her lip. I wondered if she would blush the same way if I kissed her.

"It's one of my finer qualities," she cleared her throat and smirked.

I pulled my eyes away from her mouth, glancing at my watch. It was eight o'clock already. "I think it's time to feed you some dinner. It's been a while since we had lunch."

Her stomach growled on cue. "Now that you mention it, I am kind of hungry."

"Where to? I believe based on our bet you choose the next destination."

"Drive thru hamburgers and then I want to watch the sunset with you," she answered without delay.

I pulled her into a hug, her soft body pressing into mine like we had done this a million times as I wrapped my free arm around her, my left one still clutching hers by our sides. She rested her face against my neck. "I like the way you think," I whispered against the top of her head.

"Follow me this time," she said. "I know the perfect spot." Her free arm wrapped around me, pulling us closer. Neither of us wanted to let go. The time ticking away weighed on my shoulders. We were running out of time.

Chapter 8

Matt

RILEY WAS ALREADY OUT of her car, arms full of the food she had picked up when I parked next to her at a pull-over spot on the mountain. We rested against the hood of my car as she passed me my food and then pulled out her own.

I took a bite of my burger, chewing slowly as I took in the view. We made it just in time to catch the sun just starting to dip below the horizon sending watercolor swirls of orange and pink up the sky. I shifted to take in her profile as she took in the view. Her hair had mostly fallen out of the clip she had it twisted into. Frizzy curls stuck to the sides of her face and neck. Her skin glowed in the fading golden light.

"It's beautiful," she said.

Her face turned to me "You're beautiful," the words slipped from my mouth on accident, my face heated as I blushed.

"I bet you use that line on all the ladies." It was the second time today she had responded with that sentence.

We ate in silence for a few minutes. I continued to struggle to find the right words to say to her. She kept saying things like that, like she couldn't believe anything I said to her. It was just little things peppered here and there throughout our conversations today brushing off any complements. I wondered if she kept forgetting what I had told her, or maybe she hadn't heard me. There hadn't been anyone since my ex. There had only ever been my ex.

I finished my burger and tossed the wrapper in the paper bag, shifting closer to her. "How many times do I have to tell you it's just you?" I caught a loose strand of her hair that fluttered in the light summertime breeze and tucked it behind her ear. I took my time brushing my fingers down the strand of hair and then coiled it around my fingers. Her bottom lip was swollen and red from all the times she had bitten it through the day. Her cheeks were red from heat and goosebumps appeared on her neck from the soft breeze blowing.

She had shown up for our date with her guard up in every way. She'd been beautiful enough to take my breath away outside the coffee shop, but now with her guard lowered enough to be a little messy she was the most beautiful person I'd ever seen.

I could lean in and kiss her right now.

I dropped my hand away from her, picking up my fries to keep my hands busy and shuffling to the side to put some space between us. I shoved a handful into my mouth.

"I don't think any first date could ever beat this." Riley said after finishing her own burger, her voice almost a whisper. "I think you've ruined me for all future first dates."

I choked on the fries, coughing and sputtering as I scrambled for my cup. I held a hand up to stop her as she leaned in close to me. Casual, this was supposed to be casual.

A few days of talking, a full day spent together, and I was already falling for her. Being around her was easy, like I was meant to always be around her. I had spent all day reminding myself that we were on a countdown, that we had a deadline. That deadline was rapidly approaching.

We sat in silence for a few minutes staring at the sky while I chugged half my sweet tea, willing my thoughts to slow down. I wanted another day like this with her. I wanted to ruin second, third, and more dates for her. I wanted to ask for her number. I wanted to know where she was from, I had glanced at her tag long enough to know she was from Georgia but wouldn't let myself look at the county name. She had slipped up and told me that home was a three-hour drive away narrowing down what part of the state she was from without meaning to.

Next week I would be back in Georgia, all my loose ends in Kentucky tied up. My hometown was only a three-hour drive from here too. Sure, even just north Georgia was a big area and three hours away could work for a large portion of that area. There could still be an hour or two drive between us.

Or there was the chance that home was the same place for both of us.

No, don't be dumb, Matt. I'm not that lucky. Meeting her here this week felt like I was already testing the bounds of my luck.

"While I appreciate your honesty, I'm going to have to ask you to refrain from saying anything like that again," I finally breathed out.

She poked my side and asked in a flirty tone, "Why?"

"I don't think I can answer that without scaring you away." The words flew out before I could stop them.

Her face tensed and she turned back toward the setting sun. Did she know how close I was to asking her to break her rules? How much I wanted her to prod until I couldn't stop myself from telling her that I didn't want this to end with tonight?

She scooted closer to me. The sun was almost gone now with just a few slivers of pink reaching up from the horizon. She laid her head on my shoulder as we both rested there against my car watching as those last slivers disappeared.

Darkness fully took over the sky and the first pin pricks of stars started to sparkle. We shifted at the same time, her face tilting up toward mine as I tilted mine down toward her, the same position as the photo her sister had snapped of us. I leaned back as much as I could to put some space between our mouths while still keeping her against me.

She swiped the back of her hand across her mouth. "Please don't tell me I have something on my face."

I shook my head and fought back a smile. A lump formed in my throat as I let the words I had been holding back tumble out. "I really want to kiss you. Is it okay if I kiss you?" I twisted one of her loose curls around my finger.

"Well, the thing is," she started, pausing to bite her lip. "I usually don't kiss someone until they confess their undying love to me." She forced a smile, the corners of her mouth twitching like she was fighting against a frown. For the first time today, she looked worried.

"If that's the case –"

"No, don't you dare." She cut me off and lifted my wrist to look at my watch. She held it up to my face. "We've known each other a whole nine hours."

"Are we really still counting hours? If you want to be technical about it, we've known each other for four days."

"But only nine of those have been in person."

"As I was saying," I tried again.

"No, no, no," she waved her hands in my face, the one still holding my wrist made my hand flop around.

I laughed, twisting my hand until it was wrapped around her wrist instead. "Would you please let me finish what I was trying to say?"

"I am not about to let you say you're in love with me already. This is a one-time thing, remember?" Panic flashed through her eyes, the pulse in her wrist raced against my fingers.

"Well, I hate to let you down, but I was going to say I'm not in love with you yet. I am, however, really enjoying my time with you and I like you a lot." My pulse raced with hers, but her hand relaxed in mine. Her shoulders dropped and the tension melted from her face.

She snorted. "Like me? What are we fifteen?"

"I wasn't the one almost stomping my foot a moment ago," I reminded her with a laugh. "Not too long ago you had me running from your family like we were teenagers sneaking around." The tension in the air broke at the reminder. She ducked her face and laughed.

"I think I can make an exception to my rule," she finally managed to say between laughs.

"I think I'm going to need you to tell me exactly what you mean," I said as my own laughter died in my throat. I released her hands, laying them to rest on her lap. I pulled my hands away, the feel of her soft skin too much as I tried to listen to her.

"I mean, I want you to kiss me."

"I don't know, sweetheart. I don't normally kiss on the first date." I brushed a finger against her chin, lifting her eyes to meet mine. Her breath fluttered, her eyes dropping to my mouth.

"I don't think this qualifies as a first date anymore. We're nine hours in and at location number three. At this point it has to count as at least the second," she whispered.

"Hmm, is that how it works?" I pressed a finger against her chin, directing her eyes back up to mine. I could see thoughts whirling behind her eyes. While there was an undeniable connection between us, I didn't know her well enough to know what they were. I wasn't kissing her tonight without being sure it was what she wanted.

"We're making our own rules here. By that logic, yes, that's how it works." Her voice shook as she spoke.

"Should we take a vote on that?"

She closed her eyes and squeezed her fists in her lap. Her eyes popped open and shifted between my eyes and mouth a few times. "You're driving me crazy, Matt. Are you really going to make me beg?" She shifted forward so her lips hovered close enough to mine that her hot breath tickled my lips.

"As much as you would love to hear you beg, maybe we should save that for another time." I closed the small space until our lips almost brushed against each other as I spoke, but didn't kiss her.

"There won't be another time," she reminded me, making my heart drop to the pit of my stomach.

"If this is our only chance, I guess we better make it the best first kiss in history." Panic flashed in her eyes before they fluttered closed to hide it. I couldn't do this knowing she was so unsure. I shifted to press a kiss against her forehead. "I can't just kiss you. I want more. I wish we had more time." I took a deep breath to gather the courage to pull back to study her face. Her eyes snapped open, a range of emotions rushing across her face while she studied me back.

Her eyes softened. For the first time today, I knew without a doubt that she wanted the same thing I did. She cupped my cheek in her hand and ran her thumb over my bottom lip. "We have all night. You can do whatever you want." Her face blazed red, radiating heat that I could feel against my own skin.

I shook my head, realizing she thought I was talking about sex, not a relationship. "If we do-" I closed my eyes and took a deep breath as I thought about her words. A casual date with her was already hard enough, I could feel my heart breaking already at the thought of the night ending. But sex was something else entirely. I had only ever been with my ex, and based on what she had told me I would venture to guess it was the same for her. Neither one of us were the type that could handle casual sex. "I can't keep my promise to you. I don't think I would be able to let you go."

"I wish you could keep me." She stepped out of my arms.

"I could if you'll let me." I pulled her back in and pressed another kiss to her forehead. "Please, let me keep you." We wanted the same thing. There was no point in fighting whatever was between us. We should talk about it, figure out a way that we could fit into each other's lives.

She shook her head while she took a few shaky steps away from me. Her arm brushed against the food bag sending it tumbling to the ground as she retreated away from me. "If I let you keep me one day you'll wake up and realize it was a mistake. It's better this way." Tears gathered in her eyes and one hand clutched her chest. "I don't think I would survive getting my heart broken by you."

Tears spilled down her face as she backed away from me toward her car. "I'm sorry," she whispered. "This was a mistake."

My face dropped as my own vision started to blur as her car rocketed away from me. My mind raced with my heart as I repeated our conversation over and over again trying to figure out where I went wrong.

Chapter 9

Riley

August

EMERY THREW HER ARM around my shoulder as we approached the high school. "You finally made, big sis, your first school year as teacher." She gave me a squeeze.

The call came last week that the teacher I was supposed to sub for had given birth and decided she would not be returning from maternity leave. I had been scrambling since to get everything to start the school year as a full-time teacher rather than as a sub. School started the next week and I did not feel ready. Today was Edward County schools' annual kickoff event with all employees. This was Emery's fourth year as a bus driver.

My hand lifted to brush my hair back from my face, breathing in the scent of the perfume I picked for today after I was told I would be full time this year. The subtle floral scent with a touch of musk was always my go to for when I needed to feel strong and confident in new environments. It helped that it was one I always received compliments from strangers on.

"So, explain to me what we're doing today," I said. We had been over it a few times and I had a rough idea from hearing other teachers discussing the kickoff over the course of the last week while we prepped our classrooms.

"Do a little meet and greet with all the other district employees, eat some lunch while the superintendent gives her annual pep talk, and then everyone usually breaks off by grade level to do team building shit," she said it all slowly. I knew she was tired of repeating it all to me.

It felt like being the new kid at school. Our county was small, consisting of one main town and then four smaller towns that were mostly farmland most people didn't realize were separate towns. We all called them all Mountain View unless a distinction was needed. It didn't matter that I knew pretty much everyone across the district since I had been subbing for so long, most of them were people I went to school with or had as teachers, being full-time changed things.

"Riley, you look like you're panicking," Emery said. "It's really not a big deal. You're not the only new teacher this year. I heard that there are at least two others." Three new teachers in one year was a lot around here.

"What if I mess this up, Em? I've been subbing so long I don't know if I even still have it in me to do more than follow plans that someone else left for me."

"That's it," she said, shoving me from behind. "We're not doing the self-doubt game today. You're going to go in there, meet with the other first grade teachers, and rock this."

We resumed our walk toward the front doors, joining with the crowd of teachers, bus drivers, cafeteria workers, and janitors that were lined up at the tables stationed at the sidewalk. "They really invite everyone to this," I said to Emery.

"I was told that before Mrs. Bryant took the superintendent position this used to just take place at a school level and was usually just teachers. She really likes to go all out and have everyone considered full time here." She nodded her head to the short lady with a head of gray hair standing with a door propped open greeting people.

Mrs. Bryant was one of those teachers that had taught for so long most of the school district employees had been taught by her at some point. Sometimes it seemed like she never aged. Every so often the kids would start circulating rumors that she was a vampire or witch. I had never heard anyone call her by her first name. When she was appointed as superintendent five years ago there wasn't a single person who disagreed with the decision.

The line moved forward as I twisted my neck to look back over my shoulder toward Emery only to catch a glance of a familiar profile and dark blond hair. I blinked a few times, willing my vision to clear, sure that once it did my mind one stop playing tricks on me. It had been happening all summer. I'd see someone blond and convince myself that I was seeing Matt. A second look always proved I was imagining things. Some small part of me wished that whatever greater power made sure we met in June would force our paths to cross again. It was wishful thinking. Real life didn't work that way.

My vision focused on the parking lot again expecting the figure walking up to have reverted back to being some else. He was closer now, close enough that his eyes met mine. I snapped back to facing the table in front of me and focused on writing my name and grade level on a name tag. "Emery, I need you to look toward the parking lot and tell me if you see anything –"

She squeezed my shoulders and shuffled beside me to grab her own name tag. "Riley, I think that was Matt," she said.

I closed my eyes and smoothed the name tag onto my shirt. "I'm scared to look." My heart raced against my hand on the name tag. I didn't know if I was scared that it was going to turn out that I had been imagining things or that I was right this time.

She looked back over her shoulder and then back at me beaming. "I think he noticed you."

I shook my head. "There's no way. I don't think he saw my face." He did. His eyes had focused on mine like a magnet. The corners of his mouth had started lifting into a smile. Maybe I had imagined that part. After how I left him it wouldn't make sense for him to smile at me.

"He saw mine and we look a lot alike," she pointed out.

"I think we're just imagining things. Let's just get inside." We shuffled past the groups that had formed in front of the door filling each other in on their summer.

"Riley Harrison, it's so nice to have you as a part of the team this year," Mrs. Bryant said as we approached her. She wrapped me in a tight grandmotherly hug.

"I'm really happy to be joining," I replied.

She reached for Emery. "You girls look more like your mom every year."

My mouth formed a tight smile as she ushered us through the door. All I could think about was turning around to check behind me.

"Matt Fletcher, welcome to the team. It's so nice to have you back home," Mrs. Bryant greeted the next person. That was fast. He must have pushed past everyone to be right behind us now. The false piece of hope that he hadn't seen us slipped away.

Unable to resist any more I turned around to see him there shaking her hand and giving her his sunshine smile showing those slightly too big front teeth. I felt my face light up as I watched them. He was here. His eyes met mine and everything crashed down. *He was here.*

I turned back to Emery. "What do I do?" I started walking toward the cafeteria and pulled her with me.

She looked over her shoulder. "He's following us. You could just stay put."

My head shake was more aggressive this time and my feet picked up speed carrying me away from him. Emery pulled her arm out of my hand and turned around. That was the moment my sister did the most humiliating thing she had done in the twenty-six years of her life. She raised her hand and waved Matt to us.

My stomach dipped and nausea gripped me. I looked toward the cafeteria and saw the teacher whose classroom was next to mine. We met earlier in the week while we were both there doing set up. "Kristy, hey," I said, rushing to meet up with her. The tall thin woman turned to look at me, her highlighted hair in two long French braids slinging over her shoulder as she did.

A glance back over my shoulder showed Emery covering her face and shaking her head. Matt stood next to her with the same beat down look he had on his face the last time I saw him, the sparkle gone from his bright eyes. Seeing that look on his face felt like a stab to my heart.

***

The group of first grade teachers in the district sat gathered in the back section of the auditorium. My back ached from resisting the urge to slump in the hard plastic chair. A teacher from a school on the south end of the county discussed the increasing number of students they felt were being passed through kindergarten to first grade too quickly. She was one of the few teachers I had never subbed for, I had a strong suspicion she was one of those strong believers in perfect attendance for all no matter what. She was another one of those teachers all the kids loved to spread rumors about.

Someone tapped my shoulder and I turned to see Emery. "Shouldn't you be with the other drivers?" I asked her.

"Yeah, I'm headed back there now. Mrs. Bryant was looking for you. She wanted to have a meeting with the new teachers in the art room. I told her I would let you know." Her brows were pinched together, and she flared her nostrils as she spoke, both tells I knew didn't match her light tone of voice. My sister was lying about something.

I raised my eyebrows. "Art room?"

"Yeah, um, I think it's the only classroom no one is using." She stumbled over her words and pulled the corners of mouth tight as she spoke, her eyes looking everywhere but at me.

Next to me Kristy shrugged. "It's better than listening to this." She tilted her pen toward the teacher that had transitioned to a full rant.

It didn't take any more convincing than that to stand and follow Emery out into the hallway. "Better hurry up. It took me a while to find you." She back peddled toward the cafeteria where all the drivers stayed once everyone split up after lunch.

Emery had always been a terrible liar. This was a trap, not a meeting.

The door to the art room was open but I didn't see anyone. The sound of the chair I pulled out at the back of the classroom echoed in the empty space. A break did sound appealing. I could probably get away with a few minutes before I needed to head back to my group. This time I let myself slump forward in the chair, resting my elbows on the table and enjoying the silence of the room.

"Knock, knock. I was told I needed to come to a meeting here?" The familiar voice sent a jolt through me. I looked up knowing who I would see standing at the door. His eyes were scanning the classroom and hadn't spotted me yet.

"Can I ask who sent you here?" I asked. My fingers taped hard against the screen of my phone typing out a strongly worded message to Emery.

His gaze settled on me. "I think your sister might be playing games with us," he answered.

"As I'm sure you remember, that's a habit of hers."

"I can leave." He motioned with his thumb over his shoulder. "I don't want to upset you."

"I'm pretty sure at this point if anyone gets to be upset, it's you." I laid my phone face down on the table as Emery's text messages started to flood in. "I've run away from you twice now. Hell, after how I left back in June, I would say you would be justified in hating me."

He made his way to the back of the classroom and pulled the chair from the table in front of me, spinning it to sit across from me. "I'm a little upset, but I don't hate you. I know I crossed your boundaries. I've been more worried about you than anything else." He pushed a hand through his hair making it puff up the way it did on our first date. Just like during our date he didn't try to smooth it back down. "I tried to check on you that night when I got back to my cabin but you had already deleted your profile. You never gave me your number, so I had no other way to reach you. I thought about trying to look for you at all the cabins, but I didn't want to cross any more lines."

My head dropped to the table, the cold surface felt nice against my hot skin. "This would be so much easier if you weren't so sweet," I said into the wood.

"I didn't know this is where you were from. I promise. I was very proud of how much self-control I had at not looking at your tag for any hints."

I tapped my head against the table with a huff and then looked up at him. The tag on my car would have been such an obvious giveaway.

The thought hadn't even crossed my mind. "Thank you for not being a stalker. I didn't even think about the tag on my car."

"I'm not going to make you talk to me, even though I'm really happy things worked out this way." He tapped his fingertips against the wood. He walked over to the cubbies full of paper, scribbled something down on a sheet, and slid it across the table to me. "In case you decide you want to talk, here's my number. It's up to you."

He returned his chair to where it belonged. He turned back and smiled at me. "I'm glad you got the job. I hope everything goes well."

Chapter 10

Riley

M Y FINGERS TRACED OVER the rough paper with Matt's number scribbled in his messy writing while I waited on Emery in the car. My brain and heart were battling to decide what I should do. My heart knew that I needed to give him a chance. I wanted to get to know him better and see where things could go. I could be missing out on something special just because I was scared.

My brain was being a bitch. I had been here before and it always ended in heartbreak, even when I thought that time might be different. All those times before I thought I might be missing out on something special.

He would get tired of me once he got to know me.

He would get tired of never feeling like I loved him.

He would think all my quirks were silly.

The door slammed as Emery climbed into the driver's seat. "Look, I know you're mad at me, but I had to do it. You've been all weird and quiet since you went on that date with him. You didn't see how the two of you looked at that festival." She knocked her fist lightly on the side of my head to make me look at her. "Please get out of your head."

I slammed my head back against the headrest. "I'm so scared, Em."

"I know you are, Ri. I would be too if I was you. Just because you're scared doesn't mean you shouldn't do it. If anyone has ever been good at doing things that scare them, it's you." She put the key in the ignition but didn't start the car.

I snorted. "You say that like I'm scared of everything."

"I'm not taking that bait," she said.

"What do you think about him?"

She started the car and fastened her seat belt. Music blared from the radio loud enough that everyone in the parking lot could probably hear it. I leaned forward and turned the volume down a little so I could hear her answer. "The way he looks at you makes me nauseous. I wish I had someone that looked at me like that."

I fastened my seat belt. "Is that a good thing?"

She laughed as she threw the car in reverse. "Is that a good thing, she asks," Emery muttered with an eyeroll. "God, Ri, I can't believe you. It's the best thing. My annoying baby sister senses are telling me he's it. He's the first person you've dated that I can picture as being part of the family."

"I don't feel ready. Getting my heart broken by him feels inevitable."

She slammed the car back into park and tore off her sunglasses. "We're not doing this shit," she said, shaking her sunglasses in my face. "All you're doing right now is breaking your own heart before he has the chance. I want you to be happy. You deserve someone that is going to give you the world and that man is the one that is going to do it. Stop being mean to my sister."

My arms crossed right over my chest and leaned away from her. The car felt too small all of the sudden. "I don't want the world."

"What do you want?"

I chewed on the inside of my cheek. "I don't know."

"Well, you better figure it out. I know for a fact he would wait for you but that doesn't mean you should make him."

I leaned my head against the passenger side door. "Can we just go? I have a lot I need to do for my classroom."

She put on her sunglasses, shifted into reverse, and backed out of the parking space. She was fuming more than I was. I don't know what she thought she had the right to be angry about. "I'll drop you off at your school but you're going to have to call someone else to come pick you up." She gestured toward the paper still clutched in my hand. "You shouldn't have any problem finding someone. I had something come up."

The most annoying thing about my sister was that when she said she was going to do something she did exactly that. The moment I was out of her car in front of Pine Elementary School she peeled out of the parking lot. I took a deep breath and opened a new text message on my phone.

Riley

Hi, it's Riley.

Do you want to help me with my classroom?

Matt

I would be happy to help.

I don't know if I'm ready to talk about what happened that night. Is that okay?

Whatever you're comfortable with.

> Do I get to help decorate the door? I always wanted to do that.

>> I would like that.

***

Matt

"I'm glad your sister likes me enough to keep forcing us together, but her methods are getting a little extreme," I said. The blue butcher paper felt damp under my sweaty palms. There would be two perfect hand prints left behind once I lifted my hands away. My whole body prickled with nervous sweat, had been since I saw her run away from me in the school hallway. The jittery feeling I had all day from starting the new job had been magnified by her.

I thought my eyes were playing tricks on me when I saw that familiar wild hair in the crowd of teachers. Her sister turned around and lifted her hand in a low wave hidden at her side from Riley. It was the moment I had been hoping for all summer. She wasn't just a wild dream created by loneliness at the cabin. Our date had been real. Now, against all odds, she was right in front of me. Like a man possessed I had sprinted from the parking lot, pushing my way through the groups socializing to catch up to her.

She hadn't been as excited to see me again, hadn't looked at me the same way she had outside the cafe in Copper Ridge. For a brief moment I was sure I had imagined it all after all until her sister Emery blamed it on her being nervous and assured me that Riley had enjoyed our date. "Give me some time and I'll make sure she comes around," she'd told me with a mischievous glint in her eyes.

Riley smoothed tape over the top on the backside of the door and peeked at me through the window. "Once Emery has her mind set on something nothing will get in her way, even if it's something she has no business interfering with."

"Was she really going to leave you stranded here?" I asked. I bent down enough to look at her through the window. Her breath caught as our eyes met, the sight sending a fresh wave of jitters through me. During our date I thought we had felt so connected, but now that we were back in our everyday lives the realization that we were strangers felt like a bucket of ice water. Her small reactions felt like a foreign language I had learned enough of to pass a test only to forget right after.

She shrugged shoulders, "I don't think she would have. I probably could have waited a couple hours and then told her you couldn't come help me." Her eyes dropped to the tape in her hands. She tore a few more pieces off and added them to the back of the door with slow movements.

"Then why did you ask me to come here?" My sweaty hands swiped over the fabric of my jeans without thinking and then I dropped to my knees to feed the bottom of the butcher paper under the bottom of the door. The paper kept catching on the edge of the door and rolling up. My hands were damp again and my fingers struggled to unroll the paper. The corner tore off and stuck to my palm.

Riley knelt on the other side of the door. Her fingers caught the edge of the paper I managed to feed through and pulled it tight against wood. The only sounds were my racing heart pounding in my ears and the sound of tape being pulled from the roll slowly. "I don't know what I'm doing, Matt," Riley broke the silence. A relieved breath rushed out of me from hearing my own uncertainty reflected in her voice.

I poked my head around the door. "Riley, we're going to have to talk about it at some point." Riley was still kneeling on the floor, twisting a piece of tape around her fingers. The look on her face brought me back to our last moments together at the overlook. I tried to think through anything I could say that wouldn't scare her.

"I know. It's just, I'm going to screw it all up. I'm scared and confused. You deserve so much better." She stopped twisting the tape and started rolling it between her fingers until it was a tight ball.

I shook my head and moved around the door until I was by her side. I settled on the floor next to her, leaving enough space between us that we weren't touching. She let me slip the tape dispenser from her hands and I went to work on securing the door. With the paper secured I turned back to her, reaching slowly toward her chin like I was trying not to startle a nervous animal. She didn't flinch once my hand met her hot skin, so I lifted her face until our eyes met. "Tell me what you want. Tell me what you need. Riley, if you'll let me, I'll do everything I can to give you the world." I fought the urge to cringe at myself, forcing a smile instead. Good job, Matt, that definitely wasn't too much. I dropped my hand away from her.

She had told me that day that she didn't want me to ever stop touching her. Did she still feel that way? I did. My arms itched with the need to wrap them around her, to smooth my fingers through her curls. Her hair was twisted up in the same clip she wore at the festival, wild strands escaping the same way they had that night.

She laughed, a small sound that was more nervous than anything, and shook her head. "We barely even know each other."

I stood and held out a hand to help her up. "Let's get to know each other." It was a good starting place, getting to know each other in this new environment. As much as I wanted the woman I met in June back, it was clear that we were both different from the personas we'd worn that day. I couldn't wait to see who she was here without the safety nets.

She took my hand, letting me pull her up. Her hands smoothed over her pale pink linen blouse as she looked around her classroom. To me it looked like everything was set up, but I was used to a type of room that didn't need much. The walls were covered in an assortment of colorful posters, most of which featured The Magic School Bus. The tables all had name tags placed in front of each seat along what looked like a welcome goodie bag. A bean bag chair was tucked in one corner with a short bookshelf on each side. From the wall at the back of the classroom to her desk at the front everything looked like a picture perfect classroom.

Riley bit her lip and blinked back the tears that had started to gather in her eyes. "Okay. Let's get this door done and then..." She cut herself off to take a deep breath.

"And then, we're going to get pizza and go wherever you feel comfortable enough to talk," I finished for her.

She nodded her head, her mouth lifting the first real smile she had given me today. "Sounds like a plan."

Chapter 11

Riley

MATT PULLED UP IN front of the small two-bedroom house that Emery and I shared. Emery's car sat parked next to mine, where I'm sure it had been since she abandoned me at the school. Matt's hands flexed on the steering wheel briefly before he moved to shift the car into park.

"We can go somewhere else, if you want," I said.

Matt popped his door open and then twisted to reach for the pizza in the back seat. "Is there anywhere else you would feel comfortable?" He didn't look at me as he spoke. It felt like there was a wall between us the whole time we were in my classroom and for the drive over. I wasn't sure which one of us was putting it up, but I got the sense he was just as scared of trying to take it down as I was.

I knew we could go to his apartment, he had already offered that option, but it felt too weird to ask him to take me there only to have to bring me home. I wouldn't have a way out if we went there. Here we may have to deal with Emery since she had shown she wouldn't hesitate to interfere, but I could make him leave whenever I needed him to.

I shook my head. "I just don't know what Em is going to say."

He leaned in and squeezed my hand, his touch more cautious than it had been during the summer. The small connection sent a wave of relief through me. I missed this. I missed him. "If she is as invested in us as you've told me, maybe she'll leave us alone."

I took a deep breath and exhaled as I unfastened my seat belt. Taking that as a sign, Matt came to my side of the car to open the door. He scooped up my teaching tote bag from where I had it tucked against my legs on the floor and swung it over his shoulder.

"I can carry my bag," I told him.

He smiled and took my hand urging me out of the car. "Come on, beautiful, I want a tour." Just like that, it felt like we were closer to being the two people we were on vacation, not the two nervous people that had been tip-toeing around each other all evening. Maybe we could get back to who we had been that day.

I led him to the front door. Emery slung the door open, hopping on one foot as she struggled to slide on her sneakers. Her crossbody bag hung from her neck like she had thrown it there. "I just remembered an errand I forgot to run," she said out of breath as she rushed past us. She was in her car and backing out of the driveway in a flash.

Matt and I locked eyes. We both burst out laughing, the remaining tension between us melting away. "One problem taken care of," I said.

Matt followed me in. I gave him a quick tour with a few points of my hand in each direction. The house was mostly the living room and kitchen with an arched doorway separating the two. To the left of the front door was a short hallway that led to the bathroom and our bedrooms. Emery had the master bedroom since she lived here first, while mine was the smaller one she had originally been using for storage. The TV stand in the living room held all of Emery's cookbooks and binders of recipes. Emery had opted for all black furniture and minimal décor for most of the year. In a couple of weeks the place would be overflowing with fall décor.

He placed the pizza on the coffee table as I retrieved plates from the kitchen. "I hope you're okay with paper plates," I yelled over my shoulder. Emery would kill me if we used real plates for something that contained two of her big food allergies. I should have corrected Matt when he picked pizza. In the moment I had been too nervous to do anything other than be relieved he was making the decision so I didn't have to. We took cross contamination risks seriously enough that we opted to keep the house completely free of dairy, tomatoes, and avocados. He came up behind me and took them from my hand. I grabbed two bottles of water from the refrigerator and held them up to Matt silently asking if he was okay with the option.

Back in the living room we spread everything across the coffee table and sat on opposite ends of the couch. "Are you ready to talk?" he asked. He rubbed his hands against his thighs.

"I don't want the world," I said, my thoughts going back to what he had said in the classroom.

He nodded. "What do you want?" He shoved his hands in his pockets only to pull them right back out. I was tired of people asking me that question today.

I leaned forward placing my elbows on my knees. I remembered our first rule from our date. The stakes were higher now than they were then making the rule feel somehow even more important to stick too, though more difficult. "I don't know what I want. All I know is that when I met you things felt different than they ever did with anyone else. I feel so comfortable with you, like I've always known you. I'm so scared that you're going to turn out like everyone else." My eyes burned with tears that threatened to spill over. I didn't even know why I felt like crying.

Matt shifted from the couch to kneeling on the floor in front of me and ducked his head so his eyes could find mine. His hands rested on his thighs, fingers flexing like he didn't know what to do with them. "Let me show you that I'm not them. I'm not going anywhere, sweetheart. I meant what I said that night at the overlook." Sweetheart. The term brought me back to that day, the familiarity pulling me back to the safety I had felt with him.

This was different, I reminded myself. He was still a stranger. The safety I had felt that day was the product of the perfect situation we had created. We didn't have any of that now. Anything we did now would have real repercussions.

"You mean it now but what about in a few months? Or a few years? I meant what I said too." I sniffled and tried to hold back the tears. Why did I have to be such a crier? Happy, sad, angry, nervous, it didn't matter what the emotion was, they all made me cry. "I can't handle having my heart broken by you."

His fingers brushed through my hair pushing it away from my face, familiar sparks pricked my skin at his touch. "I know you're not going to believe anything I say. I could sit here trying to talk you into trusting me but there's nothing I can say that you probably haven't heard before. I want you to be comfortable. We don't have to be serious right now. Just tell me what you need and let me meet you there."

"I want to trust you, I'm just scared." I covered my face with my hands as the tears spilled over. I knew I was making everything more complicated than it was. I liked him and he liked me. It didn't get any more straightforward than that. It felt too easy, which is why it was all too much. "I don't want to be another person that drags you along making you wait so I can sort myself out."

"I'm scared too." The cushion next to me sank under his weight as he sat next to me. He pulled me against his chest and my body relaxed into him. "You needing time to figure things out isn't dragging me along. Just make sure you tell me when you figure things out, even if you think it's going to hurt me."

"Why are you scared?" I asked.

"Because talking to you, being around you, holding you feels so right. It feels like all it'll take is one wrong move and you'll slip through my fingers." He kept one arm wrapped tight around my back holding me against him and moved the other to stroke his hand through my hair. It did feel right, like his arms were meant to keep me safe. Things had never felt this easy before.

"I'm sorry I'm making it so complicated. None of it is your fault." I pressed my face into his shirt, trying to ignore the wet smudges of tears and mascara I would be leaving behind. His arms relaxed around me, feeling less like he was scared I would push him away.

"Please don't ever apologize for how you feel," he said against the top of my head. His voice was so soft, so gentle.

"But I'm making something that's not your problem into your problem."

"How you're feeling is not a problem. It's just a little something we need to work through."

I relaxed into him more, wrapping my arms around him, and let a silence settle over us.

"Riley, rule number one," he said after a few minutes.

"Are we still playing by the rules? I'm pretty sure we already broke the others," I joked.

He kissed the top of my head and stilled the hand in my hair. "All other rules are subject to change except for rule number one."

"I want to give this a chance, but it can't be serious yet. I think we should slow down a little bit. Everything before moved so fast," I said into his shirt.

He pulled back and lifted my chin, so I was looking up at him. His eyes were bright again, filled with the sunshine from before. "Whatever you need. Tell me what slowing down looks like." He brushed his thumbs over my face, wiping away the tears. "Does it look like just going back to phone communication only?"

I nodded a little and then switched to shaking my head instead. "Mostly, maybe. I really missed talking to you. We can still see each other in person but maybe no more marathon dates."

"I missed talking to you too. I think that sounds like a good plan."

"No talking about the future or anything like that. I just want to focus on the now."

He shifted again and took one of my hands in his. He shook it and then gave it a squeeze. "I agree to your terms."

I laughed and nuzzled my face back into his chest. "Do you have any terms I need to know about?"

His hands skated up and down my back and his face pressed back into the top of my head. "No running. If you get scared, you stay and talk about it. I'll give you space if you need it, and we'll come back together to talk about it later."

I leaned back again so I could look up at him. "Agreed. I feel so bad about how I left before."

"Don't feel bad. I knew you were skittish, and I pushed you too far that night." He pressed another kiss into my forehead. I felt like I was going to melt. "It's in the past. We're going to make the now better."

"Any other rules?" I asked him.

"No kissing or touching more than what we're doing right now until we're both sure of where this is going." His eyes studied mine. "It feels like it would cloud things."

I chewed on my bottom lip and weighed this against all my past experiences. Even while we were in the purgatory stage of me trying to decide how I felt things had always moved so fast physically. Sometimes faster than I had wanted but I had always been too scared to put the brakes on. "If I can't handle talking about the future, avoiding anything that could cloud things sounds like a good idea." As much as I wanted to kiss him, to know if everything would feel as magical as his simple touches did, it did make me feel safer knowing it was off the table.

A soft smile lifted his mouth. I touched a finger to one corner. Touching him felt so natural, like a language I was born knowing how to speak. He turned his face to kiss the tip of my finger. I let my fingers brush over the stubble on his face just like I had thought about doing during our date. "You're going to make it a really hard rule to keep," he muttered.

I blushed while clearing my throat. I leaned forward and opened the pizza. "So, how about that getting to know each other you mentioned?" I asked as I transferred a piece to a plate. I shifted away from Matt to fold my legs up on the couch placing some space between the two of us.

He returned to the other end of the couch giving me the space I needed without me having to ask. "What do you want to know?"

I picked the sausage off my slice trying to think through everything we hadn't covered during our marathon date over the summer. "On your profile you said your favorite hobby was learning new things. Why is that your favorite?"

His eyes watched my hands as I continued to pick at my slice. He shrugged and finally reached for the pizza box. "Whenever I start trying to learn how to do new things I always suck at it, I've never really been a natural at anything. When I get good at things I feel really accomplished. Or when there's something I don't know a lot about, it feels really satisfying to learn everything I can about it."

"What's your favorite thing you've ever learned?"

He lit up and tilted his head down to hide his face a little. "Playing instruments," he shrugged. "Probably just music in general." It was the first time he had ever looked shy with me. His eyes stayed focused on our food rather than lifting to look at me.

I tapped his leg with my foot. "You look cute when you get like that," I told him.

"Like what?"

"Excited." I wanted to touch his smile again, trace it with my fingers until the memory of it was imprinted in my skin. I wanted this look to be the one I saw when I closed my eyes, and needed it to erase the memory of him on the mountain watching me drive away.

"Why did we get the supreme pizza if you were going to pick the sausage off it? We could have gotten something else." He gestured to the small pile of sausage on my plate.

I laughed, struggling to cover my mouth full of pizza. "Because I like all the other topping on it. I do it so often I don't even think about it anymore." I pressed my foot against his leg again and left it there. "Don't change the subject. I want to hear more about music. You never told me what instruments you play."

He angled his body toward me more, pulling one leg up onto the couch hooking his foot under my ankle. One hand ghosted over my ankle and calf over top of my jeans, up and then down over and over again. He still touched me the same way I did him, like it was something we had been doing our whole lives. It was as natural as breathing. Again I wondered if kissing him would feel the same. I tried to focus on my pizza instead of his touch.

"I started with the trumpet in sixth grade. It was okay but I always wanted to learn everything else. I was always driving the teacher crazy asking if we could learn multiple instruments. In eighth grade he let me take on the French horn. During the summer I was able to talk my parents into hiring a tutor to teach me the saxophone." He paused to eat his pizza, his fingers gently tapping in patterns as his hand continued to skate over my leg. I had noticed how he did that during our date, sometimes he would hum under his breath while he did it.

I wondered if he even knew he did it.

"It's my favorite," he added in a whispered after thought.

"How many can you play now?" I picked up another slice of pizza and began picking off the sausage, keeping my eyes on him.

"All of the marching band instruments, some better than others. I had to learn them all so I could teach them." He paused the motion of his hand and squeezed my ankle before finally looking up at me.

"Why do you love it so much?"

His face lit up even more for a moment, then he dropped it again. "Music is just so powerful. Most instruments just use a few buttons or keys in all these different combinations paired with different mouth movements to create all these notes. Then those notes can be put together in so many combinations to create something so beautiful, something that is a universal language. It's crazy to think about." His whole face was so alive despite how cautious his voice was, and the tips of his ears turned red. The way he dipped his head to conceal his smile made me wonder if anyone had ever made him feel bad about the passion he had for music, for his job. His hand started moving over my leg again.

I reached for my phone and snapped a picture, needing to be able to remember this moment.

"What are you doing?" He asked it so gently, like he was genuinely curious, not upset.

"Need a contact picture for you," I mumbled. I saved it to his contact and turned my phone toward him as proof.

I took another bite of my pizza and he snapped a picture of me. He presented his phone to me to show that he had made it my contact photo. My hair formed a frizzy halo, most of it falling out of my clip and there was pizza sauce smeared on my chin, my mouth was wide open with pizza hovering right in front of it. My eyes looked tired, a little puffy from crying earlier, but bright from happiness. My skin was oily and red, almost all my makeup faded away.

I laughed. "Did you have to take such an unflattering picture?" I grabbed a napkin from the coffee table to take care of the sauce on my chin.

"You look beautiful."

I tossed the wadded-up napkin at his face. "I look like I've had a really long day."

"Still beautiful," he said leaning forward. How had we moved so close together again? His hand cupped my face.

The butterflies in my stomach bounced around. "Keep doing that and I'm not going to be able to stick to the rules," I warned him. I gulped as he moved his hand away. My fingers fluttered at my side wanting to grab his hand and bring it back.

"Do you play any instruments?" he asked me.

"No, I thought about it, but I could never focus enough to read music. All the lines blurred together."

"What were you like in school?" He asked.

"A teacher's pet. I was always hyper focused on my grades. I tutored a lot during the year and volunteered at a lot of after school activities for younger kids when I was in high school." I smiled remembering my first time sitting in the public library helping a second grader that was struggling with reading. She'd been so excited that I let her pick out her own books. She told me at the end of our time that day that I made her feel like she wasn't stupid for struggling so much. That was the day I knew I wanted to teach.

"What made you want to teach younger kids?"

"They're just so innocent. They have so much life ahead of them and it's so much fun getting to see the world through their eyes. I love how even the simplest things are magical to them." I could feel myself smiling and wondering if I looked as cute talking about this as Matt did when he talked about music.

"You really like kids," he said. He beamed at me. The butterflies in my stomach crashed into each other as a memory from the festival flashed into my mind. I didn't know if he remembered the way he had casually mentioned how he thought he would have kids by now.

"I know we said we weren't going to talk about the future, but there's something I need to ask you." I moved my plate to the coffee table and pulled my knees up to my chest trying to think of the best way to say this. Acting like I didn't remember him saying it felt like a safe approach, even if I hadn't forgotten a single second of that day. "Do you want kids? I kind of feel like that's something that more people should talk about early on." I stared at a worn spot on my jeans and rubbed my thumb against it while I waited for his answer.

It was probably too early to bring this up. I tried not to imagine what he was thinking about me bringing up a question like that. It wasn't a conversation I'd had to have with my exes, since it wasn't something I knew we needed to be concerned about. Now it was something I knew better about. A potential ticking time bomb that would be better disarmed now rather than waiting for it to blow up in our faces later.

"I do. I want a house full." He paused before adding, "I always really liked the idea of fostering and adopting more along with having biological kids," he said.

His answer started the butterflies up again. I took a deep breath and bit my lip. My thumb nail dug into the spot on my jeans. I tossed words around in my head, not knowing how to explain my concerns to him.

I had always known something was off about my body but didn't have a doctor listen to me until I was with my best friend's brother. He went through the journey of the diagnosis with me. My best friend had been there for it too. This was the first time I was ever in a situation where I had to tell someone.

"Me too," I said. "At least the fostering and adopting part. I, um," I paused to take another deep breath. "Biologicalkidsmightnothappenforme," I blurted out as quickly as I could.

His brows drew together, and his mouth turned down. He squeezed my lower legs. "I'm sorry, Riley, I didn't catch that."

"I don't know if I can have biological kids, at least not easily. I have this thing called PCOS. It's a chronic health condition that affects a lot of things about my body but the symptoms can make it really hard to get pregnant. Most people with it need some form of fertility treatment. It can be a really hard process and, to be honest, it's not something I want to go through. I would rather foster kids." There were a lot of factors that went into the reasons why it would be hard, but it was all more than I was willing to share with him right now. It was all hypothetical until the time came. So many things were still unknown, questions I wouldn't have answers for until I was at the point of trying. For now, my doctor had only been focused on getting my hormones and insulin resistance back to healthy levels. It was possible that fertility wouldn't be a struggle for me, that I was worried about it for nothing, but it felt better to be prepared for the worst.

His hands moved up my legs and tugged on my arms to pull me to him. He shifted so my legs were over his lap and my body was tucked into his side. His hand brushed over my shoulder. I watched his jaw work as he tried to think of what to say. It was too soon. I shouldn't have told him any of that. Now I had him worrying about something that might not be an issue.

"I'm okay. Most of the symptoms are just annoying and embarrassing most of the time but sometimes they interfere more with my day to day." I lifted my hand to my chin and wonder if he could feel the rough stubble that I was sure had to be starting by now when he touched my face earlier. I was lucky enough that I only had sparse hair on my chin and jawline, but it was still enough that I had to remove it every morning. "I have a really good doctor now and she's helped a lot with getting everything to the point of being more manageable but it's not something that has a cure."

It took a while to find a doctor that would take the time to listen to all my concerns instead of just blaming them on my weight. Emery and I had tried every crash diet out there over the course of our life, but the weight just kept packing on instead of melting off like all the ads promised. It turned out to be insulin resistance and imbalanced hormones caused by PCOS. Excessive workouts and restricting my food couldn't fix those. There was a lot of trial and error with medications to help my body get to a more balanced state. After a while I was able to come off all of them and transition to holistic methods instead, which I preferred.

Even with everything under control and some weight loss, I still carried extra weight, especially around my stomach, ass, and thighs. My stomach stuck out further than my boobs just enough to have people always asking if I was pregnant, which crushed my soul every time. The little bit of weight I had lost left behind loose skin covered in stretch marks.

"I'm sorry, Riley." He pulled me against him tighter and kissed the top of my head. Being held by this man was quickly becoming my favorite thing.

I shrugged my shoulders. "It's just a thing that I have to deal with," I said.

"I'm glad you felt safe enough to tell me. I'm here if you want to talk about it, but you don't have to if you don't want to." He took it as me feeling safe with him, not as me looking for any reason I could that this wouldn't work. Guilt settled in the pit of my stomach knowing that it had been just another possible excuse for me why we wouldn't work out.

I leaned my head into his shoulder and worked my thumb against the spot in my jeans again. "Like I said, some of it is...well it's a lot. I don't know if I want to talk about it anymore than that right now."

His hand moved to cup my face, and I ducked away from it, becoming more and more paranoid about my facial hair. I wondered if I should make a trip to the bathroom to touch things up. With my makeup being rubbed off the shadow of hair would be visible if it was there.

"There's not a lot of research about it, but there's some if you want to look into it." I winced as I thought about some of the things I saw when I first started learning about PCOS. Emery had been the one to mention it to me because she had also started the process of seeking her own diagnosis. We were so much alike, of course we would have the same chronic condition. "I don't think I'm ready to answer questions about it, so maybe –"

"Wait for you to be ready to bring it up?" He asked. He brushed his fingers through my hair. "You know I only want you to feel comfortable. I won't ask you to talk about anything you don't want to."

"And don't tell anyone? It's not something that I want a lot of people knowing."

I let him lift my chin until our eyes met. "Riley, you never have to worry about me telling anyone anything you trust me with."

I bit my lip and tried to look anywhere but at his face. It was so close. Every cell in my body was focused on how close he was. "Thank you," I said.

"I have ADHD," he blurted out. My brows knitted together, my brain jolting to follow the conversation. His ears turned red. "You shared something big about yourself, I just thought I should share something too." His whole body tensed, and he rubbed a hand over his jaw. "Sorry, I probably made things weird."

I wrapped my fingers around his wrist, pulling his hand away from his face as it inched toward covering his eyes. "You don't get to take credit for making things weird, that was all me." I threaded my fingers with his and pulled our hands to my lap. "Thank you for sharing something too."

Chapter 12

Matt

"S HIT," AN UNFAMILIAR VOICE whisper yelled. My eyes shot open to taking my surroundings. I was on a couch with a throw blanket tucked around me. My neck ached. The arm of the couch dug into my side. Riley's body curled against the other side of my body, her head resting against my chest and my cheek was pressed against the back of her head. My arm wrapped around her back was asleep. My other arm rested around her soft stomach holding her in place against me. Her hair tickled my face now that it was freed from its clip and draped around us. "Y'all could have at least gone to your room," the voice said. I closed my eyes, not ready to wake up and end today.

"Emery?" Riley asked. "What time is it?"

Emery laughed and Riley shifted to sit up. Her movement sent tingles down my arm as blood rushed back through it. I let my head follow until my face rested in the space between her shoulder and neck. "It feels later," Riley said, pulling away more.

I didn't want to know what time it was. Our time together in June hadn't been long enough and our time today felt like a blink of an eye. Her hand squeezed my arm that was around her waist. I pressed my eyes closed tighter.

"You're just getting old. Is he staying the night? You could have warned me."

I nuzzled my face against her neck taking in her warm floral scent, the thought of brushing my lips against her skin flashed through my mind. She squeezed my arm again. "Matt? We've been caught."

"We're all adults. If you want to have someone stay the night, it's fine. Just a little warning would have been nice." I opened one eye to see Emery's shadowy figure kick off her shoes and hang her keys on the hook by the door.

"Five more minutes," I said against Riley's neck. She felt perfect pressed against me like this. I couldn't remember how we ended up in this position. We spent all that time setting boundaries but somehow we had ended up here, smushed together and asleep, like they didn't exist at all.

Emery and Riley burst out laughing, forcing me to give up trying to pretend like I was still asleep. I pulled my arm from around her to rub my eyes. Without my arm holding her in place Riley scooted away until we were no longer touching.

"I think we fell asleep," I laughed. We were talking, shifting slowly closer and closer together as we did. It had been daylight outside last I remembered. Now the only light was the soft glow coming from the kitchen. It had been a long day for both of us and the longer we were together the more we'd relaxed around each other. My neck and shoulders ached. It was worth it.

Emery flipped the light on, and I threw a hand over my face. "Seriously, Ri, we've gone this long without me catching you red handed. I thought you were sneakier than this." Her lips trembled as she fought to keep a straight face before more laughter bubbled out of her. "I thought you guys were just going to talk."

"I should probably get going," I said. I felt around the couch until I located my phone between the cushion and armrest. "I'll, um, text you when I get home?" I asked Riley, making sure I wasn't overstepping. Even with the boundaries we had established I still wasn't sure what was okay. Falling asleep cuddling on her couch had probably been asking for trouble. Did she still want to give me a chance after that?

"Yeah, yeah, that's fine."

I kissed the top of her head and whispered in her ear, "Thank you for giving me a chance."

She opened her mouth like she to say something only to snap it closed. She gave me a nod and a smile. I wanted to say something else; I was sure she did too. Trying to say anything felt like too much of a risk, like if I opened my mouth all the wrong words would fall out.

Emery held the door open for me. "God, big sister, you really do suck at this," she said to Riley like I wasn't even there. The door slammed behind me, blocking out their conversation.

Chapter 13

Riley

I SET THE TIMER on my phone one more time and ran back to pose with my first day of school sign. This would have been so much easier if Emery hadn't left so early to start her route. A notification flashed across the top of my phone. My eyes registered Matt's name just as the phone snapped the picture. Swiping to view the photo showed that the notification had finally managed to put a genuine smile on my tired face. I had been trying so hard to get it just right that the frustration had been clear for the last several tries.

Matt

> Good luck today! Those kids are going to love you.

His message was followed by a selfie of him giving a thumbs up in his car. I could see his backpack and lunch box in his passenger seat. His hair looked like he'd already been running his hand through it this morning and a pair of dark tortoiseshell rectangle glasses were perched on his nose. I remembered seeing those glasses in one of the photos on his profile but he hadn't worn them around me yet. He wore a burgundy polo shirt with the Grassy Middle School logo on the chest. I typed out a quick reply.

Riley

> The hot nerdy teacher look looks good on you.

I sent him the photo I'd just taken. One hand had a white knuckle grip on the sign that said, *my first year teaching!*. Today's date and first grade were written underneath. My other hand held up one finger in front of my bright smile. My oversized tote bag pulled down one shoulder of my thin pencil patterned cardigan layered over a pale-yellow maxi dress. I looked so dorky but the smile on my face was so priceless I couldn't bring myself to try for a less dorky take. I was going to be late if I kept trying.

I scrolled back to Matt's photo and smiled.

The excitement for today kept me up almost all night. Matt had stayed up with me on the phone until sometime around midnight when he fell asleep leaving me listening to his soft breathing. That brought me back to the night last week that we had fallen asleep on the couch, which led to a spiral of increasingly panicked thoughts about what we were doing. My brain had finally let me fall asleep around 3 am only to be awoken by my alarm at 5:30.

> I think that's the first time you've called me hot.

> Better be careful, that might go to my head.

My cheeks heated as I stared at the quick message I'd sent without thinking. It wasn't that big of a deal, right? We had been clear that we were both interested in the other, of course it would be normal for me to call him hot. Except, it wasn't normal for me. It was a term that my brain applied to anyone so easily.

It didn't make sense the way that we had bonded so easily, that I had become so attached to him this quickly. The butterflies and electricity I had felt on our first date had been bizarre enough. None of this was normal for me.

I didn't just take forever to fall in love. Even while sharing our relationship history with each other I had been too scared to tell him, to tell anyone ever, the whole truth. For so long I thought that something was wrong with me. There was a reason I had been confused about how quickly I found myself attracted to Matt, a reason why I always felt like I didn't understand how others could be immediately attracted to a stranger. I took a deep breath, closing my eyes as I exhaled.

I had never talked to anyone about how I identified, hadn't even really put much thought into myself until my college roommate told me she wanted to come out. It had taken me years to find the labels that worked for me, and by then telling them to anyone had felt unnecessary. My relationship history had everyone assuming I was just bisexual, which while partially true never felt like it completely described me.

I wasn't walking around experiencing physical attraction to strangers. I didn't look at people and think about dating them just because I felt a spark with them. The spark came later, sometimes not even until after I was looking for it.

All my friends used to think I was lying when I told them I didn't have crushes when we were younger, when I didn't join in conversations about how hot boys were. It wasn't until I was an adult that I heard the term demisexual for the first time that I felt like I finally understood all the things I had been so confused about. Demisexuallity, like all other sexualities, is a spectrum that can be different for each person. It was dumb to feel embarrassed about, but the feeling always crept up when I even thought about trying to explain it to someone. Up until now my experience had always followed the same formula, but meeting Matt had thrown everything off. There was no doubt in my mind that the few days we spent texting before ever meeting helped to build the emotional bond that I needed, otherwise meeting him for the first time would have gone differently.

It still didn't make sense that the connection had formed so fast. I couldn't explain that part. My brain felt scrambled as my thoughts raced. This was such a stupid thing to be panicking over. I called him hot, so what? I was attracted to him enough to enjoy the way it felt when he touched me innocently, to think about kissing him.

I focused on remembering the way I felt when he touched me. It was nice, electric and comforting at the same time. He made me feel safe and heard. It didn't stir up any other thoughts. No pressure between my legs or desire to rip off his clothes. There was nothing past wanting to be around him and continuing with the physical contact we frequently shared. Realizing that was comforting, a reminder that who I thought I was hadn't just flown out the window because things were moving faster than I was used to.

This was so much easier when it was just going to be a one-time thing.

Gotcha. No more compliments.

Ugh, you look like such a nerd.

winky emoji

My hands shook as I reached for my thermos filled with an embarrassing amount of espresso shots and a touch of hazelnut creamer. I thought I was going to need every bit of this to get through the day, but talking to Matt gave me more of a zap of energy than caffeine ever could.

***

Matt

Have middle schoolers always been this mean?

Riley

I think they get worse every year.

Those kids are fearless. Consequences mean nothing to them. There's a reason I prefer elementary school age kids.

I don't think I got bullied this badly when I was in middle school.

For the record, I was a nerd. I was bullied A LOT.

I think we already established that you're still a nerd.

You can't let them see you get upset. If you don't give them a reaction, they get bored.

I think my mom told me that once.

It doesn't work. I wear my heart on my sleeve.

Do I need to come defend your honor? We made pirate swords during craft time. We could ride to your rescue after recess.

My hero! *swoon*

Chapter 14

Riley

"MATT, OH MY GOD, I'm so sorry." I yelled out of my open window while pulling into the driveway. He leaned against his car, legs stretched out in front of him and crossed at the ankles, a bouquet of flowers in his hands.

He smiled and pushed his glasses up with the back of his hand as he approached my door. I scrambled to unbuckle my seat belt, shut off the car, and open the door. The lack of sleep had caught up to me, leaving me shaky as I ran on nothing but caffeine and the adrenaline of the first day.

I was going to sleep so hard tonight.

I'd had after school care today on top of it being the first day of school and the parents of the last child had been running late. Then I ended up being caught in the worst of rush hour traffic on my way home.

He pulled my car door open and leaned down, holding out a hand for me. I let him help me out of my car only to be wrapped in a hug. My body melted into his, a wave of peace washing over me. We hadn't seen each other in person since the district meeting, both of us doing our best to take this slow. We had agreed to celebrate the first day of school together tonight, something I had been looking forward to every day since I last saw him. I didn't realize how much I had missed his touch.

I thought back to this morning, examining every detail of the way I felt. It was still the same. Safe, peaceful, nice. No burning desire.

"Hi," he said against the top of my head.

I pulled back so I could look at him. "Hi."

He cupped my cheek and rubbed his thumb against the corner of my mouth. I smiled into his touch, earning a smile from him that showed all his teeth. We stood there staring into each other's eyes wrapped up in the moment. I wondered if he missed me as much as I missed him. Being back in the classroom today meant we were limited on how much we were able to respond to messages. The few minutes we had been able to spare had left me with butterflies for the rest of the day.

He gave me another squeeze and stepped back presenting the bouquet of yellow flowers. "I realized I never asked you what kind of flowers you like, but I saw these and they made me think of you."

I took them from his hand, letting my fingers linger against his. "They're beautiful. Honestly, I don't really care what kind they are. I like all flowers." Like was understating it, I loved flowers. I love being gifted them. I loved buying them for myself. I loved looking at the wildflowers that grew all over our area. I couldn't think of a time anyone had given them to me just because.

He walked toward the passenger side of my car and retrieved my tote bag and then turned back to pull two grocery bags from his car. "I thought we could try out a recipe I found. You were up so late last night I didn't know if you would feel up to going out tonight."

I ran my eyes over him. His hair was messy and falling over his forehead, a mix of flat and puffy from him running his hands through it all day. He still wore his school polo tucked into a pair of grey trousers, meaning he went straight from school to the grocery store and then here. I had kept him up late last night but here he was thinking about me.

I blushed and stepped closer to him so I could kiss his cheek. The brush of my lips against his stubble covered skin made my cheeks blaze harder. "You better be careful; you're going to spoil me."

He pressed a finger to the bridge of his glasses and pushed them up. "I seem to recall you calling me hot and then offering to defend my honor today," he laughed and started toward the front door. "I think you're the one doing the spoiling."

I rolled my eyes as I followed him. I hadn't stopped thinking about how I called him hot at all today. The word kept turning itself over and over in my head. So no, I didn't mean the word hot in the context that he was so attractive I felt this burning desire to have sex with him. It was more of a fact that I liked the way he looked, simple as that. "I was just stating a fact."

He stepped behind me giving me room to unlock the door. "Is it the glasses? I didn't know you would be this into them." His breath felt hot against the back of my neck and ear. My fingers fumbled the key as the thought of him leaning forward just a little more to brush his lips against my skin crossed my mind. Still no burning desire.

This would all be so much easier if I felt that desire, right?

Calm down, Riley. This is only the third time you've seen this man in person. We're taking things slow, stop with all the pressure.

I shrugged my shoulders. Oddly, glasses were the one thing all my exes had in common. I didn't realize I had a type until that moment. "Why are they just now making an appearance?" I asked once I was able to push open the door.

"I ran out of contacts over the weekend and still need to find an optometrist around here." He sat the grocery bags on the counter, his free hand now pushing up his glasses again. "Had to break out the back up glasses in the meantime."

My shoulder rested against the kitchen doorway and I watched as he pulled ingredients from the bags.

"Riley," he said without looking up from the grocery bags. His head turned to me after a beat of silence. "You're too far away."

I joined him at the counter and bumped my hip against his. "Is this better?" I tucked my hair behind my ears as I looked over the ingredients he had laid out. I remembered the flowers were still in my hand and turned to grab the empty vase from the table. "I should probably change before we start cooking."

The heat of Matt's gaze followed as I moved around the kitchen adding water to the vase with the flowers and returning it to the table. His hand caught my wrist, my dress fluttered against my legs as he spun me back around and pulled me tight against him. My eyes met his, registering how blown out his pupils were. His mouth tensed and his throat worked in a swallow.

"What?" I asked.

He shook his head. "I don't think I can answer that question."

I raised my eyebrows. "Rule number one."

" Mhmm, but it breaks other rules."

I swallowed hard, redirecting my eyes to the floor as my heart started to race. I wanted to ask what rule his thoughts were breaking, but my brain felt full of static. More information might make it worse.

"I'm going to go change, okay?" I told him with a shaky voice as I kept my eyes on the floor.

He stepped back, loosening his grip on my wrist but not letting go. "Yeah, okay. I have a change of clothes in my car. I'm going to grab those." He squeezed my wrist. "You look so pretty in that dress," he said in a lowered voice as his hand slipped away.

My thoughts swirled making my chest tighten.

He said I looked pretty. He looked like he wanted to kiss me. He brought me flowers. He was thinking about breaking the rules. It was clear that Matt was light years ahead of where I was in our relationship. He had no idea that I was holding back because it terrified me that there wasn't anything to hold back, not because I just wasn't there yet.

He wanted to cook dinner together, something about coming home from work and doing something so simple felt so domestic. He was thinking about breaking the rules. Which rule?

What would it be like to come home to that smile every day, cook dinner with him every day? Would he always bring me flowers just because?

I made a mental note to ask him what he was thinking another time. Another time when we were past all these rules. That made my chest tighten more. I sat on my bed forcing myself to take a few deep breaths until the bands closing around my chest loosened.

I heard the front door open and close followed by the bathroom door closing. I took a few more deep breaths as I changed into leggings and an oversized t-shirt.

"So, chef, what are we making?" I asked once we both returned to the kitchen.

Matt had changed into a black T-shirt and jeans. He held up his phone to show me a recipe. I recognized the blog it was from; it was one of my favorites for PCOS friendly recipes. One of the hardest life changes I had made since my diagnosis was adjusting my diet. I had been so used to focusing on the typical diet trends that I had to completely relearn what healthy really meant, and the ways different foods affected my body.

"Pecan crusted salmon," I read aloud. "I haven't tried that one yet. Emery hates fish so she refuses to let me cook with it."

While I have always been willing to try anything, Emery was always a picky eater. She was also the only one of the three of us with food allergies, which made everything worse growing up.

"Oh, I brought enough that we could share with her."

I tapped my fingers against the sides of my thighs. My hands itched to reach for him, but I still felt on edge from his earlier comment. Not only had he thought of me, but he also thought of Emery. He must have remembered when I told him that we usually alternated nights cooking dinner. "I think she had other plans tonight."

He narrowed his eyes toward me. "You okay?"

"Yeah," I nodded a little too hard. I pulled the scrunchie on my wrist off and busied my hands with tying back my hair.

"I freaked you out, didn't I?" He laid his phone down on the counter but didn't move any closer to me.

I turned toward the cabinet with the cutting board and pans to pull out what we would need. The weight of his gaze pressed down on me. "A little bit. I think I just need a few minutes to calm down." My skin buzzed and my chest tightened again.

He moved closer to me. I stepped back, the counter digging into my hip. Touching him right now didn't seem like a good idea, not while I wrestled with confusion from the way his touch made me feel. I should tell him that I'm demi. No, that felt more intimidating than telling him about my PCOS. Was it because telling him wouldn't be out of looking for another excuse for things to not work between us? Yeah, that was it. The need to tell I was demi came from wanting to tell him how confused I felt about how quickly I was developing feelings for him. Sure, he made me feel safe and heard, but that was more vulnerability than I was ready for.

"Sorry, um," I rubbed a hand over my face. "Can we just cook without any physical contact for a few minutes?" The bands around my chest tightened more. I pulled out my phone to find the recipe he had shown me so I could avoid looking at him.

"Yeah, that's fine. Whatever you need." There was an edge to his voice. Anger? Hurt? I wasn't sure. It amazed me how it could feel like we had known each other our whole lives but at the same time we were strangers, still learning how to read each other.

"I just feel a little overwhelmed. It's not that I don't like when you touch me, because I really like it." A nervous laugh escaped as I tried to find the right words. "Sometimes touch calms me down when I'm panicking, but sometimes it just makes me feel claustrophobic."

He blinked at me like he couldn't make sense of what I was saying. I couldn't even make sense of what I was saying. All I knew was that if I let him touch me right that second, I was going to melt and give in only to spiral more because of it.

My thoughts spiraled back to thinking about everyday being like this. I knew if I gave in to letting his touch calm me, the thought of taking that leap would stop feeling so enormous. But once his touch was gone it would loom over me again.

Not yet, I'm not ready, I told myself.

"I'm sorry, I know it doesn't make sense." My scalp felt tight. I pulled the scrunchie from my hair and gathered it back up into a loser ponytail.

"What did I say about apologizing for how you feel?" He gave me a gentle smile. He pressed the buttons to set the oven temp to preheat.

"You can tell me I don't have to all you want. It doesn't mean that I'm not going to. It's frustrating enough for me having to deal with my confusing brain, so I know it has to be frustrating for you." I pounded the bag of pecans with a rolling pin to crush them up. "Can we change the subject?"

He moved to the sink to wash his hands. "Sure. I want to hear all about your first day of teaching, Miss Harrison. Start with why you let a group of six-year-olds have pirate swords."

I laughed and told him about how the swords we made were related to the book we read during story time. The whole day was pirate themed as a way to get them all excited to be back at school. We used goldfish during math time, and I gave them each a gold coin for behaving during story time. We did ice breakers sharing what they did over the summer and chose pirate names. I was more grateful than I expected to be for the breaks PE, lunch, and recess gave me. Keeping twenty kids entertained and ready to learn was harder than I thought it would be.

Matt told me that he started the sixth grade band classes with a test to see what they knew about music, only to find that the majority of them knew nothing. He knew he would have to spend the first couple of weeks teaching them how to read music and about each of the instruments but didn't realize how arduous the task would be. He gave the seventh and eighth graders benchmark tests to see where they were starting the year at. He knew there would be a few that didn't pick up their instruments during the summer, but he wasn't expecting it to be almost all of them. The amount of catching up he would need to do with all of them felt overwhelming. The eighth graders would be spending a day in October touring all the feeder elementary schools, something they did every year as a way to get the kids interested in joining the band once they were old enough, and they were already behind on being ready for that.

"I forgot how many kids take band class just because they have to choose between it or chorus," he told me. It was a requirement our district had always had for middle schoolers to encourage the fine arts.

Less than half would choose to continue on once they reached high school.

"If anyone can turn them into band nerds, it's you," I offered as encouragement.

He shook his head as he plated the food. "What makes you so sure of that?"

"The way you talk about it." I smiled as I remembered the excitement and passion that had been all over his face when he first told me about why he taught it. "Middle schoolers may be cruel and act like they don't like things, but they pick up on which teachers are genuine."

He groaned. "Riley, they made fun of everything about me."

I pushed the hair hanging over his forehead back. The tension in my body had loosened while we cooked and shared about our day. At some point we had slipped back into our casual touches without me thinking about it. "It's just because you're new. They're going to test you just like you test them. They'll warm up to you."

He pushed his glasses up. "I think I failed today. I tried to act like they weren't bothering me, but I know I was beet red all of class. I kept struggling to keep them focused and forgetting what I was trying to tell them." He lifted the plates and carried them to the table. "This is a lot harder than I thought it was going to be. I was so much better at being an assistant director."

I pulled him into a hug, squeezing as hard as I could. "It's a difficult age group, but it'll get easier. You're going to be their favorite teacher by Christmas break."

***

Emery came home to a cleaned kitchen and us on the couch with some of his teaching materials spread across the coffee table. I had convinced him to teach me to read music while I pretended to be a bratty preteen constantly interrupting him.

"It smells like fish," she said, wrinkling her nose and walking to the kitchen.

I looked over to the candle I had lit to cover the smell to make sure it still burned. The only noticeable smells in the room to me were the vanilla candle and Matt's cologne. "There is no way you can smell it; we scrubbed everything down three times. Salmon doesn't even have that strong of a smell."

Matt gathered his things up. "You missed out. We were going to save you some, but it was so good we decided to split your portion."

Emery stood in the doorway with her arms crossed. "Don't forget I'm on your team, if you keep breaking the no fish rule I might change my mind."

Matt laughed and pulled his backpack onto his shoulder. I followed him to the door for a quick hug. "Text me when you get home," I told him.

"I will," he replied with a kiss to my forehead.

"What is going on with you two?" Emery asked after I closed the door behind Matt.

I shrugged. "We're still figuring it out."

"What did you guys cook tonight?"

"That salmon recipe I've been telling you I want to try. He surprised me with it. I didn't even tell him about it."

"What I'm hearing is he researched recipes based on something you shared about yourself – since I know you showed me where that recipe was from - and came over here to cook dinner with you after you both had a long first day of school. The chemistry between the two of you is so strong I'm sure people a mile away could feel it. This place reeks of it." She shook her head as she sat down on the couch, then patted the spot next to her for me to sit down. "I can't figure out why he didn't kiss you when he left. Is it because I'm here? I could have –"

"No, that's not why," I cut her off. "We haven't kissed yet."

She laughed. "That's a joke, right? You two maintain constant physical contact like you've been together for years, but you haven't kissed?"

My back pressed into the armrest as I pulled my knees up to my chest. "We were going to kiss on our first date, but then he stopped and said it wasn't a good idea since we'd probably never see each other again. Then last week when we talked things over, we decided that maybe it would be best to wait until we knew where things were going with us."

Emery stared at me.

"What?"

"What happened before he changed his mind?" She asked.

"I joked about how I had never kissed anyone until after they confessed their love for me. We were flirting back and forth, and he said something about if we kissed, he wouldn't be able to stop."

"Is that true, that you never kissed anyone other than your exes and not until after they confessed their love for you?" She drew her eyebrows together like the information didn't make any sense to her.

I nodded and pulled my knees tighter against me.

"What about other things?" Emery and I discussed a lot about our lives, but sex was a topic we normally avoided.

"Things usually progressed pretty fast after their love confessions, even when they were still waiting on me to decide what I wanted."

Her eyes narrowed and she rubbed a hand over her face. "Did you want things to progress that fast physically?"

I shrugged. "I didn't not want it. I mean, I wanted it because they wanted it. But I always enjoyed things more after I figured out my feelings." Truly, I hadn't really wanted to, but went along with it because I didn't want to upset them. I may not have been to the point of feeling that attraction to them yet but it had never stopped me from going along with things. Sure, it had hindered my enjoyment of the experience. Often I struggled to orgasm until I got to the point where our bond was strong enough to trigger my desire. But once the switch flipped my sex drive would go from nonexistent to always high, the change usually bringing up questions I couldn't answer. I didn't know how to explain it to them without making them feel bad.

I stared at Emery's shocked face, eyes wide and mouth tight. Even though I hadn't been ready to tell Matt about it earlier, thinking about this so much today had me wanting to tell someone. Emery seemed like a good start. This conversation seemed like a perfect opening to admit it. So what if she thought it was weird? It's not something that her opinion on really mattered. "I'm demisexual," I confessed. It wasn't just the first time I had told anyone; it was the first time I had ever said the words out loud. It felt like a weight lifted off my shoulders to finally say.

Emery slapped a palm on her forehead. "Oh shit." Her face tensed as I watched the wheels turning behind her eyes.

"I always felt like something was wrong with me because I didn't experience the same things around dating that you and all my friends did growing up."

Emery took her time processing the information, nodding slowly as she did. "I feel so stupid," she finally said. "I've been pushing you into this and not even thinking about any of that. I'm so sorry, Riley."

I stretched out my legs and tapped hers with my foot. "It's okay, you didn't know. You weren't wrong that there's something there between me and Matt."

Emery smiled and wiggled her eyebrows. "Does that mean that you want to kiss him and all that?"

"I definitely want to kiss him, but I don't know about everything else." I pulled a throw blanket off the top of the couch and draped it over myself. "I think I may want to, but maybe not yet. I feel so much more comfortable and connected to him than I ever did with my exes, but it's all so fast."

"Sometimes things just click and happen fast. It doesn't have to take years to build."

I pulled my knees back up to my chest and pinched the throw between my fingers, rubbing them over the seam on the edge. Again I thought back to this morning when I called Matt hot. It had just sort of slipped out without me even thinking about it. In the past I had maybe used the word hot to describe any of my exes less than five times, and all those times had been prompted. I smiled to myself. Not only had it been so easy, but it had made me feel happy to say it, at least until I thought about it more and then freaked out.

A throw pillow smacked into me. "Hey!" I yelled.

"You are so lovesick already," Emery said.

I threw the pillow back at her. "No, I'm not."

"Do you remember the first time Milo told us about Jenna? You have the same look on your face that he did."

This was all happening too fast. Within just a few days Matt was fitting into my life like he had always been here, making me feel things that have always taken years to build with anyone else. It made me feel like I had been wrong for all those years about my own identity.

It shouldn't be this fast. It shouldn't be this easy.

For the first time since that date back in June I started to think harder about everything Matt had said about his ex. He thought he was going to marry her; they had been together for ten years and he thought he had already found his happily ever after. I was the first person he'd try to date since her. He said he was all in with me, that he would be patient for as long as I needed. What if it's all just him wanting to get married, not about how he feels about me?

"I'm right, and you know it. I'm placing a bet now that you'll be engaged in less than a year," Emery stated.

Tears started to sting my eyes. When it was just the two of us together things felt so real, so simple. There was nothing to question. Now, with the smell of him lingering on my clothes and my body craving to have his touch back, it all felt too good to be true.

"Riley, talk to me," Emery's voice broke through my thoughts.

"You don't think it's all too fast? It feels too fast." I swiped the back of my hand under my eyes to catch the tears that were falling. With a sniffle and a deep breath, I launched into telling her everything I knew of Matt's past then followed up with a word vomit of all my worries. Emery stood quietly from the couch and disappeared into the kitchen. A cabinet opened and I heard pots clank together, the sound of the refrigerator opening followed. I sighed and paused mid sentence while I waited for her. There was a thud that sounded like her moving the Kitchen Aid mixer to the counter.

My phone lit up with a message.

Matt

Thank you for letting me come over today.

Riley

> Thank you for dinner. Cooking together was nice,

> I enjoyed it too. Maybe it's something we can do again?

> I would like that. I'm going to hang out with my sister for a little while. Can I call you later? I promise I won't keep you up so late tonight.

My phone was pulled from my hand and the throw blanket yanked off me. Emery tugged me off the couch. "Come help me," she pleaded.

"What are we doing?" I asked.

She blinked at me and let out an exaggerated sigh. "We're making cookies. You have big feelings we need to work through." She shifted her hands to my shoulders and shook me. "And we still need to celebrate your first day as a teacher!"

Chapter 15

Matt

September

Matt

Do you have any plans for Labor day?

Riley

What do you have in mind?

Go on a hike with me?

There's a waterfall I want to show you.

I promise it's an easy hike. I went there a few times over the summer. We can pack a picnic. It looks like it'll even be warm enough to swim.

Are you going to get us lost?

I promise I won't. I've been enough times I think I've got it down.

I only get lost on new trails sometimes.

> Only sometimes?

I'd never take you somewhere I might get us lost.

Trust me?

I'll keep you safe.

> Okay. BUT if you do get us lost, I'm never letting you live it down.

Deal.

I opened the front door of Riley's house to see her sitting on the floor in front of the couch, Emery on the couch behind her braiding her hair. Riley's eyes lifted to mine, her face lighting up as she did. I felt my own face light up, my mouth widening into a bright smile that only happened when I saw her. Her eyes dropped to the small bouquet of daisies in my hand, then raked over my athletic tank top and swim trunks.

Emery pulled Riley's harder than necessary as she braided, eliciting a sharp grunt from Riley. "You're going to have to stop bringing so many flowers. You're not even giving them time to die before you bring more. We're running out of places to put them," she said to me.

I shifted my weight from one foot to the other, my empty hand dropping to tap lightly against my thigh. Riley smacked Emery's knee and she responded with another rough tug. "Don't listen to her," Riley told me. I knew she had a point, they were running out of surfaces in their little house. There were flowers on the kitchen table, kitchen counter, coffee table, Riley's nightstand, and even the bathroom. Riley telling me she liked flowers that day, the look on her face each time I brought her some, had unlocked something inside me. I was addicted to seeing that look, to doing anything that would make her happy. I had even made sure I had fresh flowers for her the one time she had been to my apartment. The look on Riley's face right now told me I could cover every inch of this house in flowers, and she would still be happy to receive more.

"At least start bringing vases with them. We had to resort to using cups." Emery wrapped a hair tie around the end of the braid.

I rushed to Riley, putting out a hand to pull her up. It felt like the longest we had been in a room together without touching each other. I knew that wasn't true, but it still felt like it. Anytime we were together our bodies were like magnets drawn to each other for any contact we could get. "I can do that," I said to Emery.

She rolled her eyes. "Please don't, I'm just messing with you." She stood and went to her room.

"Hi," Riley said as I pulled her into me for a hug. Her soft body relaxed into me the way she did each time I hugged her. I was addicted to that feeling too. She smelled different almost every time I saw her, like she wore different perfumes or maybe used different body wash. Today she smelled like peaches, just like she did on our first date. "Thank you for the flowers," she whispered.

"You look so beautiful." I kissed the top of her head and pulled back to look at her. She wore workout shorts that hit right above her knees and a long tank top, the straps of a swimsuit peeking out. It was the first time I had ever seen her without makeup, and she couldn't hide her blush as I looked at her. The baby hairs around her face were frizzy, forming a soft halo. I smoothed my fingers over them. Her eyes dropped like they always did when I called her beautiful.

She pulled her bottom lip between her teeth and chewed it, her most obvious tell when she was nervous. Her eyes locked on my shoulder, her fingers coming up to trace the series of music notes that started at the top couple inches of my bicep wrapping around and then trailed up to my shoulder where they disappeared under my shirt. "You have a tattoo," she whispered.

"Yeah...um...I...um." I cleared my throat while I watched her fingers. I wanted her to keep following the trail under my shirt, to feel her touch everywhere. I pushed the thought out of my mind, these swim trunks weren't going to hide anything.

She brushed the top of my tank top where the notes disappeared. "How far does it go?"

My face warmed and I cleared my throat again. "You'll see later."

She raised an eyebrow at me.

"When we're swimming," I added.

She smiled softly, her eyes flashing briefly with panic as she took the flowers from my hand, turning her back toward me as she said, "I have two." She added the flowers to the cup on the coffee table. Emery had said she was kidding about the lack of vases, but I had been around her enough to know that wasn't true. I made a mental note to pick a few up after school tomorrow. "You can see them later," she said. "When we're swimming," she added with a wink.

My brain sputtered, all thoughts of vases going poof. "You're going to kill me," I muttered.

***

I spent days researching this trail, making sure I understood the map so I wouldn't get us lost. I had hiked this trail a couple times during this past summer. I knew where we were going.

All my prep work didn't make a difference. I forgot the name of the trail we were on and followed the wrong sign when we came to a crossing point. My confusion may have involved a large dog that was hiking with its family. It was wearing a hat and a little backpack. How could I not get distracted by that? We wandered down the wrong trail for half a mile before the trail brought us to a steep incline that I didn't remember from my previous trips.

"I can't believe you got us lost just because you wanted to pet a dog," Riley said once we reached the crossing to return to the correct trail. Her tone was light and soft, but her words still sent a jolt of embarrassment through me.

"Tell me he wasn't cute. He even had his own backpack," I joked. I poked my bottom lip out at her.

"I'm not saying he wasn't cute."

I shrugged. "I don't know what point you're trying to make." I tried to keep how stupid I felt out of my voice, off my face. If I failed, she didn't let on.

She fell into step behind me as I led us down the trail, trying to keep my face hidden from her. "Just that you got us lost because of a dog."

"He was such a good boy." I stuck my hand behind my back needing to touch her. I opened and closed it a few times, beckoning for her to take it.

"Remember how I said I wasn't going to let you live it down if you got us lost?" She hung back a couple steps.

I laughed. She had said that in our messages. There was something about being teased by her that made me feel less like she was trying to embarrass me, and more like she was letting me know it was okay to have fun together. "I am okay with my fate. He was the goodest boy I've ever had the honor of petting." I glanced over my shoulder as I opened and closed my hand again. She still didn't close the distance between us. I stopped and turned around to face her. "I'll make it up to you."

She laughed and finally placed her hand in mine. "If you make it up to me, I won't get to bug you about it forever. I fully intend this to be the thing I bring up to annoy you for years."

For years. That was the first time she had given me any clue that she saw this lasting. It was small, and I wasn't sure if she even knew she had let it slip, but from her it felt like a giant leap. She might as well have told me she wanted to marry me. I smiled as I tugged on her hand until she collided with my chest. "Promise?"

Her whole face turned red as she pressed it against me. I could feel her heart pounding against me. Her shoulders tensed as she took a deep breath. She must have realized what she said. She was barreling straight toward another panic attack.

"Can I ask you a question?" I pressed a kiss into the top of her head, my arms tightening around her silently begging her not to run.

"I, uh, I didn't mean to," She started to say.

I kissed her forehead. "Why do you smell different every time I see you?"

She laughed so hard that she choked. I rubbed small circles on her back as she worked to catch her breath.

"Sorry, that was a weird question." I watched her laugh, tried to focus on that, but all I could think about was how we had been tip-toeing with the boundaries we had set. I wanted to push her to blow right through it, but I would do anything to make sure she didn't run away this time. It had been the only thing I could think of to change the conversation.

More laughter poured from her as she bent over and rested her hands on her knees. "I don't smell different every single time," she managed to say.

"Not every time, but most of the time."

She wiped the corners of her eyes with the back of her hand and straightened. "I like perfume. Most people have one, maybe two, that they wear all the time. I like to wear different ones depending on my mood, what I'm doing, and the time of year." She smiled at me then reached for my hand, squeezing it as she pulled me to keep walking. My jaw loosened and my shoulders relaxed as I let go of the worry.

"The one you're wearing today, is that the one you wore on our first date?"

She nodded. "It's my favorite for summer and outdoors when it's warm." Her head was down watching her feet as she stepped along the well-worn trail. "This is the first time I've worn it since that day."

"Why?"

"Because every time I thought about wearing it all I could think about was you." She paused. I couldn't see her face but I knew she was chewing that bottom lip again. "It made me sad," she added a few minutes later.

I picked up my pace until I was beside her and bumped my shoulder against hers. "Why did you wear it today?"

She shrugged. "It just felt right."

We walked in silence until the distant sound of rushing water reached us. I picked up the pace to an almost run, pulling her along behind me. We rounded a bend, and the falls came into view. It was small but still took my breath away every time. There was a cool breeze blowing off it that tickled my warm skin. "Wow," Riley said.

"Come on, let's swim first. I want to cool off before we eat." The predicted high for today was in the low nineties and with the sun beaming down on us for most of the hike I currently couldn't even think about eating anything. I led the way across a series of large rocks off the side of the trail until we reached a large flat one perfect for spreading out a picnic. I dropped the cooler backpack I had been carrying at our feet so I could sit down to pull off my shoes and socks. My back was to Riley as I pulled off my shirt revealing the music notes that trailed up the back off my right shoulder and then down the top of my back where they disappeared just below my left armpit. There was another trail that started on my right side close to the midpoint of my ribs and led to my lower rib cage on the left side. I slid into the water, which was only waist deep, then turned to face her so she could see how the notes trailed across my chest, ribs, and abdomen. I spun around giving her the opportunity to put the pieces together. I pushed away the self-conscious thoughts about my body that were at the edge of mind. I had a strong body from all the different physical activities I had hyper fixated on over the summer, but I also had a soft stomach that folded slightly over my waistband and the layer of fat that hid the definition of my muscles.

Riley sat on the rock to pull off her shoes. I moved in the water until I was in front of her, planting my hands on either side of her against the rock. She reached out to trace the notes on my shoulder with her fingers again, following the trail further than she had been able to earlier. Her brows were knit together in concentration.

"Tell me what that look means," I said.

She slid her bare feet into the water and moved her fingers across the trail of notes on my chest. "What look?"

"Do you think it's stupid?" I ducked my head to watch her hand. "Liz thought it was stupid." When it started on my arm and shoulder, she hadn't said anything, but as I had added to it over the years, she had started letting me know what she thought about it.

Riley's brow knit together harder, making me realize I had never called Liz by anything other than my ex in front of her. "My ex," I said, answering the unasked question.

"It is very you," she told me, letting her fingers follow the trail down across my ribs. "I think she didn't know what she was talking about."

I caught her hand and brought it to my mouth where I planted a kiss on each fingertip. I wanted to lean forward and catch her red bottom lip between my teeth. One day I would get to, but not until she was ready. "Are you going to show me yours?"

Riley swallowed hard and goosebumps sprouted over her exposed skin. She took her time easing the hem of her shirt up like she was nervous.

"Are you teasing me?" I asked.

She shook her head and then dropped her hands away from the hem of her shirt. She twisted her fingers together in her lap, her eyes fixating on her hands. I cupped her cheek with my hand, almost urging her to look at me, but opted instead to dip my head to meet her eyes. "Talk to me," I coaxed gently.

"I'm not exactly confident in my body." She leaned into my hand.

I lifted my other hand to smooth down the growing halo of hair around her face. "I promise you that no matter what you look like, I'm still going to think you're beautiful. Nothing is going to change that." Her eyes darted away from mine. "Sweetheart, I'm self-conscious about how I look too," I admitted.

"You're just saying that."

"Are you calling me a liar?"

She shook her head as she closed her eyes. Her hands wrapped around each of my wrists and she moved my hands to the hem of her tank top. I wanted to yank it over her head, but not here and not now. Not until she trusted me enough to watch me.

"You don't have to swim if you don't want to. Or, if you want, you can swim with this still on. I'm just happy you're here with me," I told her, twisting the fabric between my fingers.

She lifted her arms up, her eyes still closed and nodded for me to lift up. I reached for her hands, pulling them back down so we both held the hem. "Do you trust me?" I asked her. Her eyes popped up, a mix of emotions flashing across them. "I want to see you, Riley, I really fucking do, but not if it makes you uncomfortable. We're not doing anything you don't 100% want to do." I dropped my hands to her full thighs, squeezing them three times before I pulled my hands away.

She closed her eyes again, but this time she pulled her tank top over her head, tossing it on top of where mine lay on the rock. Her swimsuit was bright yellow, a one piece with cutouts on her ribs. There was a tattoo of two flowers tied together with a bow on her left side.

"You have flowers on your ribs," I said, brushing my fingers over the lines the same way she had done to me. Of course she would have flowers. With how much she loved them I was surprised she wasn't covered in them. Goosebumps bloomed across her skin under my fingers. Her face brightened with a smile as she opened her eyes.

"It's mine and Emery's birth month flowers. I lost a bet, and she made me get a matching tattoo with her," She explained.

I chuckled lightly, letting my eyes linger over her exposed skin as I lifted them to meet her eyes. I wanted to tell her how beautiful she looked, but she still looked so nervous I thought it might be better to skip putting any attention on her body. "What was the bet?"

"That my dad wouldn't happy cry the first time my brother brought Jenna and Aaron over to meet us all. She had been asking me to get matching tattoos for years. She showed me this design the day that Milo had asked all to meet at my parents' house because he had something to tell us. She knew I wouldn't be able to say no to this one, but I still wanted to give her a hard time over it. Our dad is a crier so I picked a bet that I knew I would lose."

She rested her hand over where mine covered the tattoo, smiling softly at the memory. "My dad is one of those people that never meets a stranger," she said with a dreamy look on her face. She paused as she smiled at our hands, stroking her thumb over the back of mine. "My dad would like you," she added in a whisper.

"I can't wait to meet your family," I told her, flipping my hand over so I could weave our fingers together.

Her forehead scrunched and she started to blink rapidly. Between blinks I noticed her eyes growing red. "Not yet," she breathed out.

"When you're ready." I gave her hand a reassuring squeeze before I pulled away from her. I let my eyes roam over her body again, not bothering to hide it, searching for the second tattoo. "I thought you said there were two tattoos," I said with a raised brow when I couldn't see another one.

She stood up on the rock and my hands shot forward to steady her without thinking. She tugged her shorts down her legs. I helped her step out of them before running my hands over the curves of her hips and thighs, flicking my eyes up to her to make sure it was okay. She gave me a subtle nod. My eyes dropped back down to find the line art of a bus on her left thigh with the outlines of Ms. Frizzle and Liz visible in the driver's seat.

"Is that the magic school bus?"

She threw her head back as she laughed. "Ms. Frizzle was my idol as a kid. I got it in college."

I lifted my hand up to her hips and urged her to join me in the water. I could spend forever staring at her, taking in the sight of her in nothing but her swimsuit, but if I didn't stop soon, we would be blasting right past all our rules. Every time we were together all I could think about was what it would be like to kiss her, to touch all of her. Then I remembered the flash of panic in her eyes that night at the overlook, remembered that she wasn't ready yet.

She crouched down and let me pull her in. I wrapped her hand in mine to lead her toward the base of the waterfall. We swam and splashed each other, playing around until the last of the nerves on her face were gone.

Matt

Thank you for going hiking with me today.

Riley

I had a lot of fun, even though you got us lost.

Petting the dog was worth the detour.

I always have fun when I'm with you.

I might get us lost a little more often.

If you want to spend more time with me all you have to do is say so, no getting lost required.

I always want to spend more time with you.

Sounds like someone has a crush.

Sweetheart, this is more than a crush. I'm head over heels for you, and you better not let yourself think anything different.

Fuck. Was that too much?

Does your silence mean you fell asleep or did I scare you?

Good night, beautiful. I hope you sleep well.

I have a crush on you too. Sorry, I nodded off there for a few minutes. It's late, so we probably should go to sleep.

Good night, Matt. Thank you for today.

Chapter 16

Riley

I DREAMED ABOUT OUR hike. In this version Matt traced the lines of my tattoos with his lips. He had stood in the water with his hand rubbing over the ink on my ribs just like he'd done in real life, only this time he'd closed the distance between us. I didn't care about how my body looked or what he thought of it. His mouth against mine had been electric and soft, flooding me with the same sense of being home that his touch did. There were no rules, and all my fears were gone.

We fell asleep in my bed, him whispering good night in my ear. I could feel his body wrapped around mine holding me close. His arm around my stomach pulled me closer, squeezing hard enough to send a jolt of pain across my lower abdomen.

I jolted awake with another cramp clenching my abdomen shooting making my head spin. The feel of dream Matt's body against mine and the ghost of his scent still lingered as my senses struggled to catch up. I reached for my phone as I curled into a ball, clutching my stomach as another cramp hit me.

Yesterday I felt bloated during our hike, a detail that rattled my already precarious self image when the time came to let Matt see me in nothing but a swimsuit for the first time. According to my tracking app my period was right on time based on the data I had been diligently entering for the past year. Yet somehow it always caught me by surprise. Why did my body have to give me such a harsh reminder that I was doing a great job at taking care of it? I'd much rather be told, "Hell yeah, you're doing such a great job being healthy and balancing your hormones! Here's a gold star."

My phone buzzed with the sound of my alarm as the realization that today would be the first time I would have to teach on the first day of my period, the pain was intense enough my thoughts weren't able to spiral about the dream I'd been woken up from. The first day was always the worst, not because of the bleeding, but because of the intense cramps that made me feel like something was cutting its way out of me along with the nausea triggered by them. The intensity would dull some tomorrow, enough to be just severe but not debilitating. Through years of trial and error I had discovered the combination of menstrual discs and menstrual underwear to handle the heavy bleeding. The discs were a more comfortable alternative to a menstrual cup that could be worn for a full work day, which worked well for the limited restroom breaks I had, and the underwear absorbent enough to prevent any leakage from staining my clothes. When I worked as a sub, I always opted not to take on anything the day my period started, though during that time it had been few and far between. It was only in the last few months that we were able to get my cycles regulated even if they still ran long.

Matt's picture popped up on my phone as it vibrated with an incoming call. I smiled as best as I could through the pain as I answered.

"Good morning, beautiful," he said in his husky morning voice. He had been calling me to tell me good morning for a week now instead of texting. It had started when we fell asleep on a late-night call and woke up to find the connection still going. In my early morning sleepy haze,

I had told him that starting my day hearing his voice made me happy and he had agreed.

"Good morning," I gritted out through another cramp.

"Are you okay?" he asked, his voice switching from sleepy to fully awake in an instant.

I tried to steady my voice and shifted to sitting on the edge of my bed. "Yeah, it's just...um...bad cramps. I need to get up and deal with them so I can get my day started."

I stood and moved to pull the basket from my closet that I had dubbed my period kit. It was filled with both reusable and disposable discs, menstrual underwear, overnight emergency pads, Midol, nausea meds, a microwave heat pack, and sticky heat patches. I also kept an emergency stash of dark chocolate at the bottom. I shifted to hold my phone between the side of my head and shoulder as I pulled out everything I would need for the day.

"Anything I can do to help?"

"Not really, I have everything I need."

The only sounds coming from Matt were the sounds of him moving around getting ready for the day. I could picture the way his face must be scrunched in thought, the way he would be running his hands through his hair. I could practically hear the gears turning in his brain.

"Are you thinking about all the things you're going to bring over later anyways?" I asked him.

He stayed silent.

"Matt, I promise I don't need anything. I'm going to go to work, go to therapy, and then come home and watch a sad movie until I fall asleep on the couch because period exhaustion is no joke."

"Are you sure? Anything you need I can –"

"You can come over if you want, but I'm not going to be any fun. I promise I don't need anything."

"Okay, okay, I'll see you after school."

***

Tears blurred my vision as I pulled into the driveway and saw Matt's car already there, because of course he was. Even though he knew I would be getting home later today, I was willing to bet that he had left school and raced over as soon as the students were gone. Today was my first therapy appointment and I promised Emery I wouldn't cancel, even when having it on the first day of my period felt like cruel torture. I stopped by the store on my way home for crackers, bananas, and Gatorade. A handful of dark chocolate bars also found their way into my basket. The nausea had been worse than I expected, and I had barely managed to eat anything all day, which only made things worse.

The comforting smell of Emery's chili flooded my nose as I opened the door. It was the first thing I had smelled all day that didn't make me immediately gag, probably because it had been such a staple comfort food in our house growing up. The AC blasted making the house feel like a refrigerator compared to the end of summer heat wave outside. Matt sat on the couch, his elbows resting on his knees and his hands rubbing together. He had pillows and blankets covering almost all of the couch. My heat pack lay next to him and a steaming thermos cup of what I assumed was tea sat on the coffee table with a metal straw. He jumped up before I could make it all the way through the door. I dropped my work tote and the grocery bag by my feet as the tears rolled down my face.

Matt's arms wrapped around me. "Happy or sad?" he asked me. His fingers combed through the curls around my face, massaging my scalp as he pressed a kiss to the top of my head. I pressed my face against his shoulder, inhaling his scent as I let my body relax against him. "I don't know." I tensed as a cramp tightened my abdomen, Matt's arms squeezing around me tighter as I did.

"Don't touch the thermostat," Emery yelled from the kitchen. "It's September and I want chili. I'm over this heat."

"Em, it's still summer for a couple more weeks. You're going to freeze up the AC having it set this low." My voice was muffled against Matt, and I knew she didn't hear me.

"Don't ruin her fun," Matt said to me.

I pulled back and rolled my eyes. "You're supposed to be on my side."

"I talked her out of putting up the fall decorations. The first thing she did when I walked in was ask me to get them out of the attic." It was surprising to me that she had asked for his help at all. Typically Emery would have had the decorations covering the house before the end of August. The décor used to be stored in my room before I moved in with her so maybe that was the problem. Emery had always stressed that me taking the spare room wasn't an imposition but I couldn't help the guilt at the possibility of me being in that space being the reason she hadn't decorated yet.

I forced a laugh, then winced when another cramp hit me. "I'm going to go change," I said with a hand clutching my stomach.

He reached for the bags I had dropped. "I'll be right here. I have your heat pack ready to go and Emery made you some sort of tea concoction. I think she put three different kinds in there. Do you want me to find a sad movie for us to watch?"

More tears streamed down my face, and I swiped them away with the backs of my hands. Stupid hormones. All I could do was nod softly. It was one thing to have my sister here to take care of me on days like today, a favor I always returned during her period, and a whole other thing to have Matt here. Not only was he here without me having to ask, but he had followed all of Emery's instructions to help me. I was willing to bet that he had asked her to tell him what to do.

I changed into loose sweatpants and an oversized t-shirt and pulled my hair up into a messy bun before I removed the makeup that hadn't already been washed away from my tears. I tried not to look too long at my reflection in the mirror knowing that my face was puffy and red from the combination of my period and crying. The fresh flowers on the bathroom counter pulled a few more tears from me.

Matt pulled me onto the couch in a spooning position once I returned to the living room. He piled pillows under us enough that I could still sit up to drink what Emery referred to as her period potion – a mix of green, ginger, and cinnamon teas – before tucking an arm around me to hold the heat pack in place.

"I promise I'm not like this every day of my period," I told him as I settled back against him.

"I wouldn't care if you are. I just hate that you're in pain."

"I'm a mess."

"I like messy you."

"Ewww," Emery yelled from the kitchen. "I'm going to my room. The chili needs to simmer for a little while."

I sipped my tea to hide my laugh. "What movie are we watching?"

"Well, we have two options. Do you want to go with a sad Disney movie or something a little different?"

I sipped more of the tea while I weighed the options. My eyes already felt heavy, and I knew no matter what I picked I wouldn't make it through. Disney would be the best option. I had seen them all a million times so it wouldn't matter if I fell asleep, but I was intrigued to know what the other option he offered was.

"Let's go with something a little different, but I'm not promising to stay awake," I answered.

He pulled up something called *The Last Five Years*. "It's a musical," he explained. "If you like what little bit you watch, we can always watch the full thing some other time.

"You would pick a musical," I said as I shifted until my legs were curled up enough to trap the heat pack in the perfect position. I pulled his arm up a little until I could twine my fingers with his.

"Matt?

"Yes, sweetheart?"

"Will you pull down the fall decorations before you leave tonight? I give Emery a lot of shit about that stuff, but it makes her happy."

He kissed the side of my head. "I may have done that earlier when she asked, and she hid the evidence in her room." The image of boxes full of décor crammed into Emery's bedroom filled my mind. Fall was her favorite and she had enough themed décor to fill several houses. It all took up the majority of our attic leaving only a small corner for the handful of Christmas decorations.

Not only had Matt come over ready to take care of me today, but he also made multiple trips up and down to the attic to help Emery. It wasn't anything new. He was always doing whatever he could to help the two of us despite only knowing us for a month.

Emery and I had always been close friends, but since I moved in with her, we had become a package deal. I hadn't realized just how much all my exes had avoided her in the past. I hadn't realized until then just how important it was to me to have someone willing to be part of both our lives, not just mine.

I twisted as much as I could so I could see him and squeezed his arm to me. "I really like that you take care of both of us." He planted another kiss on my forehead. "I should warn you, the chili she is making is going to taste a little different from what you're used to," I added as I twisted back to face the tv.

"Tomato free, yeah, she already warned me. I'm not sure I'd call what she's making chili, but it still smells good." The recipe was one that Emery and my mom had worked on for years, adjusting it as Emery's allergies changed over time. Growing up I was so used to the food modifications we made at home because of Emery's extensive list of food allergies that anytime I ate outside of our house I was always thrown off by what things were supposed to taste like. Sometimes it felt like cheating to be able to try all these things that my sister could never have.

I snuggled in closer to Matt. We were lucky to have him, this incredible sweet man that took care of us and ate weird food without complaining. I fell asleep safely in his arms during the first song, my heart overflowing.

Chapter 17

Matt

> We're having a thing today for my mom's birthday. Want to come?

Riley

> I think it's too early for me to be coming to family dinners.

> It's family and friends. We can tell everyone you're just a friend.

> I don't think I'm ready. Maybe another time?

> Okay, I understand.

> I'll come over after?

> You're always welcome to come over. Emery and I are going to put up her fall décor today.

> Can't wait to see it.

I knew she would say no, if I had thought there would be any chance of her saying yes, I would have asked her during the times we were together this week or even while we were on the phone this morning. The hopeless romantic part of me couldn't stop thinking that maybe, just maybe, if I asked her, she would prove me wrong. The thought drove me crazy as I got ready until I had texted her while sitting in my car ready to leave my apartment like a coward.

She responded immediately, making my heart race with hope and then crash as I read her response. dropped my phone in my cup holder, drumming my fingers on my steering wheel the full fifteen minute drive to my parents' house as I thought over what to say, only texting her back once I was in their driveway. I had to remind myself that we'd only really known each other for a month, that I shouldn't rush things. She needed to take things slow. Hell, I should probably be taking things slow. We were good together, there was no denying that. Being impulsive and pushing her would just scare her off, I'd already done it once.

I pressed my head back against the headrest and scrubbed a hand over my face, letting out a disappointed sigh. My phone buzzed in my lap. I unlocked the screen to see a photo of Riley surrounded by an assortment of pumpkins. Her hair was piled on top of her head and twisted into a bun, baby hairs frizzing around her face. A small peek of orange in the bun caught my eye. I zoomed in, a chuckle escaping me as I took in the small pumpkin nestled inside her bun.

> How long do you think it will take for her to notice this one is missing?

From what I had learned this week hearing Emery take inventory of her collection, she was going to be tearing their house apart once she noticed it was missing. I didn't know how long it would take her to notice, but it was going to be hell once she did. Another picture popped up in our messages. This time Riley had stuffed a tiny scarecrow in her bun, the legs hanging out.

> How many things do you think I can fit in my hair?

She had so much hair she could probably fit several tiny pumpkins and scarecrows in there. A third picture came through with more legs hanging out of her bun. I could see Emery behind her with her arms crossed. I chuckled again.

> I think I've been caught.

> You're so cute.

A knock on my window startled me and my phone tumbled from my hands down into the space between my seat and the center console. My finger fumbled in the space until I caught one corner enough to push it forward onto the floorboard. I turned to see my youngest sister standing outside my car with her arms crossed and her eyebrows raised. Her bleach blonde hair was pulled back in a tight ponytail that made her face look more intense. She popped my door open.

"Everyone is waiting for you," she said. She dropped her eyes to where my phone rested on the floorboard. "Who is she?"

"How do you know it's a she?" I swung my legs out of the car, forcing her to take a step back, and then leaned down to scoop up my phone.

"I guess it could be a he. Or maybe a they? But it's definitely someone." She pinned me with a glare, reminding me how much she and Emery were alike. No wonder Emery and I were able to slip so easily into a sibling relationship. She motioned with her pointer finger, drawing circles in the air. "You have that look."

My phone vibrated in my hand, and I fought the urge to look, shoving it in my pocket instead and stepping around Shelby. The front door of the house swung open, my nieces and nephews sprinting outside. My knees hit the pavement and my body braced for impact, arms spread wide as their tiny bodies crashed against me. I wrapped us in a group hug, swaying us all side to side just rough enough to draw giggles from them.

***

I dropped into a camp chair to take a break. "Uncle Matt, we're not done yet," my oldest niece, Melody, said. She tapped her foot on the ground as her siblings and cousins gathered around her.

"Uncle Matt is too old for this," I answered. They hadn't let me sit down once in the hour since I arrived, barely even giving me a moment to greet my parents and sisters before pulling me into a game with rules that changed every two minutes. I didn't know what was happening other than it leading to me running around the large back yard for an hour. "What if we play a different game?" I suggested.

"How about hide and seek?" My oldest sister suggested sitting in the chair next to me. She urged the kids to go hide while I counted to a hundred. I covered my eyes dramatically, counting at the top of my lungs until I heard their giggles drift away. Madison tapped my arm. "I think you're all clear," she said.

I dropped my hands. "Thanks. Smart move on picking one hundred," I said turning toward her. Her highlighted hair was shorter than the last time I saw her, just grazing her shoulders, and the creases around her eyes were deeper. She looked more like our mom every time I saw her.

"Should buy you a long break."

I pulled my phone out of my pocket, checking for any messages from Riley. She sent several progress photos of the decorations, including one with a garland of leaves wrapped around her like a scarf.

"She's cute," Madison said, leaning over my arm to see my phone. "Shelby mentioned you were seeing someone."

I locked my phone and shoved it back in my pocket. "It's new," I answered. I clamped my mouth closed to hold back all the information I wanted to share about Riley. There hadn't been a chance for me to talk about her to anyone yet, but doing so felt like getting my hopes up. I had fallen hard for her on our date in June, and even more so in the time since we reconnected. I was in this more than she was and letting anyone know how I felt about her seemed like a great way to curse the whole situation.

"Is she why mom keeps complaining about you not coming over much?"

I cocked an eyebrow at her. Despite all the time I spent with Riley I had still been making time to stop by at least once a week since school started back. "I think I just spoiled her with how much I was here over the summer," I answered. During the summer I had practically moved back in with them, helping my mom babysit my nieces and nephews. Shelby had moved out at the beginning of summer and my mom had been struggling with the adjustment.

"Why didn't you bring her with you?"

"It's complicated."

I braced myself for her to ask why, tried to gather the words to explain it without her thinking that Riley was just like Liz. Instead, Madi nodded once as her eyes scanned the yard for rogue children. "Is there anything you can tell me about her?" she asked me, her eyes locking on a child peeking out from behind a tree. She lifted a finger to her mouth in a shushing motion.

"Fifty!" I yelled as if I had still been counting. "Her name is Riley," I answered my sister, trying not to cringe at how lovesick my voice sounded when I said her name. "She's a teacher." I paused to choose what else I could tell her, my mind flooding with options but I didn't want to share a single one. I wanted to keep them all to myself, to enjoy her being just mine, not my family's, for just a little longer.

We fell into silence as we watched our family around the back yard. Mom and dad stood in front of the grill, dad's arm around her as they swayed back and forth. They touched each other the way Riley and I did, effortlessly. A pang of jealousy shot through my chest, a longing to have her with me and my arm around her in front of everyone.

Don't rush things, Matt, just let it happen. I tapped my fingers against my leg in time to the music flowing from the Bluetooth speaker on the back porch. The music stopped, changing over to children's music after a pause. I looked over my shoulder to see Shelby shoving her phone into her pocket. "Oh no, Matt, I can't believe you. I guess I'm it!" Shelby yelled dramatically as she sprinted past us. She paused in the middle of the yard and turned in a circle, covering her eyes with her hands. "One hundred!" she yelled, dropping her hands to her sides. "Ready or not, here I come!"

"Looks like you're off baby-sitting duty," Madi chuckled beside me.

"Good, I'm getting too old for this."

"How's the new job?" she asked.

I shrugged my shoulders and suppressed a smile. "It's harder than I expected. Middle schoolers are kind of evil."

"But you like it?" she prodded. Her head swiveled again, watching as the kids frantically changed hiding places every time Shelby had her back turned.

My lips twitched as the smile I fought back won, spreading across my face as I dropped my eyes to my shoes. "I do." Then I remembered all the times Riley told me she liked the way I brightened when I talked about work. Most people would argue that I wasn't teaching the kids anything useful, that it was less important than the core subjects, but to me it was more important. Kids needed a creative outlet and that's what I was giving them. I gave them a classroom to come to each day that was just about having fun, without the pressure all their other classes put on them. I liked to think that I was changing their lives by just being that fun safe space.

"I think I'm starting to get into the groove of things now," I said.

Madi's hand clapped on my shoulder. "I'm glad you're happy and back home. We were getting worried about you for a minute there."

A chorus of hello echoed from the porch, followed by the kids coming out of hiding and running to greet the new arrivals. I looked over my shoulder to see my best friend and his siblings filing out of the house. Oliver had been my best friend since the day he stood up to another kid in our class for stealing the blocks I had been playing with when we were in kindergarten. He spent more time at my home than his own, something I later learned was due to a rough home life. Somewhere along the way when things were at their worst my family had welcomed his siblings into our lives, becoming a second home for the three of them.

Shelby stopped where she was to scowl toward them, crossing her arms over her chest. Oliver's cousin Wade stood at the back of the pack, slouching down like he was trying to hide his tall frame behind his much shorter cousins. I watched as he shifted under the weight of Shelby's glare.

"Well, I guess this party just got a lot more interesting," I said to Madi. I slapped my hands against my thighs as I stood up.

"I still can't figure out why she hates him so much." Madi jumped up and grabbed a kid that was scaling the side of the porch instead of using the stairs.

I pulled my phone out, remembering that I hadn't texted Riley back. I couldn't hide the smile on my face as I looked through her last few progress photos before typing out a quick reply. Oliver took Madi's place next to me as I typed, lifting his hat and pushing back his shaggy hair.

"How are things at the shop?" I asked him without looking up from my phone and returning to my seat. Out of the corner of my eye I could see the dark circles and bags under his eyes. He always had a permanent look of exhaustion but over the summer I had noticed that it was getting worse and worse. I'd offered several times since I moved back home to help out. During my last haircut his sister Ava spent the entire time telling me how worried she was about him.

He huffed and slumped in the chair. I flipped my phone over on top of my leg and shifted to look at him. God, he looked bad. The man needed a break, a long vacation, or maybe a year long hibernation. I don't think any of those were words in his vocabulary. "Dude, you need to hire some help. Or at least let me help on the weekends." I was getting sick saying those words to him. We had this conversation every time we saw each other. Ava said it was a conversation she and the others had with him daily.

"It's fine. Aubrey has been dealing with some stuff lately so she's been out a lot. It's fine. I've got it under control." He always had it under control. Even when he was drowning, he had it under control. Ava was the same way. They both complained about each other but couldn't see that they were doing the same thing. Some things never changed. Aubrey was Ava's wife who started helping at the shop almost two years ago when her chronic pain became too much for her to keep working as a stylist. I knew all about her struggles with seeking a diagnosis, how she'd been going around and around with doctors hoping one would finally listen.

My eyes shifted to Shelby chasing kids around the yard. This was the first family event she had been able to attend in months. She was juggling two fast food jobs that kept her working constantly. She needed something stable, something that would pay well enough she wouldn't need a second job. She needed it soon before she burned herself out. "What if you hired Shelby?" I suggested.

Oliver adjusted his cap on his head and huffed. I could hear the no on the tip of his tongue.

"Let her cover the front so you don't have to worry about when Aubrey is out. Weren't you saying you need someone to help with marketing? She could do that too." Shelby had been going to school for a degree in marketing before she dropped out. Even though she didn't graduate I knew she was a natural enough at the work that she would be able to help out. It would be better than the absolute zero marketing they were doing now. The shop may be thriving on word of mouth and repeat customers but eventually the lack of new customers was going to catch up to them.

Maybe if they were a little busier Oliver wouldn't have a choice not to hire a couple more mechanics instead of insisting on doing the work of three people all on his own.

Oliver looked between Shelby and where Wade was hunched over away from everyone else with Drew. "I brought Wade on as a mechanic. Do you think the two of them would be able to work together?" It was a good point. Shelby and Wade used to be inseparable as kids, even before Oliver and his siblings had melded in with our family. We all used to joke that they would end up married. Then one day they just stopped talking. Shelby would roll her eyes whenever I asked about Wade. Wade would walk away from a conversation if Shelby was mentioned.

"Maybe give it a try? You'd be helping her out as much as she would be helping you." It was a mean move to mention that Shelby needed help, but I knew he wouldn't be able to say no to that. Being unable to resist helping the people we cared about was a quality Oliver and I both shared.

He pretended to think about it, picking at his nails while he did. "You're not going to give up on this, are you?" he asked.

I shook my head, my leg jiggling as I did. My phone plopped to the grass landing face up. At least there weren't any fresh cracks on the screen. "Either hire her or let me start helping," I told him.

"Fine, I'll talk to her about it, but if she says no I'm not pushing the issue."

My phone chimed in the grass. I couldn't hide the way I smiled seeing a new message from Riley light up the screen. Oliver glared down at my phone and then up at me. "Who is that?" he asked gruffly. All this extra work was turning him from regular grumpy to bitter.

I flipped my phone over with my foot. Not only was I hiding my relationship with Riley from my family, but I was also hiding it from my best friend. I almost told him several times about our date over the summer, chickening out because I knew what he would have to say. I didn't want him to get a negative impression of her when I hoped one day things between us would be real. I wouldn't be able to handle my best friend hating my future wife just because we'd had a rocky start.

"Matt, everyone you talk to is here. Who is that?" Oliver hated Liz, always had, but it had been worse right before she and I broke up. He'd never been a relationship guy, something I blamed on his parents. The only time he'd been in a relationship he was convinced she was the one, we were all convinced she was the one even though I never met her, but she'd broken his heart. He'd thrown himself into work even harder after that. He tended to take his bitter views on love out on the rest of us.

My phone chimed again, my fingers itched to pick it up. I was an addict when it came to Riley. All I wanted to do was see her every day, spend every free second with her. When I was away from her, I couldn't stop myself from needing to be constantly available. I regularly accidentally forgot to respond to messages from my friends and family, but when it came to her, I never forgot. Oliver really needed to let me help at the shop, it would make it easier to keep my distance from her.

Oliver narrowed his eyes. "You're grinning like an idiot right now. Who is it, Matt?"

I tried to school my face into a blank expression. Riley telling me that she liked my goofy grin popped into my mind. She had blushed when she said it, her own goofy grin spreading across her face. My grin spread wider thinking about her.

He looked down at my phone, leaning forward like he might try to snatch it from under my foot. I could see him calculating if he could get away with it. Riley's tear-filled eyes when I told her I wanted to meet her family filled my mind. I knew she wasn't ready for anyone to know about her yet. Madi could keep a secret. No one would believe Shelby if I didn't offer information to back up her claims. If I told Oliver, it wouldn't be long before everyone else knew. The girls would have her tracked down before I knew what was happening.

"Do we have to talk about this?" I asked in a lowered voice.

Oliver settled back in the chair, his fingers going to the chain around his neck. He rubbed the rings on it through his shirt. "Be careful, okay? I don't want you getting hurt again." I wanted to ask him about the girl that broke his heart. Aside from knowing that there was one, and the few details his grandmother had shared with me, we hadn't talked about her much. I didn't even know more than her nickname. All I knew was that it was the only time anyone had seen Oliver be more than the closed off man that made it his mission to put everyone before himself. Whoever she was had balanced him, brought him out of the hard shell he built around himself.

I hated her, whoever she was. She had broken his heart and soon after his grandparents had passed away leaving him the hollow man sitting beside me. Lately I hadn't even been able to make him smile. I was at my wits end with him; we all were.

Maybe I should take a page from Emery's book and start meddling in his life more. It's what Granny would have done if she were still around.

Chapter 18

Riley

W E WEREN'T VERY GOOD at sticking to the rule of limiting the amount of time we spent together. At my suggestion he started coming over every day after school to cook with me, or if Emery insisted on cooking that night, he would just hang out with us and help me with the cleanup. It wasn't an open "hey you should come over every night" invite. It was me asking him if he wanted to come over after school during our morning phone call every morning. Or Emery asking him each night if we would be over the next day so she could plan dinner.

If I thought too much about it I would panic, tell myself that I need to press the brakes. Take a couple of days off from seeing him. Then each morning I would wake up thinking about how I couldn't wait to see him.

The weekends become a time when we would swap out whose place we were at to get chores done that were neglected through the week. We had fallen into the pattern easily, spending almost all our free time together.

"I want to take you on another date," Matt said, wiping down the counter as I loaded the dishwasher. Last week Emery asked Matt what one of his favorite comfort foods was because she wanted a new challenge of adapting something to fit her restrictions. Dinner had been chicken pot pie with kitchen sink cookies for dessert. She watched him like a hawk asking detailed questions about the flavors and textures, taking notes of every little reaction. It was still unclear if his feedback helped any considering that Matt was the least picky eater we've ever met.

"You say that like we don't have dates all the time." I rested my back against the counter and watched the way his arm flexed as he worked, the way his shirt clung to his chest. The sleeve of his t-shirt had ridden up enough to show the bottom of the lowest placed note of his tattoo. "We've seen each other every day since Labor Day."

"Sweetheart, that's just doing life together. I want to take you on a real date again."

"It's spending time together. Isn't that all a date is?" What my partner and I did during a date never really mattered to me in the past, I've always been the kind of person that preferred the small moments over the big ones. Quality time was quality time regardless of what we were doing. Every moment spent with Matt felt more important, more meaningful than even bigger moments of romance from my past. Helping each other with lesson plans, watching movies while cuddled up on the couch, cooking together – those were all dates to me. No pressure for romance, just time together.

Matt reached for the trash can and raked a pile of flour into it. It looked like Emery dumped more flour on the counters than she had used for the pie. She claimed she had cleaned as she worked, but the evidence stated otherwise. She lived in denial about how messy of a cook she was.

"Name the last time we went out," he said.

"On Sunday we went grocery shopping and had a dance party while we cleaned the house." I smiled at the memory of walking hand in hand down the aisles while he pushed the cart. Emery gave us the list of everything she needed for what she had planned this week and we filled in the blanks with our plans for our nights to cook. Sure, it felt a lot like treading too close to making things real. I kept catching myself thinking about how one day it could be us shopping just for the two of us. The two of us cleaning our house, dividing up the chores. I'd pick up the things that had been scattered around through the week because he hated it and always ended up distracted by something else during the process. He'd sweep and mop because it was my least favorite. We'd clean out the refrigerator together as we made our weekly meal plan. It would always be fun because it was the two of us.

It was all so easy to picture.

He laughed and shook his head, his hair falling onto his forehead. "Riley, that isn't a date."

I crossed my arms. "A date is spending time together and having fun. We did both. I don't understand how it's not a date." Any time spent with him was the time of my life. Even if it was just us on the couch, his head in my lap so I could play with his hair while he told me about his day at work. I wanted to know every detail about his day and he was always willing to share.

Matt laughed again and stepped closer to me, pressing me against the counter. His long fingers stroked the hair that had fallen from my clip at the side of my face. "Have I told you how much I love spending time with you?"

I gulped as my heart started to race. "I think you've mentioned it." *I love spending time with you too, it's the best part of my day.* We didn't live together, we weren't even a real couple, but for the past couple weeks it felt like we were pretending we were. The past couple of weeks were perfect. I pressed my hands into the counter behind me, the edge biting into my palms keeping my thoughts from spiraling.

"It doesn't matter what we're doing as long as I get to spend time with you. I'm happy with the little things, but I really want to take you on dates too." He trailed his hands down my arms until he reached my hands, taking them into his. "I promise I won't get us lost in the woods again." He lifted our hands to his mouth, flipping them so he could press a kiss against my palms. "Do I need to get on my knees and beg?"

I rolled my eyes. "What kind of date do you have in mind?"

"We're going to start by getting dressed up and going to dinner somewhere," he said, placing my arms around his neck. He pulled me away from the counter to the middle of the kitchen and started swaying to a song in his head. "After dinner we can flip a coin to pick our next destination or activity." It was clear he'd been putting a lot of thought into this already. Normally Matt processed everything out loud, telling me half formed plans in bits and pieces until he worked out all the details. Often he would start mid thought leaving me scrambling to catch up. He moved one of my hands from around his neck and swung me out, following up with a tug to spin me back into him. His free hand tapped against his thigh.

"I have a question I need to ask you," I told him. He moved his hand to my back and lowered me into a dip, his fingers tapping against my back now. "Why are you always tapping your fingers in patterns like that?"

His fingers froze and he knitted his brows together. "I don't even notice I'm doing it most of the time."

"Are you playing along to the song in your head?" I knew enough about ADHD to know that it was probably his go to stimming behavior. I had also watched him talk about work enough, let him start teaching me to play different instruments for long enough to recognize that sometimes the tapping happened in patterns similar to the finger placements on them.

He tilted his head and bit his lip as he thought, the tips of his fingers moved slowly against my back. "I guess so," he finally said. He moved my arms back around his neck and started swaying again. "Now answer my question. Can I take my beautiful girl on a date?"

"Matt, I'm not –"

He cut me off with a finger pressed against my lips followed by another dip. "You don't have to say anything. Please, just let me call you mine for a little while." He pulled me back into him, wrapping his arms around me in a tight hug. "I'm yours, whenever you're ready to let me."

Chapter 19

Riley

"E MERY, I DON'T KNOW about this dress." I twisted in the mirror, my hands hovering over my stomach. The dress Emery shoved in my hands as soon as I told her I didn't have anything to wear was a black bodycon maxi dress with a square neckline that hugged every curve of my body. The things it did for my boobs, hips, and butt were nothing short of magical, but I couldn't get over how it did nothing for my stomach.

"You'll change your mind as soon as Matt sees you." She moved my hair behind my back and sprayed the soft curls she spent the last half hour working on with more hair spray, fixing the spots that had been ruffled while I dressed. She pinned the top half back to show off my favorite pair of small chunky silver hoop earrings. "I have an idea."

She disappeared into her room and returned with a cropped leather jacket. The addition helped, but my eyes kept going straight to my stomach. Emery turned me away from the mirror and added a dainty silver necklace around my neck. "You look great," she told me. "Now go, Matt's been waiting."

"What? When did he get here?" I asked as she shoved me out of my room.

"I let him in while you were changing."

Matt jumped up from the couch when his eyes met mine, the bouquet of red roses across his lap and his phone dropping to the floor. "Riley, wow you look..." his words trailed off as I got closer to him. "Fuck," he said as he bent to pick up the roses and phone.

I laughed and took the flowers from his hand and passed them to Emery. He pushed a hand through his hair as his eyes moved over me. I pulled his hands to my waist, needing his touch. "Hi," I said to him.

"Hi." His hands moved down my hips and then back up.

"Do you like the dress?"

He nodded. "You look amazing in everything, but wow."

I laughed again and brushed a kiss against his cheek, light enough that the rosy pink lipstick I wore didn't transfer to his skin. "You clean up pretty well yourself." I ran my hands over his chest, my breath caught at the feeling of how hard his heart beat against my hand, and then smoothed my fingers over his blue tie.

"I can't decide if I want to show you off like this or if I want to keep you all to myself." His hands clutched my hips, rocking me forward until our bodies were flush against each other. Heat flooded my body. I've always felt like I couldn't get enough of his touch, but for the first time I felt like I couldn't get close enough to him. The way his eyes traveled over me, the way his fingers dug into me, I thought maybe he felt the same way.

We had rules to keep, boundaries we couldn't break yet no matter how much we had been blurring them lately.

"You're going to take her out and show her off," Emery yelled from the kitchen. "You better not bring her back home before sunrise." I didn't know if she was kidding or not. Quite frankly I didn't care. All that mattered was the way Matt looked at me.

I slipped my hand into Matt's, fighting back a whimper at the loss of his fingers digging into the soft curve of my hip and pulled him toward the door. We needed to leave before we both decided staying home was a better idea. "Come on, I believe you promised me a real date."

***

Matt drove with his right hand on my thigh right above my knee, alternating between tapping along to the radio and squeezing. Sometimes his fingers would drift a little high before he would catch himself and move his hand back down. I could see his mouth moving but I couldn't hear the words over the pounding of my heart. Every squeeze of his hand made it hard to breathe. I covered his hand with mine and threaded our fingers together.

All the time we've been spending together felt so easy, so natural. This felt like too much. This dress felt too tight. The seat belt felt like it was digging into my skin. The jacket was smothering me. The way Matt looked at me felt so good, but all I could think about was what would happen when he stopped looking at me like that.

I wanted the romance of the small, everyday things. The dancing in the kitchen, fresh flowers every day, cuddling on the couch after work, the way he smiled at me. I knew how he sounded in the morning, the way his eyes sparkled when he was excited, the way his mouth twitched to fight back a yawn when he tried to hide how tired he was because he wanted to stay just a little longer. We'd gotten good at those things over these few weeks.

I didn't know how to do romantic date nights. I didn't know how to act when all I could think about was how this fabric stretched over my stomach. I didn't know what to do when he decided that me being bad at this meant I wasn't enough.

The car stopped and I jolted, looking around the empty parking lot. Matt unbuckled his seat belt and twisted in the driver's seat to face me.

"Where are we?" I asked.

He unbuckled my seat belt and moved his hands to his lap. "You're panicking."

Panicking. That's what this was. Why was it so hot in this car? I pushed the jacket off and laid it over my lap.

"Riley, please talk to me. Tell me what you need." I looked at his hands clenched into fists in his lap. I couldn't tell if he was mad or if he wasn't fighting the urge to touch me until I gave him permission, all because I told him once that sometimes touching me when I was upset could be overwhelming.

"What are we doing?" I asked him. I couldn't take my eyes off his hands. Why were they so far away?

"I'm taking you on a date, sweetheart." His voice was calm and low, it didn't match the tension in his hands. That had to mean he wasn't mad at me, I tried to reassure myself. The realization hit me that I didn't know what he was like when he was mad. He could be, and I wouldn't know because I had never seen it.

"I don't know how to do this kind of date." I couldn't take it, I needed him to touch me, to know that he was here with me. I pulled one of his hands to my face.

His lips lifted in a small smile as his fingers stroked my cheek, the tension melting from the hand still in his lap. Seeing his smile loosened the pressure crushing my chest. "It's the same as all our other dates. We spend time together and have fun, like always."

I shook my head and bit the inside of my cheek. "This feels different."

"It's just us. Remember our first date? It's just like that." His hand moved the back of my neck and pulled me toward him. "Is it okay if I hug you?" Was it just like our first date? That one had been practice, no risk. There were risks now.

I leaned into his pull letting him wrap me into a soft hug. The pressure gripped around my chest melted away, the pounding in my ears slowed. His arms felt like home. "This just feels like so much more pressure than the first date."

He combed his fingers through my hair. "Just us sweetheart," he whispered into the top of my head.

"I really like you." *I think I'm falling in love with you.* "I'm so scared you're going to change your mind."

He pulled back until he could look in my eyes. "I like you too and I'm not going to change my mind." His hand cradled my cheek again, his thumb brushing the corner of my mouth. His eyes dropped to my lips, then back up to meet mine. His thumb at the corner of my mouth pressed against my lip. I dropped my eyes to his mouth, noticing how his mouth parted, and his top teeth scraped lightly over his bottom lip. "I really want to kiss you," he whispered, his cheeks turning pink.

"But your rule," I said, meeting his eyes. I didn't give a shit about that rule, hadn't for a while. I knew that we didn't need it anymore, that he wouldn't push me to do something I didn't want. I thought about kissing him constantly lately. Were his lips as soft as they looked? What would it feel like to have his smile pressed against my mouth? Would it feel like home too?

"Just one kiss."

"You'll mess up my lipstick." I knew I was just making excuses, giving him time to change his mind. It was his rule after all.

His hand slid down my face and settled on the side of my throat. "Riley, I think about messing up your lipstick every time you wear it." He leaned closer, his breath mingling with mine. "Tell me if I can kiss you."

I tangled my fingers in his hair and pulled him forward, closing the distance between us, bracing for him to pull away like he'd done in the past. I couldn't go another second without knowing what his mouth against mine felt like. I've been fighting the urge to ask him to modify the rule constantly lately. Our mouths collided without hesitation this time.

Kissing him felt like hot chocolate on a snowy day. Like walking into the AC after spending all day outside in the summer heat. Like coming home after a long day. We were both pulling on each other, trying to get closer as our lips moved together. His teeth scraped along my bottom lip before his tongue slid against mine. All I could think about is how right this felt, how this must be what people mean by true love's kiss. I'd been kissing wrong my whole life up until this moment.

If this is what kissing him feels like I can't imagine what more would be. More. Did I want more?

We broke apart, both breathing hard. He pressed himself back into his seat and pushed his hand into his hair. "Fuck, I'm going to need a minute," he said. My eyes flicked down to his lap, and I saw that, yes indeed he was going to need a minute.

"That was – wow," I started but I couldn't find the words to finish the sentence.

"That was us, sweetheart. Do you see what I mean now?" He pushed his head back against the headrest, turning toward me and flashing that beautiful smile. One of his hands twisted a strand of my hair around his fingers. "We're something special together. This isn't something people just walk away from. This is what people fight to keep."

I pulled a napkin from the center console and wiped the lipstick smudged on his mouth. "That's why I'm scared."

Chapter 20

Matt

I PULLED A COIN from my pocket when we parked in front of the restaurant and held it out to Riley. "Okay, we have two decisions to make." I pressed the coin into her outstretched hand. "Choice number one, heads we get food to go and tails we eat here."

She tossed the coin in the air, and I caught it, covering it with my hand. My eyes fell to her mouth, lips still a little swollen from how hard she kissed me, pink lipstick faintly smudged around the outline of her mouth despite her efforts to clean it up. She smiled when I moved my hand away to reveal the coin. My eyes dropped to the way the fabric of the dress hugged her chest. I forced myself to look away, reminding myself that the rules said I couldn't touch her there yet, no matter how much I wanted to. I looked at the coin in my open palm, heads face up. "Guess I'm going to have to find another way to show you off." I placed the coin back in her hand and pulled out my phone to pull up the restaurant website.

"What is the second decision?" She asked me as she ran her thumb over the metal.

I kept my eyes fixed on my phone, too scared to see how she would react. She had practically slammed her mouth against mine when I asked to kiss her earlier without any hint of fear in her eyes, but I couldn't shake the fear that she may have changed her mind in the time since. "I get to kiss you whenever I want to tonight or we go back to the rules, you call it."

Out of the corner of my eye I saw her shake her head. "I want you to kiss me whenever you want to." There was no hesitation in her response, just blunt honesty. I looked over at her, forcing my eyes to stay on her face and not any lower. God, that dress was so distracting. Her mouth pulled tight with worry. I brushed my thumb against one corner of her mouth until she relaxed.

"Just for tonight. Tomorrow, we'll revisit the rule," I said.

Riley shook her head again. "Just for tonight, if you want. Starting tomorrow, we get a kiss hello and a kiss goodbye, at minimum. We're not going back to nothing." Her eyes were on my mouth, her tongue flicking out over her lips.

Fuck it. Fuck these rules. I wanted to toss the rule out completely, to kiss and touch her however we both wanted without a stupid rule. The only rule should be that we did whatever the other was comfortable with. But Riley struggled with setting boundaries, and I knew the clear rules between us made her feel safe. "Okay, kissing whenever we want to from now on. The rule changes to nothing more than kissing." I offered my hand to shake on the rule change like we had done during our other discussions setting rules for whatever this was.

She laughed and leaned over the center console. "Kiss on it or no deal."

I met her over the console but kept my mouth away from her. My hands smoothed over the goosebumps on her arms and shoulders, my thumbs teasing the thin straps of her dress while I studied her face for any sign of being uncomfortable. She scraped her teeth over her bottom lip, pupils flaring as she stared at my mouth. I twisted one thumb in a strap, fighting the urge to drag it down.

"Matt," my name left her lips as a breathy whine, and she twisted my tie around her hands to pull me forward to close the distance. Did she have any idea how sexy she sounded, how she was making me feel? "Please."

I fought against her tug to pull me closer, drinking in how much she wanted me, how unashamed she was about it because she felt safe with me. I love her, the thought crashed through me. I swallowed hard to keep the words to myself. Riley was it for me, and I wished she could see that. I wish she understood that she was safe to fall, that I wasn't going anywhere. "I just need to take in this moment," I said.

Her eyes flashed with panic before dropping away from me. Did she know what I was thinking? "I need you to kiss me again," she finally said, lifting her eyes to meet mine again.

"Whatever you need." I started with a soft peck of my lips against hers, pretending to pull away after. Riley made a noise of protest and leaned into me, her mouth chasing mine. I let her draw it out into a soft languid kiss.

"I could sit here and kiss you all night, but I would really like to move this date past being in my car," I said, forcing myself to pull away from her again. I untangled my hands from her hair and dress, reaching for my phone and the coin in my lap, shifting to hide that I was hard again. "Heads you pick our food, and tails I pick."

***

I drove with my right hand squeezing Riley's soft thigh while she flipped the coin to decide which way we needed to turn next. She was all smiles this time, not even a hint of the panic from earlier on her face.

We pulled into the city park filled with people with blankets spread over the grass all facing a giant screen.

"Hmm, movie night in the park. I feel like you planned this," Riley said and reached for the door handle.

"Wait!" I jumped out and came around to open her door. I lifted the food bag from her hand and sat it on the roof of the car so I could pull her into my arms. I kissed her, relishing the feeling of her pressed against me completely this time. Like everything always did with her, it felt like something we had done a thousand times. My body buzzed from the relief of having her back in my arms. Kissing her, holding her, made me feel like I didn't even know what a real kiss felt like before her.

"I planned for the possibility," I admitted when we broke apart. Riley wrapped her arms around herself and shivered slightly. I pulled her jacket from her seat and wrapped it around her shoulders, holding it steady as she slipped her arms into the sleeves.

Riley watched me, her hands clutching her jacket to hold it closed over her stomach, as I pulled blankets and pillows from the back seat of the car. She looked down at the heeled shoes she wore, grinding the edge of one heel against the pavement before she bent down to her tote bag on the floorboard. She supported herself against the roof of the car as she kicked off the heels and replaced them with simple flats.

Once everything was gathered in our arms, I led her to a spot as far away from everyone else as we could get. I spread the blanket across the softest patch of grass I could find, then helped Riley sit down. I sat behind her, my legs stretched out on each side of her and pulled her back to rest against my chest.

"Are you going to be able to eat like this?" she asked. She pulled the to-go containers from the bag.

I wrapped my arms around her shoulders and pressed a kiss against the crown of her head. "I can make it work," I assured her. I pulled a piece of creased notebook paper from the pocket of my shirt, smoothing it out and laying it on the blanket next to us. The words were smudged from how many times I had folded and unfolded the page, adding things to the list as I thought of them.

"What's this?" Riley picked it up.

"Everything I've been meaning to ask you."

She squeezed my leg before twisting around so we were facing each other while she looked over the list. It was mostly getting to know you things, like questions about our parents and childhood, bucket lists, travel dreams, and various favorites. After our first date we had skipped a lot of learning about each other, never revisiting the subjects we hadn't covered that day.

"How have we not talked about all of this?" Riley's eyes were wide when she looked up at me.

"I don't know. Sometimes it feels like we skipped over all the early dating subjects and straight to acting like people that have known each other forever."

We'd slipped into a routine focused on the now and only filled in the blanks of the past when necessary. I didn't know her parents' names, or the names of her brother and sister-in-law. I had never told her about Oliver or my sisters and their husbands aside from the fact that they existed. I didn't know her middle name. We hadn't talked much about what our childhoods were like.

"Matt, what's your middle name?" Riley asked, the paper fluttering from her hand back to the blanket.

"My middle name is Matthew." Her eyes were so wide they looked like they might pop out of her head. "I go by Matt, but my first name is Rupert," I explained.

"Holy shit. I should have known that already. How did I not know that?"

I shrugged and smiled. "I think that's more my fault than yours." I wrapped her right hand in mine and shook it, her arm flopping around as I did. "Hi, I'm Rupert Matthew Fletcher Junior. What's your name, beautiful?"

She tried to fight back the laugh that bubbled out of her, the look of panic wiped from her face. "Riley Elaine Harrison. I'm not a Junior but I do share my mom's middle name."

We recapped our parent's names and professions for each other. I told her about Oliver and how we had drifted apart when I moved away but were closer now that I had moved back. I told her how my parents never shied away from showing their kids the good and bad sides of marriage and always used any moment they could to teach us about healthy relationships. That they were strong believers in PDA and that's probably where I'd gotten it from.

Riley's parents were the opposite. They had married young and had all three of their kids early in their marriage. They both came from divorced parents and struggled with a lack of communication skills. They tried their best to hide it from them, but there were many nights of Emery climbing into Riley's bed because of their fighting. It wasn't until they were all in high school and her parents on the verge of divorce that they finally tried marriage counseling. Their marriage was stronger now, but it took a lot of work and left Riley with a lot of unsavory memories. Talking about her parents made Riley's eyes glisten with tears.

I moved her food from her lap and pulled her into my arms. "Riley, I'm so sorry," I said into her hair. I had learned at a young age how lucky I was to have the parents that I did, that more people had a story similar to Riley's than mine.

"Explains a lot, huh? My therapist said it did when I told her last week." The fabric of my shirt was wet from her tears. She pulled away and I could see tear stains and mascara smudges on my white button down. "Matt, your shirt."

I lifted a napkin to her face, gently wiping away the tears and smudged makeup on her face, pretending I didn't see the smudges on my shirt. "It's just a shirt."

"I wish I didn't cry so much." My heart ached as I watched her open her phone camera, using it as a mirror while she swiped at the dark smudges under her eyes. She did cry a lot, with almost every emotion. I had never met another person that showed their emotions as strongly as she did, that didn't fight back their tears. Riley cried as easily as I smiled.

"It just means that you feel things deeply," I told her. "It's one of my favorite things about you. I mean, not that you're hurting, but how deeply you feel." The two of us both wore our hearts on our sleeves, it was like we were made for each other.

The tears started again, happy this time. Tears gathered at the corners of her mouth as she smiled at me. I brushed them away with my thumb.

"You're amazing," she said to me through her tears.

I rolled my eyes and tried to fight back the grin lifting my mouth. I love her. My brain scrambled for something else to say. "I know I am, but it is nice to hear you say it," I joked.

She kissed me, more confident than she had been earlier. Her hands rested lightly on my forearms, not clutching me like she thought I might run away. Maybe she was starting to see that I meant it when I said I was here when she was ready.

"Careful, Riley, we're in public," I whispered in her ear. I was hard again just from kissing her. I really needed to get that under control.

My fingers teased the strap of the dress on her right shoulder where the jacket had slid down.

"You really like this dress," she whispered.

Fuck yeah, I did. She looked sexy in it, especially as the evening went on and she grew more comfortable in it, hiding less and less under that jacket. "I do. Tell Emery that you're keeping it."

"How do you know it's not mine?"

I leaned away from her and picked the list back up. "Riley, there's a lot I still need to learn about you, but I know how you act when you're uncomfortable. You've been pulling at that dress all night and keep pulling that jacket closed over it. You never do that in your clothes. I hate that you're uncomfortable, but I wish you knew how incredible you look in this." I reached out and moved the jacket from where she had started to pull it closed across her stomach. I knew that was the part of her body that she felt the most self-conscious about. It was soft and stuck out further than her boobs, and she often hid it behind her arms or objects when she could. I slid my hand under the jacket, cupping her side just below her ribs and brushed my thumb over the swell of her stomach, keeping my eyes on her face for any clue I needed to stop. "Also, you never wear all black."

Every visible patch of skin blushed at my words. I watched her work through her thoughts as she absorbed my words, fighting back the urge to ask what she was thinking.

"What's the next question, Rupert?"

I wrinkled his nose in feigned disgust at the sound of my first name. "That's Matt to you, missy. The only person that calls me Rupert is my mother when she's mad at me."

"Excuse you, my name is sweetheart, not missy," she teased.

"Sweetheart, gorgeous, beautiful, my dear, honey, baby," I peppered her face with kisses as I listed off every pet name I could think of until we're out of breath from laughing and lying back on the blanket. I had to remind myself we were in public surrounded by families, trying not to think about how she felt under me.

I pulled the list of questions from under Riley's back and asked the next one, forcing some space between us so my body would calm down. Soon we ran out of questions on the list and transitioned to asking each other anything we could think of. We laid there, side by side, hands intertwined, and lost in the world of just the two of us until the sounds of car doors pulled us back. We sat up and see up see we're the last ones left on the grass.

Riley pulled the coin from my shirt pocket and held it up. "Where to next?"

Chapter 21

Riley

A FEW COIN TOSSES later we found ourselves in his car parked in the Walmart parking lot eating cookie cake with a game of battleship set up between us.

"You have to be cheating," Matt said as I sunk another of his ships. He only had one remaining while he had only managed a couple hits on mine.

"I think you're underestimating how competitive Emery and I were as kids."

"I've seen you together, trust me, it wasn't just when you were kids." He turned to look at his window, no doubt checking to see if his board was reflected in it. "I grew up with three sisters, remember? I know all about how competitive they can be."

"You're just salty because I'm better at board games and arcade games."

"I'd be less salty if you would be my secret weapon for family game night." He held up a hand before I could say what I was thinking. "Forget I said that. I mean, unless you want to think about it, but I know you're not ready to meet them."

I chewed on my bottom lip and leaned back against my door. "One day, I promise, I do want to meet them. I just need to work through my problems first."

He moved the game boards from between us and onto the dash. His hands squeezed my legs. "I know, Riley. I don't want to pressure you. Sometimes I just get excited thinking about how you're going to fit in with them. They're going to love you."

I'm sure I'm going to love them too.

"Can I see a picture of your family? I don't think you've shown me any." He had framed photos all over this apartment but I always stopped myself from looking at them. It was too much of a reminder that I was scared to meet the people that were important to him.

He reached for his phone, stopping to check my game board. I had the aircraft carrier, cruiser, and submarine all lined up horizontally two columns over from the middle. My battleship and destroyer were each horizontal a column to the left and right. "I won't forget this," he said, squinting his eyes as he tried to twist his face into a serious expression.

I cleaned up the pieces as he scrolled through his phone for a family picture.

The first thing I noticed when he showed me the picture was that he had his dad's smile and gentle eyes. His nose and blonde hair came from his mom. They all gathered around a Christmas tree and wore ugly Christmas sweaters. His youngest sister, Shelby he told me, looked the most like him. Matt stood behind her trying to give her bunny ears, her head tilted back with laughter because she noticed, and she had a hand up knocking his hand away. He wore both a Santa hat and reindeer antlers.

His older sisters, Madison and Grace, sat in their husbands' laps on the floor. Grace held a baby and there was a toddler climbing her husband's back, her little hands pulling his hair. Three kids gathered around Madison and her husband, the oldest looked around five.

"This was Christmas last year," he told me. "The older everyone gets the harder it is to get us all together, especially when I was living in Kentucky. My favorite part of being back here is that I can see them whenever I want."

I stared at the photo and tried to picture myself there with them. It was easy to see myself there beside Matt with his arm around me as I leaned into him laughing at Shelby. I wondered which of his parents he learned to give such great hugs from.

Matt brushed a strand of hair back from my face. I turned to see his eyes fixed on me. I wondered if he had been watching me this whole time. "I can't wait to have a family photo with you by my side."

"Matt, no talking about the future."

His smile turned sad, his eyes dropping to where his fingers brushed my neck. "I know, but it's hard not to when all I can think about is a future with you." He gestured to the game and cookie cake on the dash and then to his clothes. "A future full of nights with adventures like this."

Warmth flooded my stomach, because I could see it too. A future full of talking for hours on end and forgetting the rest of the world existed. A future of him holding me while I cried one moment and having me rolling with laughter the next. Sitting in his car dressed up and playing board games while having the time of our lives, because anything with him felt right.

The panic didn't creep in until he asked me what I was thinking.

"No talking about the future," I told him. It's too soon, you can't know you want this already, I told myself.

He nodded and started the car. My eyes flicked to the clock, and I had to pull out my phone to double check the time. "Matt, it's almost midnight."

"Are you ready to call it a night or do you want to see what else we can find to do?"

"I think the only thing open at this point is Waffle House and I'm not feeling that tonight." I frowned at my phone as I scrolled through increasingly more aggressive messages from Emery telling me not to come home tonight. Matt rubbed his jaw when I showed them to him.

"Your sister scares me sometimes."

I laughed. "She gets like this with people she cares about. She likes you and wants me to be happy."

"Stay with me tonight."

I blinked at him, not sure that I heard him right.

"I'm serious, stay with me. I'll blow up the air mattress in the living room and we can build a blanket fort. We can stay up all night together."

It all sounded so nice. I wasn't ready for the night to end, I never was. Even if we didn't do anything more than talk and sleep, the idea of it all felt more than casual. We were more than casual, and had been for a while. What would he think when he saw me in the morning? I couldn't even say I loved him, how could I let him see me with my messy morning hair and stubble covered chin? All my morning supplements were at home. It wouldn't hurt to miss just one day, but it felt like a big deal after being so diligent about never missing a single one for so long.

"I don't have a change of clothes or anything," I said instead of all the worries clouding my head.

"I have something you can wear." Matt wasn't a small guy, but he wasn't big either. Would I even be able to fit in any clothes he had to let me borrow?

I bit the insides of my cheeks and tried to stop my head from spinning.

Matt bracketed my head with his hands and kept my eyes on him. "I know you're scared right now, and you're thinking about all the reasons this is a bad idea. All you need to decide is if you want this. It doesn't have to be anything more than us just having more time together. The rules still apply. No funny business."

I swallowed and tried to focus on his eyes, tried to remind myself of all the mornings I had dreamed of waking up next to him. Maybe this could be a good thing. We could try this, and if things went sour then we would know that this wasn't what we thought it was. We could rip the band aid off before we got any deeper into whatever this was.

"Okay, but just for tonight." The way his face lit up made me think maybe I had made the right decision. I wanted to always be the reason for this look on his face.

***

I stood in Matt's bathroom staring at the pile of items he left on the counter for me. There were brand new bottles of my body wash and face wash, a pack of my favorite kind of scrunchies, even a tube of my deodorant, an electric toothbrush identical to the one I use at home. There was even a brand-new razor. I had been so worried about what I would do in the morning since I knew Matt didn't shave, he just trimmed his beard hair down to barely there stubble when it started to get long because he didn't like the way shaving irritated his skin or the way a full beard felt. There was a worn t-shirt folded up with a pair of my favorite sweatpants. The print on the t-shirt was faded but I could make out the words Mountain View High.

He had been in my house enough I shouldn't be surprised that he noticed any of these items. I had several pairs of these sweatpants and wore them all the time around him. But I was surprised, because he didn't just notice, he remembered. He remembered and made sure he had them on hand.

"Matt?" I call from the bathroom door.

"Everything okay, sweetheart?"

I opened the door to let him in. "What is all of this?" I asked, pointing at the pile. "Why do you have all this?"

A mix of emotions flashed across his face. "In case you needed it."

I clenched my eyes shut and took a deep breath determined not to add any more crying to the night. "But why?"

"Riley, I don't think you're ready to hear the answer to that question."

Because he loves me.

He, this gorgeous sunshine man, loves me.

He's been telling me for a while now, with the way he touches me, the way he looks at me. With the flowers he never forgets to bring me. He kept my favorite snacks in his pantry even though we didn't spend much time here and had a list of recipes to try together from all my favorite blogs. The way he was okay with spending more time at my place than his because it makes me more comfortable. He told me in all the soft ways that no one else ever did.

I saw it every time, but it's different to hear it. He's right, I'm not ready to hear it just yet.

His hands held the sides of my head, and his thumbs brushed the clenched corners of my eyes. "You know how much I want to keep you around. I just wanted to be prepared for anything you might need while you're here with me."

"I don't deserve you."

He slowly planted kisses all over my face until I opened my eyes. "Please don't ever say that again."

Chapter 22

Matt

MY BACK ACHED, BUT the pain faded away as I noticed my bed smelled like Riley's hair products. Something tickled my nose. My eyes popped open to see messy curls on the pillow in front of me. Last night rushed back to me, talking until she had fallen asleep with her head on my chest. Now I was curled around her, one hand over her side with my fingers brushing her stomach under the fabric of her shirt. Not her shirt, my shirt. It was my marching band shirt from high school, oversized because someone mixed up my size when ordering.

Riley groaned softly and then her body stiffened against me. I stilled my fingers against her warm skin, afraid to move and spook her. She jolted into a sitting position next to me, my arm falling away as she did. Her hands went to her hair, patting it and trying to smooth it down. She flipped her pillow up, looked under it, and then lifted the covers. The scrunchie she had used to twisted her hair into a bun on top of head last night was caught between my shoulder and pillow. I offered it to her. She started to gather her hair into another bun, her face scrunching up as she worked. The curls tangled around her fingers, and she let out a little adorable frustrated noise.

I lifted a hand to her, tugging her arms down. Her face turned to me finally. She had creases on one side of her face from the pillowcase. Her cheeks were blazing red. I looped my arms around her and pulled her back to lay against me.

"Is this real?" she asked.

I shifted us so she was on her back, and I was on my side propped up on one elbow so I could look down at her. I dropped my face to the space between her neck and shoulder, nuzzling against her and smiling against her skin. "I hope so."

I started to trail my nose up her neck and then across her jaw. Her face tilted away from me and her eyes clenched shut. I lifted a hand to catch her chin, her skin there rough against my fingers, and turned her face back to mine. I kissed her slowly, careful to make it easy for her to move away if she wanted. She settled into the kiss, her body relaxing against mine as I tangled my fingers in her hair. "Good morning, beautiful," I said against her lips before kissing her deeper. Her hip moved closer to me, settling against my aching hard on.

She broke the kiss, her eyes widening as she noticed. She tried to sit up again. This time I leaned back, the hand in her hair dropping to her neck.

"Please, just stay here and wake up with me for a few minutes." I shifted away so she wasn't pressing against me anymore. "Ignore that."

Panic flashed through her eyes, then her brows scrunched. She rolled her bottom lip between her teeth as she settled back to laying beside me, her hip pressing against me. "What if I don't want to?" Her hand cupped my jaw as she pulled me in for another kiss.

"I promised you no funny business," I reminded her. I pulled back enough to see her face.

She pressed back into her pillow and rubbed her eyes with the heels of her palms. She dropped her hands from her face and twisted the sheets around them. "What if I want funny business?" Her tone was teasing, but the look on her face was uncertain. Her eyes jumped from my face to look over my shoulder.

I combed my fingers through her hair slowly, trying not to pull at the tangles. "Look me in the eyes and tell me you want to."

Her eyes flicked to mine and then back over my shoulder. I rubbed my thumb over her bottom lip, coaxing it out from between her teeth. She opened her mouth to speak but then quickly clamped it closed.

"Sweetheart, I'm not doing anything with you that you aren't 100 percent sure about," I reassured her.

She rolled her eyes, then snapped them back to meet mine. "I'm never 100 percent sure about it at first," she whispered. Her jaw clenched and she blinked rapidly. She turned to stare up at the ceiling.

"Riley?" I swallowed the lump forming in my throat. I knew her exes hadn't been the best, that they had been impatient with her. But surely that hadn't forced her into anything she didn't want.

Next to me Riley sucked in a deep breath, throwing one arm across her eyes. "I like you a lot, you know that right?" she asked. She peeked out from under her arm to see me nod. "And I'm attracted to you," she added slowly.

I pulled my brows together as I reached her arm, nudging it slightly so I could see her eyes. "Riley, it's okay if you're not ready for sex yet. We don't have to rush into any of that."

She blew out a breath. "Sometimes it just takes me a while to get to that point." She paused to chew on her lip again. "And I might want to do other things, but not necessarily want to jump straight into sex."

"I'm never going to push you for something you're not ready for, Riley. You tell me what you want or need, and I'll take care of you." I dropped down against my own pillow, looking up at the ceiling.

Riley rolled onto her side, this time pushing herself up on her elbow, so she was hovering over me. "What if I change my mind? What if I'm okay with something once and then decide that I'm not ready for that?" Her words were slow as she spoke, like she was struggling to put them together.

"Then we stop or don't do it again. I'm following your lead with this. Okay?"

She nodded and then shifted to rest her head on my chest. "Okay."

I pressed a kiss to the top of her head. "This is enough for me," I said. "Just being with you like this is enough. We can keep all the other things off the table until we're both sure what we want. We can keep that rule if you want."

I rubbed small circles on her back with one hand as she hid her face against my chest while the other brushed through her hair. Her hair scrunchie lay abandoned on the bed next to us. I reached for it and stretched it onto my wrist. I went to work on gathering her hair up. I could feel the racing of her heart slow as I worked on her hair, her body relaxing against mine more. "Tell me what you're thinking," I whispered softly as I worked a knot loose that had twisted around one of my fingers.

"I think you're right; we should keep the rule." Her fingers traced the faded lettering of the t-shirt I wore. "But what is the line we need to cross before we decide it's no longer in effect?"

I weighed her question as I finished my mission of tying up her hair. When we both wanted it was the obvious answer, but if it was that clear to her, she wouldn't be asking me. I could tell her we needed to wait until we were in love, but that felt like putting too much pressure on her to get there. Maybe just when she could admit that we were in a relationship? When she was ready to put a label on us? Again, it felt like putting too much pressure on her.

I felt impatient to get to that point with her, I could admit that. I was a hopeless romantic ready to have my happily ever after. The need felt stronger now than it ever had, and I knew it was because I already thought I had it once only to find out I was wrong.

Riley wasn't Liz. She carried baggage she wasn't ready to tell me about, we had only known each other a couple of months so it made sense that she wasn't ready. She was scared and still learning to trust me. How could someone win the trust of someone as sweet and cautious as her only to turn around and leave?

I had been ready to jump in headfirst from the beginning. I knew it was a flaw of mine to be all in so quickly. To hand a stranger my heart without a doubt.

"Matt?" Riley looked up at me through her lashes, her chin and jaw smushed against my torso so I felt more than heard her.

"I don't think we should set that line just yet. I think when we're there we'll both know it." I smoothed a finger over the lines on her face from the pillowcase. "Let's not put any pressure on ourselves."

Emery

What are your intentions with my sister?

Matt

I think that's a conversation that needs to be between me and her.

Emery

You better not break her heart.

I've never seen her like this with anyone else.

Matt

I fully plan to love your sister for the rest of my life, if she'll let me.

Emery

Don't let her get scared and break her own heart.

Chapter 23

Riley

Hot Nerd <3

> Come with me on a road trip this weekend.

Riley

> Where are we going?

> Did you change your name in my phone?

> There's an overlook I want to kiss you at.

> I want to drink coffee with you while we watch the sunrise on a porch in the mountains.

> Matt, did you do what I think you did?

I have a lot of regrets about how things went over the summer and I can't stop thinking about them.

I want to see your crazy morning hair against the backdrop of Smoky Mountains painted by the sunrise.

You're so cheesy.

You know you love it.

No funny business, I promise.

We left Friday right after school to make the three-hour drive to Copper Ridge. He drove the whole time with his hand on my leg, graceful fingers tapping to the radio, while we shared stories of our family vacations. He told me that his and Shelby's birthdays are in June, so his parents always let them each bring a friend along for their vacation instead of having a party. I panicked, realizing that we never shared our birthdays with each other.

"June 9th," he told me as he squeezed my thigh and smiled. He knew what I was thinking before I could ask him.

The date rang a bell. I pulled out my phone and checked my calendar to see if it would tell me why. That was Sunday when my family and I were at the cabin. "That's the day we first texted," I exclaimed as I squeezed his wrist.

"Best birthday gift ever." He glanced away from the road to grin at me.

"Mine is April 29th." I never did anything big for my birthday, but this past one had been smaller than ever before. Emery had baked me a cake and insisted on doing the cooking and cleaning. She made me wear a crown and blow out candles for a few pictures.

"Good, I didn't miss it. I'm going to spoil the shit out of you for your birthday."

"You already spoil me enough." I wasn't just trying to brush him off, he did truly spoil me better than anyone ever had in my life. All the little everyday things he did felt grander than anything big ever did.

I shared about the time Milo told Emery and I ghost stories about the Appalachian Mountains around the campfire after our parents went to bed one night when we were teenagers. The two of us had been so scared that we stayed up all night cooking and baking to distract ourselves. We didn't want Milo to know that he scared us that bad, so we told everyone we were starting a new tradition. Every year since the two of us stayed up all night our last night there and treated our family to a full four course breakfast the next day.

We always made Milo do the dishes.

"Have you and Emery always been this close?" he asked me after he stopped laughing.

"She's always been my best friend. We're only a year apart and sometimes it feels like we take turns being the older sister. Things were rough when we were teenagers and there were a few years not too long ago when we were distant. We were both going through a lot at the time. I think we're the closest we've ever been now." I left out how we both lost ourselves in our romantic relationships during those years and stopped making time for each other. Sometimes I wonder if I could have kept her safe from whatever she went through during that time if I hadn't been so focused on trying to make my exes stick around.

"Your sister really loves you in her weird aggressive way," he said. He moved his hand from my thigh and intertwined our fingers, his thumb stroked the back of my hand. "If I ever accidentally do anything to get between you two, please tell me."

I knitted my brows in confusion. Matt had been so amazing about accepting Emery and I as the package we are and making sure I still have time to spend with her.

"Matt, I don't think you would ever –"

"I know, Riley. You just got extremely sad talking about how you lost touch. You don't have to tell me what happened back then. Just don't ever let me be a reason it happens again. Okay?"

I bit my lip and nodded.

He told me about how much he regretted losing touch with Oliver when he moved. About all the trouble the two of them used to get into as kids. Oliver was like a brother to him. He'd been looking forward to reconnecting when he moved back only to find out that Oliver had been through the wringer the past few years.

As I laughed about his stories, I couldn't help but think about how unfair it was that he was so great to Emery, and I wouldn't even give him the chance to introduce me to anyone important to him. The thought of meeting his family felt like something big, something high stakes. Meeting his friend felt a little lower stakes. Plenty of people introduced their friends to people they were dating before things got serious.

"I think I want to meet Oliver. Do you think I could meet him before I meet your family?"

"Really? Yes, absolutely." His voice was loud as a grin stretched across his face. "Are you sure?"

I laughed as his face lit up. "Yeah, let's do it."

"He's always busy with work nowadays, but I think I can figure something out." His hand squeezed my thigh tightly. "He's kind of grumpy, but I promise he's a good guy."

***

The sun had already set when we made it to the overlook where I left him four months ago. Anxiety clutched my chest like a fist as that night flashed across my mind. I took a deep breath and focused on how different things were this time.

He helped me from the car and led me to the railing of the overlook. He pulled me into his arms and tilted my face up to his. The early fall breeze blew my hair into our faces, and he laughed as he brushed it back, tangling his fingers with it to hold it back. I reached up to push his glasses up onto the top of his head so I could see his eyes better. He started wearing his glasses more than his contacts once he figured out I liked them.

"Hi," I whispered.

"Hi," he breathed back, his lips hovering over mine like they did the last time they were here. "I owe you a kiss right here."

"Are you going to change your mind again?" I asked as I moved to bring our mouths closer together.

"Are you going to run away again?" My heart pounded as the look on his face that night flashed through my mind. His tone was light, but it still felt like a stab to the pit of my stomach.

"Are you still not sick of me?"

"Jesus, sweetheart, I could never be sick of you."

He kissed me like he needed to prove it. He told me with every movement of his mouth against mine that he loved me, that he was mine. He took my fears and told me I was home, that he'd be my safe place if I let him.

"Matt, I'm still scared," I said into his mouth. I wanted to, but I couldn't do it. I couldn't let him be mine.

Just because he believes he won't change his mind later, doesn't mean he still can't. Maybe not tonight, or next week, or even next year. It might be ten years from now. One day he is going to wake up and see that I'm not everything he thought I was.

"Tell me what I need to do to prove it to you. What do you need?" He broke the kiss but kept his mouth hovering over mine.

"I don't think you're the one that needs to prove anything. I need to prove it to myself."

The words felt like a bomb going off in my head. My therapist had said it during our last session, but it didn't resonate until that moment. I had baggage to unpack, and he wanted to help. We could have this discussion a thousand times, it felt like we'd already had it a thousand times. Until I could figure out how to open the zipper to let him in, we were just going to keep coming back to this suitcase stuck between us.

"I want everything with you, I really do. I just don't know how to let myself have it."

I love you. Please hear me. I love you more than I've ever loved anyone before. You make me think I didn't know what love was before I met you. I love you so much it hurts.

***

The smell of coffee woke me up. Next me the other side of the bed was empty but still warm. My t-shirt was pushed up over my stomach and one pajama leg was all the way up to my knee. I laid there trying to decide if I should get up or wait for him to come back. The door to the back porch slammed closed. I sat up and pushed the curtains aside to look out the window of the bedroom. There were two steaming mugs of coffee on the table between the two rocking chairs barely visible in the low light of the sun just starting to peek over the horizon.

"Sorry, that door closed harder than I expected." Matt's voice was huskier than normal from how late we had stayed up talking. He still wore his pajamas. I felt like we had just fallen asleep. He crouched beside the bed and stroked his fingers through my hair. "I tried to let you sleep in until the last minute." He pushed his glasses up on his nose. The front of his hair stood up pointing to the left. It wasn't fair that he could look so cute with bedhead.

I reached for his face, guiding his mouth down to mine, and tried not to think about what my chin looked like or my morning breath as I kissed him. "I think kissing you good morning is my new favorite thing."

"Mine too. One of these days you're going to agree to let me do it every morning." His eyes fluttered closed for a moment as I ran my fingers through the strands of his hair that poked up. His head tilted into my touch.

My brain was too clouded with sleep and happiness to panic at his words. "One day," I said as I threaded my fingers through the other side of his hair, making it stand up to match.

He pulled the blankets back and lifted a pair of thick socks from his duffle bag next to the bed. He spun my legs around until I sat up on the edge of the bed and straightened my clothes, goosebumps covering where his warm fingers brushed my skin. "I can do that," I told him.

He slipped the socks onto my feet before scooping me into a bridal carry. "You can let me take care of you."

He sat in a rocking chair with me in his lap and wrapped a blanket around us. Temperatures in the mountains were always lower than at home, but this morning felt even chillier than a normal early October morning. He freed the hair that had remained in my bun from the scrunchie.

"Did you know that you move around a lot in your sleep?"

I picked up a mug and let it warm my palms. "I always assumed so with how my hair looks in the mornings. Did you know that you're clingy in your sleep?"

"Beautiful, I'm clingy when I'm awake too." He tightened his hold on me to prove his point. I leaned into him and breathed in his scent. His normal spicy citrus was mixed with smoke from the fire we built last night because he insisted on showing me the right way to roast marshmallows at 1 am.

"I like how clingy you are." His touch always made me feel so grounded, so wanted.

He nuzzled my cheek with his nose turning my attention to the sunrise. We watched the sun creep up the sky, flooding it with colors.

"You weren't kidding about how beautiful this is."

"Breathtaking," he said.

I turned back to see his eyes fixed on me. The look on his face reminded me of when he told me about how much he loves music. A blush heated my face. "Why are you looking at me like that?"

"Like what?"

"Like I'm your favorite thing."

He laughed and his eyes flicked down as his face reddened. God, he was so cute like that. "Because you are."

"I look like a mess." I sat the mug back on the table and reached for the scrunchie he'd put around his wrist with one hand while the other gathered up my hair.

He peeled my fingers from my hair and moved my hand to his face. "You look like my favorite version of you."

I snorted. "Your favorite version of me is a mess?"

"The version that's only meant for me." He brought my mouth to his and kissed me until the sun was all the way up. Then he pulled the blanket tighter around us and we planned our day while we drank our coffee.

It was all so perfect I had only one thought on my mind the whole time.

Fuck, I love this man.

Chapter 24

Matt

"RUPERT MATTHEW FLETCHER JUNIOR, are you trying to kill me?" Riley huffed from behind me. I spun back to see her bent over with her hands planted on her thighs as she struggled to catch her breath.

My own breathing was heavy, and my legs ached from the rocky uphill hike. It wasn't as bad as the trail I hiked on my own during the summer, but it wasn't as easy as the description I'd read had promised.

"Did you get lost again?" She wiped the back of one hand against her forehead.

The chilly morning had quickly warmed up to the mid-seventies, which wouldn't have been a bad thing if we were doing anything other than this. We had both dressed in sweatshirts without checking the weather forecast for the day. I had been so excited to show her this overlook. After a quick breakfast at a small diner in town we swung by the café where we'd had our first date to grab sandwiches to pack for lunch. I adjusted the strap of the cooler backpack filled with our lunch on my shoulder.

There were three trails that led to Griffith Overlook, each one increasingly more difficult. We were supposed to be on the easiest one, which would also be the longest because it was a much slower elevation gain. This was not a slow elevation gain.

"You saw the trail marker, we're on the right one." I swung the backpack around and pulled out a bottle of water, passing it to her.

She took it and let it hang in her hand by her side while she still struggled to breathe. "Matt, if this was the trail you meant to go down that day, I really don't ever want to find out what the one you ended up on was like." She struggled to laugh as she rubbed her side. "Are you sure this was beginner friendly?"

I pulled out my phone and squinted at the trail map I had saved. The three trails were marked with yellow, orange, and red. There were a few places where the paths crossed early on. I zoomed in on the first junction of the three, my eyes widening and my smile dropping. "Please don't be mad."

Riley stood up straight and sipped the water. "We just hiked two miles uphill and I only slept like three hours last night. I don't think I have the energy to be mad." Guilt filled me as I looked at the exhausted way her shoulders slumped. I had kept her up most of the night, excited and nervous to have the whole weekend with her. I had just kept thinking of more and more things I wanted to tell her, nervous that if I went to sleep, I would wake up the next morning back at home and realize this trip was just a dream.

I passed my phone to her. "The easy trail was the yellow one." I pointed to the key on the map over her shoulder. "I forgot which one it was when we got here," I pointed to the first junction as I spoke, "and took the wrong turn. We're on the middle one now."

She sipped the water slowly, flipping the bottle cap in her hand as she did. I lifted my ball cap and ran a hand through my hair, my shoulders slumping in anticipation of her response.

"You know, you're lucky you're cute." Her laugh was exasperated. She brushed a few loose hairs away from her face. "New rule. The map is my responsibility in the future." She zoomed in and out on the screen and then glanced around us.

The pit of my stomach ached as I watched her. I should have known better than to try to bring her here. This was the second time she had trusted that I knew what I was doing, and I managed to mess it up again. Just like always I was too excited about the idea and didn't pay enough attention to the little details. I pulled my cap down low enough to partially hide my eyes. "I'm sorry," I apologized, stuffing my sweaty hands in the pockets of my jogger pants and kicking a loose rock. In my pockets my hands fisted the fabric, and my thumbs ran across the seams.

Riley looped her arms around my waist, pulling me against her, and kissed me, her forehead knocking against the bill of my ball cap. She lifted a hand to my cap and spun it around. Her hand trailed softly down the side of my face before settling on my jaw. "I'm not mad. I'm not going to promise I won't be tomorrow when I can't walk," she laughed. She pushed the corners of my mouth up with her forefingers until I smiled. "To be honest, I should have known better."

"Yeah, that's on you. I did warn you before we met," I tried to joke with her. It didn't ease the guilt that had filled me.

"I wouldn't call it a warning, per say, but it should have been a sign." She pointed to a wooden sign behind me. "It's just another mile to the overlook, we're over halfway there. Let's finish this." She motioned to the trail and poked me in the side. "At least it'll be an easy walk downhill on the way back."

I pulled her against me and pressed a kiss to her mouth. "I don't know what I ever did to deserve you." Her brows knitted together, and her lips moved with silent words. Her eyes ran over my face as she worked through something in her head. "Please tell me what you're thinking," I whispered.

"We all have our strengths," she answered. "It just so happens anything to do with directions is not yours."

The weight on my shoulders pressed down and I slumped forward more. "Oh yeah? What are my strengths?"

She smiled lightly as she pushed my shoulder. "Are you fishing for compliments?" She slipped away from me and started forward on the trail.

Yes, I was fishing for compliments, anything to convince me that she wasn't mad. I caught up with her and then moved in front of her, spinning to walk backwards up the trail. "Sometimes a guy needs to hear what his girl thinks he's good at," I answered with a shrug. We reached a set of worn stone steps, and I stepped up on the first one. I rested my hands on her shoulders as I blocked the steps.

She crossed my arms over her chest and rolled her eyes in mock annoyance. "You're so full of joy and passion. You never do anything halfway, and you always light up a room." Her answer was so quick it caught me off guard. It took me a second to process, my pressure against her shoulders relaxing enough that she stepped up onto the bottom step and forced me to step backward up to the next one.

"That last one might have more to do with you liking me than it does anything I do," I choked out.

"You should see the way everyone perks up when you walk into a room. Your happiness is so contagious." She stared up at me, brown eyes wide as her tongue flicked over her bottom lip. I mirrored the movement and swallowed thickly.

I leaned forward to whisper in her ear, "No can do, I'm too busy watching the way you light up when I walk into a room to notice anyone else."

She buried her face in my shoulder. "Stop being cheesy," she said. Her neck was pink, just like I'm sure her face was.

"I'll stop being cheesy when you stop reacting that way to it." I wrapped one of her hands in mine and started up the stairs, pulling her behind me. The guilt and worry lifted each time I looked behind me to see her smiling face.

***

Riley collapsed on the bench at the overlook and swiped the sleeve of her sweatshirt over her face to wipe away the sweat gathering on her forehead while she fanned herself with the other hand. "I should have known better than to trust a cold October morning," she groaned. At her words a slight breeze blew around us. Riley sighed and her body relaxed with relief as she felt it, her reaction almost cartoonish. I grinned at her, watching as her eyes opened and settled on the view.

If we had been a couple weeks later in coming up here the trees would be near peak color change. For now, they were all still green with the occasional small orange spec. The sun shone bright and the sky a clear blue. A stronger breeze blew, whipping Riley's loose hairs around as it passed over her. She smiled softly, standing from the bench to lean against the railing. The view was nice, but it was nothing compared to watching her take it in.

Happiness bloomed in my chest and my cheeks ached from how hard I grinned. I fumbled for my phone in my pocket, swiping up quickly to open the camera. I needed a photo of this moment, of Riley being so effortlessly herself before she noticed. Before she felt the need to be anything other than herself.

She turned to look at me just as I pressed the button to snap the photo, her smile still soft and eyes heavy from lack of sleep. "Are you laughing at me?" she asked, her eyes narrowing. The breeze whipped her hair across her face again and she struggled to brush it away.

I shook my head and somehow my smile grew, my vision narrowing as the smile forced my eyes to close slightly. "Just admiring the view," I answered.

"You can't even see it over there." She held her arm out and motioned for me to come to her. I leaned against the tree next to where the trail let out to the overlook and crossed my arms. I lifted my phone slightly, snapping more pictures of her without looking at the screen.

"Matt," she pleaded.

"I can see plenty over here," I answered.

She moved in front of me in a flash, tugging at my arms. "At least take one of us together." I let her pull me toward the railing but pretended to drag my feet. I pulled her against me as we turned with our backs to the railing and I held my phone up, angling it to get as much of the view behind us as I could.

"Y'all need some help?" a voice asked from a picnic table on the other side of the clearing around us. Riley and I both jumped at the sound, neither of us having noticed there was anyone else up here with us. I turned to see a woman with hair a mix of red and orange holding up a camera as she stood from the table. A man with blonde hair long enough to brush the collar of his jacket sat across from her, his chin resting on his hands as he studied notebooks spread across the table. His jacket had the logo for a local outdoor tour agency.

"If you don't mind," Riley answered her. I nodded and shoved my phone in my pocket. The woman took a few photos of us, directing us into various poses as she did. A few times I caught the man grinning behind her.

"You two are so cute," the woman said as she showed us the photos on the tiny screen of her camera. I wrapped my arms around Riley, pulling her against me and resting my chin on her shoulder as I looked at the screen. "How long have you been together?"

Riley stiffened against me. I squeezed her closer. "It's still new," I answered. It was the only answer I could think of that might not send Riley into a panic.

The woman's eyes lifted from her camera, and she studied us. "Oh, you just give off this vibe like you've been together forever," she said with a shrug. "Can I get your email to send you these?" she asked, moving on quickly.

Riley snapped out where ever she had drifted to in her mind and exchanged contact information with the woman. As they chatted, we learned that the woman was a travel blogger who grew up locally.

We settled back on the bench later to eat our lunch. Riley scrolled through the woman's posts about the area, excitedly showing me things we could do this weekend. Her eyes were bright as she pointed things out, saying she had no idea some of them existed. I pulled her close and said yes to every single one, struggling to plan it all out in my head to make sure we had the time.

"We need to come back here in the summer," Riley mumbled. I looked down at her screen. There was a list of the top ten underrated summer activities for the area. We need to come back. Us. Together. Did she know she had said it? My heart raced and my face hurt as I fought back a smile.

Don't get excited.

You're going to scare her.

She just suggested making a plan for something nearly eight months away.

Would It just be us? Eight months was longer than we had known each other. Maybe by then she would be okay with meeting my family. Maybe I will have met her family. It could be all of us together.

Thoughts of a hypothetical family vacation filled my mind. After a day of family activities Riley and I would sneak off for time together. We'd recap all the ways that our families fit together. We would talk about the silly things our nieces and nephews did that day. How Emery bossed everyone in the kitchen around, until her and Shelby started arguing like sisters. We would talk about how much had changed in the past year, that it was hard to believe a chance match on a dating app had turned into this.

"Yeah, we should," I said, my voice cracking a little as I spoke.

I braced myself for her to stiffen beside me, for her to backtrack when she noticed she was dancing on the line of making plans for the future. She surprised me by lifting her head to smile shyly at me and pulling the arm I had around her tighter. For a split second I could see in her eyes that we were thinking the same thing. For a split second she looked just as excited as me. For the first time I didn't see any flicker of fear

Chapter 25

Matt

Riley

It looks like the leaves are starting to change on the mountains. Emery is losing her mind over it.

Matt

We could go for a drive to look at them this weekend.

The apple festival in Fairview is the weekend. Emery won't let me forget it. She made a calendar invite and everything.

Come with us?

Of course I will, as long as she is okay with it. I don't want to crash your time with your sister.

She'll be okay with it. She likes hanging out with us.

We could make it a double date. Give her a taste of her own medicine. You could bring Oliver so I can finally meet him.

I'll see what I can do.

She won't kill me for this will she? You know I'm afraid of her.

Her bark is bigger than her bite.

I'll tell her it was my idea.

I KNEW OLIVER WASN'T going to go for the idea, but I couldn't tell Riley that. If he was the only person in my life she felt comfortable meeting then I was going to make it happen no matter what it took. He was a good friend and would do anything for me, but he was also stubborn. Since his grandparents passed away and left their auto shop to him the shop had completely consumed his life. Ava had been driving me crazy trying to get him away from the place more. Even Shelby frequently told me how he seemed to walk around with the weight of the world on his shoulders.

The guilt of how much I had neglected our friendship in the years I had been gone ate at me constantly. Oliver would do anything for me, but I never did enough to return the favor.

That's how I found myself at the shop after school. I knew there would be questions from everyone about Riley, questions I didn't have answers to, but I also knew that everyone would help me put pressure on Oliver to say yes. The man was there six days a week and often worked shifts longer than twelve hours. We caught him working Sundays when the shop was closed a few times.

Pop would be disappointed in him if he knew.

The team was lined up in front of the shop, varying looks of irritation on their faces as Shelby called instructions to them from behind her camera. Oliver stood in the middle, arms crossed and jaw clenched. Aubrey was next to him, rubbing one shoulder and saying something I couldn't hear. Wade was to his left scowling as Shelby told him that hadn't been smiling enough. Drew leaned against the shop on the other side of Aubrey playing on his phone.

"What's up?" I asked, walking up behind Shelby.

"I'm trying to get a group shot for the website, but no one wants to cooperate," Shelby whined in response.

"You got the shot fifty takes ago. We have work to do," Oliver grunted.

"Oliver be nice or I'm calling Ava. Let Shelby do the job you hired her for." Aubrey held her phone up, Ava's contact pulled up as a threat. Oliver let out a huff and let his arms drop. Ava was a force no one wanted to mess with.

I watched as Shelby instructed everyone into several poses. The second she lowered her camera, everyone broke apart, rushing back to the cars they had been working on.

She huddled next to me so I could see the small screen on her camera as she scrolled through all the photos she had taken today. I couldn't help but laugh as I watched the progression of irritation on everyone's faces in the group photos. There were also an assortment of candid and posed photos of the guys in the shop working. No wonder they were all so annoyed with her. It looked like she had been taking photos of them all day.

"Give me a second to get a bay cleared and I'll pull your car in," Oliver hollered from the open bay door next to us.

I shook my head. "I'm actually here to ask you for a favor." I walked into the shop, Shelby following behind me. Wade and Drew kept working, both wearing headphones, but Aubrey and Shelby stuck close by. Maybe the two of them would be all the backup I needed. "How do you feel about a double date this weekend?" I asked.

He turned his back to us, focusing all his attention to arranging the tools in his toolbox. "Don't have time." He lifted his ball cap and ran a hand through his dark wavy hair. It was the longest I had seen it in years, a step away from long enough to tie back. He always hated having his haircut and would grow it out until it bothered him enough that he had to get it cut. This was past that point. Guilt for not noticing how much he had been neglecting himself ate at the pit of my stomach.

"It's on a Sunday," I offered in the most upbeat tone I could muster. "You won't have to miss any work, man."

"You should go, Oliver. You haven't been on a date in years," Aubrey offered from beside me.

He rubbed a hand over his beard. "I'm really not interested." It was the least like himself he'd ever sounded. The Oliver I knew had never been one to say no to a date. Relationships had never been his thing, but he had always been a serial dater. I didn't think he'd gotten bad enough he wouldn't even consider a date.

"We won't call it a date then." I paused and leaned in closer to him, lowering my voice like I didn't want the girls to hear. I wouldn't hear the end of this from Shelby, but it was the only card I had to play. "Remember that girl I told you about?" I asked.

He nodded, turning his back to lean against his toolbox and crossing his arms.

"Do we get to meet her?" Shelby asked.

I shook my head. "Sorry, Shelby, she still isn't ready for that." I turned back to Oliver. "She's okay with meeting you."

There was a collective gasp from Shelby and Aubrey. "You have to do it, Oliver. I need to know all about her," Shelby said. At the same time Aubrey said, "you need the break." It escalated from there until Aubrey had her phone out in a threat and the two of them were talking over each other so much I couldn't understand a word that was being said. Oliver glared at me from under his hat like he wanted to murder me. I shrugged and smiled like it didn't bother me.

It bothered me. I was a shitty friend that hadn't been there for him when he needed me because I was too wrapped up in my own life and now I was asking him to do something for me. *It was for him too*, I told myself. He needed to get out of this shop.

"She's the one, Oliver. I know it this time. You've got to meet her. She's bringing her sister. It doesn't have to be a date. Just come with us and have some fun." I waited for him to call me out. How many times did I say Liz was the one? He had every right to point it out. I had been so sure then and look at where I had ended up.

Riley was it, though. I had known it from the first time I saw her in front of that café. I had known it the days leading up to that date. Everything with her was easy. Everything with her just felt right. Being with her was the kind of love I had wished for growing up and watching my parents together.

"Why me?" he asked.

"Because you're my best friend." I could already see him starting to fold, his shoulders relaxing and the tension in his forearms fading. "You're like a brother to me," I piled on. His jaw worked as he clenched his teeth and then rubbed his hand over his beard again. He dropped his arms.

"She doesn't want to meet Shelby?" He was reaching for an excuse.

I shot Shelby an apologetic look. She nodded softly at me, seeming to understand the situation. After Oliver she was my next closest friend despite our four year age difference. "Of course she does, but not yet." I rolled my lips together trying to decide how to explain the situation. "It's just complicated."

His arms crossed back over his chest, and he narrowed his eyes. "Explain," he barked. He slipped into what I always called his guard dog mode growing up. Protective older brother mode. My heart raced at the thought of him having anything bad to say about Riley.

"We're just taking things slow."

"Snail's pace slow," Shelby added.

I shot her look that said she wasn't helping.

"I know you don't want to see him get his heartbroken, Oliver. How are you going to do that if you aren't willing to meet her?" Shelby added with a smirk. She poked her tongue out at me and subtly flipped me off with the hand holding her camera.

"I can work some extra hours this week to make sure we don't get behind," a quiet voice said beside me. I turned to see Drew had joined us; one earbud clutched in his hand. I clapped him on the shoulder. "He really does need a break," Drew whispered to me. He shoved the earbud back in his ear and spun on his feet to get back to work.

"Baby bro has spoken, man. It's worse than I thought," I said to Oliver. He uncrossed his arms and recrossed them a few times before running his hands through his hair again. "Let Ava cut your hair before then, okay?"

Oliver would do anything for the people that he cared about, but his biggest weakness was Drew. He was the youngest of the family and took everything that happened with their dad the hardest. Oliver's protective instinct over me was nothing compared to the lengths he would go through for Drew. While the rest of us had to bully him into taking care of himself, Drew just had to ask.

"One date, that's it." Oliver shoved past us to climb in the driver's seat of the car he had been working on, effectively ending the conversation. Aubrey gave me a thumbs up as she headed back up to the lobby.

Now I just had to hope that Emery didn't murder all of us for this. Or worse, that her and Oliver didn't team up to murder me.

Chapter 26

Riley

I TUGGED THE BOTTOM of the berry-colored plaid shirt dress Emery had forced me into a little lower and twisted in front of the mirror. The outfit was cute, I couldn't argue with her there. The dress hit me mid-thigh, just short enough for the bottom of my tattoo to peek out as I moved. She had paired it with semi-sheer black tights, a cropped corduroy shirt, and dark brown Chelsea boots. The corduroy shirt would most likely end up tied around my waist by mid-morning due to the heat. She had braided my hair into a crown around my head. I looked more like an Instagram post about fall outfits, and less like I was going to an apple festival in the mountains.

I heard a car door close in our driveway and rushed to meet Matt at the door. His eyes moved over me slowly, his smile disappearing and eyes darkening the longer he looked at me. The paper around the bouquet of sunflowers he held crunched as his fist tightened around it and I couldn't stop myself from focusing on the way his forearm and hand flexed. My breath caught as my eyes moved up his arm and I noticed he wore the same outfit he wore on our first date with a lightweight black bomber jacket over top, the sleeves pushed up to his elbows. He wore his glasses again, his eyes crinkled behind them as he smiled at me.

How was it possible that this man could be more gorgeous every time I saw him?

"I should go change," I said with another tug at the bottom of the dress.

Matt shook his head and took one of my hands in his to spin me around for a full look at my outfit. "Please don't." The way he looked at me told me this would be another dress Emery would not be getting back.

I glanced over his shoulder at the friend he brought with him. He was slightly shorter than me with short wavy dark hair that looked freshly cut, a short beard, and a stocky frame. He wore an army green button down open over a white T-shirt and dark wash jeans. "You must be Oliver," I said to him. He nodded and smiled softly at me. I knew this wasn't really a date, that we didn't expect Oliver and Emery to hit it off even though I still secretly hoped they would. Seeing Oliver in person now told me that it was pointless to hope. He was so practically the opposite of her type.

Matt's fingers rubbed over the hem of the dress and pulled my attention back to him. The way his hand brushed over my thigh made it hard to breathe. "Em, hurry up, they're here!" I yelled over my shoulder toward the kitchen.

Matt pulled his attention away from my dress and placed the bouquet of sunflowers in my hand, folding my fingers around it like he needed an excuse to touch me. His hand moved up my arm and over my shoulders until he cupped the back of my head while his other hand lifted my chin pulling me in for a kiss. "Hi," he said against my lips before our mouths joined.

"Riley, can you come help me for a second?" I jumped and turned around to see Emery in the doorway of the kitchen. Her jaw clenched, and her eyes fixed on Oliver. She forced a smile when her eyes flicked to mine.

I placed the flowers in the vase I had prepared on the coffee table, something I had started doing any time Matt was coming over without even thinking, before joining her in the kitchen.

She gestured to the three dairy free pumpkin spice lattes in paper to go cups decorated with fall leaves on the counter. "I only made three," she told me. "You didn't tell me that someone else was coming with us."

"Oh yeah, I thought we could make this a double date. I know you probably get tired of third wheeling with us all the time. Just make another one."

She sighed as she started the espresso machine. "That's not the point." She reached for a cup and worked quickly adding ingredients to it.

I twisted the bottom of the cropped shirt and focused on the cup instead of Emery's face. "I thought it was time for us to play matchmaker for you."

She rolled her eyes and focused harder on the latte she was making.

I looked into the living room to check on the guys. Oliver looked around at all of Emery's décor. Matt's focus was on the kitchen doorway. He smiled when he caught me looking. I looked back at Emery. "Just play along. If you don't like him, that's fine. Just be nice, okay? He's Matt's best friend."

She finished the latte and then handed two to me, picking up the other two and making her way to where the guys stood in front of the tv stand. I followed behind her. Oliver pressed the button on the front of the musical haunted house figure and jumped back in surprise as lights flashed and it started to play creepy music overlayed with monster noises.

Matt shook his head at him, "I told you not to touch anything."

"Matt, aren't you going to introduce us?" Emery asked, coming up behind them.

Both men turned to face us. Oliver's eyes widened when he saw Emery. Matt didn't notice. His eyes were fixed on where I stood behind Emery. "Yeah, um, Emery, this Oliver. Oliver, this is Riley's sister Emery," he said with a quick wave of his hand between them. He moved around Emery to reach me, and I wasn't sure if he wanted out of firing range or if he just needed to get his hands back on me. It was probably both.

Oliver stuck out a hand like he was going for a handshake but transitioned to a small wave when he noticed her full hands. "Hi, Matt's told me a lot about you," he said.

"Don't listen to anything he says. I promise I'm not as bad as he probably told you." She held one of the lattes out to him. "Any food allergies?" she asked. She always asked people that the first time she offered them any food. She said it always bothered her that no one ever considered if the person they were giving food to might have food allergies and be too scared of speaking up.

"You are going to drive me crazy in this dress," Matt whispered in my ear.

"There's still time for me to change," I whispered back.

"Don't you dare." He traced my lips with his thumb making my heart race. "I'm regretting our rules right now."

I swallowed hard and flicked my eyes to his lips. "Rules can change."

He shook his head and took a cup from me. The unspoken words between us weighed heavy in my chest. All I had to do was tell him what he meant to me, what I really wanted.

"I'm driving," Emery announced. She pointed at Matt before adding, "I'm not going to be in a wreck on my favorite day of the year because you're too busy eye fucking my sister."

I met Emery's eyes, checking to see if she was okay. She always demanded to be the one driving. She hadn't always been that way. Two years ago, she told me she hated being a passenger because she would get car sick if she wasn't the one driving. She would never tell me why it was something that she hadn't mentioned sooner.

Matt threw an arm around me. "That's fine. We could use some time in the back seat being chauffeured around."

Emery made a gagging noise as she walked out the door.

***

"They have pumpkins," Matt said, pointing to a stand further down the field from where we were. "We should get some to carve."

"I don't know if Emery is going to leave any room in the wagon for that." Emery added another apple to the plastic bag in her hand. There was already one in the wagon Oliver pulled for her. The wagon also carried various jellies, preserves, and cider.

"What is she going to do with all of that?"

I laughed. "We're going to be test subjects to a lot of new recipes for a little while."

Matt licked his lips. "I can't complain about that. Everything she has forced us to eat so far has been amazing." He pulled me against his side and planted a kiss against the side of my head. "You're a good cook too, sweetheart."

"She's the better cook, you don't have to humor me." Emery had been helping our mom in the kitchen since she could stand on her own. My mom said it started out to help Emery work through the food anxiety she had developed soon after switching to solid foods and having multiple anaphylactic episodes. My parents learned about her milk allergy when she was a newborn but introducing solids led to the discovery of several other food allergies. She was always more likely to eat something if she had helped with preparing it, even at that young of an age. I would help sometimes but never had the same passion for food that Emery did. She had outgrown the majority of her allergies, but milk, tomatoes, and avocado were all still severe and required her to carry an EpiPen.

Emery paid the vendor and added the second bag of apples to the wagon. Oliver followed behind her as she joined us. "I want to check out those pumpkins," she said. She continued on to the stand with pumpkins that Matt had pointed out to me without waiting for a response from us.

"Is she mad at us?" Matt asked me. Emery had been short with us since leaving the house. While we were getting ready, she hadn't shut up about all the recipes she had planned and how excited she was for the festival. After meeting Oliver, she switched to only communicating when necessary. I had noticed the two of them exchanging tense looks when they thought Matt and I weren't watching. Oliver had still barely spoken.

"Probably." I tugged his hand. "Let's go get pumpkins. Then I want to get some pictures with those." I pointed to the photobooth of painted scarecrows with the faces cut out.

***

"I need a break," Emery said, taking a seat at the only empty picnic table. She took the handle of the wagon from Oliver, his hand flinching away as their fingers brushed. If Emery noticed she didn't show it, pulling the wagon in front of her and digging through it.

"Anyone ready for lunch?" Matt asked.

I glanced at Emery to gauge her reaction. There were several food trucks here but eating anywhere she couldn't vet beforehand always stressed her out. I didn't know if she had been able to do any research on them beforehand. "Do you want to try to eat here or were you planning to eat somewhere in town?" I asked her when she didn't look up at Matt's question.

She looked over at the food trucks barely visible through the crowd. She chewed her lip and reached for her phone. "Last year the crowds in town were so bad we were stuck waiting for hours," she said.

"We can take the risk here, if you want."

She chewed on her lip more, eyes flicking between the trucks. I could see the wheels turning as she decided if it was worth trying to get accurate allergen information from the vendors.

"You could do a hamburger, right? I'm sure we could get them to show us their ingredients," Matt offered.

She gave a cautious nod.

"But the tomatoes. How big of a cross contamination risk would that be?" Oliver asked.

Matt, Emery, and I all snapped our attention him. "I, um, mentioned it while we were looking at preserves," Emery tripped over her words as she dropped her eyes to the wagon.

My eyes caught Matt's. "I don't believe her," I tried to tell him with my eyes. He shrugged but his eyes widened, and I saw a flash of panic.

"Shit," he mouthed silently.

"Let's go get in line and see what we can do. If I can't get a straight answer, we can go somewhere else." I pulled Matt with me leaving Emery and Oliver alone at the table.

"She's lying about something," I told Matt once we were far enough away.

"Riley, I think I messed up," Matt said over me. I lifted a brow at him. "I've been so focused on you I didn't even register how they were acting toward each other."

I came to a stop and crossed my arms while I waited for him to explain. "I thought she was just taking out her anger with us on him but then he said the thing about tomatoes, and it clicked. Oliver has an ex that he never told me her name. On our way over I was telling him about Emery, and he sort of flinched when I said her name."

"You think it was her?"

"Maybe. It was a couple years ago, so I never met her or anything. He wouldn't even show me pictures of her. All I know is that she broke his heart. He's still pretty messed up over it."

I looked back to the table, trying to catch a glimpse through the moving crowd. I could see Oliver rubbing a hand over his beard. Emery fidgeted with her necklace. Both wore tense expressions.

"Emery's relationship history is rough, but she won't talk to me about it. Three years ago, she and her fiancé broke up." Emery's ex-fiancé was the only one of her exes I had ever met. Mostly only at family gatherings. He never interacted much with us, but I had never liked the way Emery was around him. Her whole personality changed. "It wasn't Oliver," I added to clarify for Matt.

"You think they met after?"

I nodded, still watching them through the crowd. "She wasn't herself around that time."

Matt moved forward with the line, pulling me behind him. "I'll ask him about it later."

I kept my eyes on them as we moved with the line. There was a split second where Emery's face lit up as Oliver tucked her hair behind her ear. I squeezed Matt's hand, trying to direct his attention to them. The moment didn't last long enough for him to see. Matt turned me forward gently and tucked me into his side.

"Everything is going to be okay," he said to me.

"I know. I just want my sister to be as happy as I am." I buried my face against Matt's shoulder hiding the blush that covered my face.

His hand stroked my jaw but didn't force me to look at him. "You make me happy too, sweetheart."

The line in front of us moved quickly and I took a few deep breaths to prepare myself for the interaction. The woman at the window was patient as I told her about Emery's allergies and asked questions. She showed me the package for the burger buns so I could check the ingredients myself. As I looked over it, she shared that her son had food allergies, so she understood the struggle. She let us come around to the door of the truck so we could watch them prepare our food and advised that the lettuce came pre-shredded so it would be safe for Emery to have lettuce and pickles, but she would need to skip the onions since they were prepped at the same time as the tomatoes. They opened a fresh bag of lettuce and jar of pickles in front of us so there would be zero risk of cross contamination. I couldn't believe how thorough they were and made a mental note to find their social media pages so I could leave a review.

My mood deflated when we made it back to Oliver and Emery. They sat so far apart I wasn't sure how they were both on the bench seat, the tension so thick it felt like walking into a wall.

"You kids having fun?" Matt asked in a forced old man voice and pulled his glasses down to sit at the edge of his nose, right when I lifted my apple cider slushie to take a sip. The freezing liquid shot out of my nose and dribbled down my face. It wasn't that funny, but the air was so tense at the table I couldn't help myself. I was too shocked to react, my sinuses burning and making my eyes water. "Oh my god, sweetheart, I'm so sorry." He grabbed a wad of napkins and dabbed at my face.

I laughed and took the napkins from his hand to clean myself up. I looked at Emery to see her holding back a laugh for the first time since the guys showed up. "I'm glad you think this is funny," I said.

She looked down at her burger and started pulling it apart to check for any visible cross contamination. Matt filled her in on our experience at the truck. I caught Oliver sneaking glances at her as he listened.

"Hey, Matt, I forgot to grab mayo packets. Could you go get me one?" I flicked my eyes to Oliver and back to Matt.

"Yeah, sure. Oliver, you should come with me. There, uh, was something over there I wanted to show you."

Oliver's brows pulled together clearly seeing through whatever Matt and I were trying to do. Matt stood and waited for Oliver to follow him.

"Spill," I said to Emery once the guys were out of earshot.

"I don't know what you're talking about."

"You're not as sneaky as you think you are."

"Admit you're in love with Matt and I'll tell you how I know Oliver." She crossed her arms in front of her and raised her eyebrow as a challenge.

I smirked and picked at my fries. "That's all I needed for now."

"He's not my type, you know that. He's too short." She narrowed her eyes, the corners of her mouth twitching like they always did when she lied.

I shrugged and chewed a fry. "Okay."

"And he's too nice," she added. That was an interesting observation. He had been so reserved over the course of the morning I wasn't sure how she could say he was too nice. I expected her to say he was too grumpy. Then again him being grumpy would make him her type. He did have a patient air around him, and from what Matt had told me he was a nice person. At least, he was nice to the people close to him. Matt had also shared that he hadn't been himself recently and warned me he might not make the best impression today.

I struggled to keep my face straight and shoveled in a couple more fries. "Fascinating. Tell me more."

"He doesn't have any tattoos."

I snorted. "That's an interesting thing to know considering he's in jeans and a long sleeve shirt. He could be just as covered as you are."

Emery's mouth moved as she tried to speak but no words came out. Matt and Oliver returned before she could gather herself. Matt gave me a low thumbs up as he walked toward us.

"Oliver, Matt's told me that you might have some embarrassing stories to share about him," I prodded. I knew all about how much of a nerd Matt had been growing up, about how much he had been bullied. He'd shared a few stories, even shown me a few photos of his awkward years. Every time we talked about it he said the stories would be better if I heard them from Oliver.

"Tell her about the trombone one." Matt tapped a finger against the bridge of his own nose in the same spot where it looked like Oliver's had been broken.

Oliver chuckled. "I don't know, man, do you really want me to tell her about that? Shouldn't I be telling her stories to make you look cool?"

Matt put on his best serious look, his mouth twitching and shoulders shaking as he held back a laugh. "You know as well as anyone there is no making me look cool."

"That ship has already sailed," I added.

Matt clutched his chest. "Ouch," he groaned. "Here I was thinking you liked me."

I patted his head. "It's okay, we all know I like you because you're a giant dork."

Chapter 27

Riley

I STEPPED BACK TO look over our trunk or treat set up as Emery made a few more adjustments. We went with a haunted pumpkin patch theme this year. We were both dressed as scare crows.

She stepped back and shook her head before shifting a pumpkin ever so slightly it didn't even look like she had touched it.

An arm landed around my shoulders and Matt's scent washed over me. I turned to my side to see him wearing a white sheet with holes cut out for the eyes, his glasses and a black top hat on top holding it in place. His car was parked next to us and decorated with several sheets over clothes hangers with black circles drawn in marker to look like eyes. It looked like he had pulled in, popped the trunk, and hung the hangers up in less than a minute. There was one ghost that appeared to be a sheet thrown over a pile of pillows sitting in the center of his trunk with a saxophone propped against it. "I think mine is better," he said. He lifted the sheet up with one arm, pressing a quick kiss to my mouth.

Emery wrinkled her nose in disgust when she looked over at his car. "You could have at least put in a little effort."

"It took forever to get the eyes right on all those sheets," he shot back.

I laughed as they stuck their tongues out at each other. I tugged his arm down so the sheet dropped back over him before they devolved into making gestures children shouldn't see. Emery was still upset about him bringing Oliver to the apple festival a couple weeks ago. "Is anyone coming to help you? Things get a little crazy once the kids get here. They always move in mobs and get scary if you don't hand out the candy fast enough."

I looked around at the high school parking lot to see that almost everyone was done setting up. All the teachers and other school systems employees set up at the two high schools in the county for trunk or treat the Saturday before Halloween. Most parents preferred to bring their kids around to these set ups rather than true trick or treating. It was safer and they didn't have to worry about being out late on a school night.

"Oliver is on his way," Matt answered.

Emery stiffened and then turned away from us to make more adjustments to the decorations. "Maybe we should swap. Can't have two newbies handing out candy, we might end up with a riot. I could help you, and Oliver could help Emery."

Emery whirled around so fast I jumped even though I had been expecting it. Her eyes blazed. Matt swallowed hard beside me. Even with a sheet over his face he looked scared.

"Emery, calm down. I was just joking." I knocked my hip against Matt. "She's not that scary."

Cars started to pull into the lot and the sound of excited kids filled the air just as Oliver appeared running toward us with a sheet over his arm. He saw Emery's glare and stopped at Matt's car, throwing the sheet over himself, securing it with a pair of sunglasses and a Franklin Auto Shop branded ballcap, then picking up the bowl of candy.

Matt had managed to get Oliver to admit that Emery was the ex that he thought she was but hadn't been able to get more information than that. The way that Emery glanced at him during breaks between groups of kids had me wondering if there might still be some lingering feelings.

Matt and Oliver ran out of candy within an hour. They were in a frantic discussion over if Oliver should try to make a run to pick up more if they should just call it and close up the trunk early.

I poked Emery in the side. "I know you have extra candy. Could we give them some?" She always bought twice as much as we would go through. The last few kids to come by our trunk in past years had ended up with all the extra. I'm sure their parents hated us.

"They're giving out too much to each kid and they keep sneaking pieces."

"That doesn't answer the question."

She grabbed four unopened bags and tossed them to me. "That's all they're getting. Tell them to make it last."

"No need to panic, boys," I said as I waved the bags at them. Matt threw his sheet off and pulled me into him when I walked over to their trunk.

"My hero," he gasped with an exaggerated swoon.

I laughed and emptied the bags into their candy bowls, showing them how many pieces to give out to stretch out for the next two hours. "I hope you learned your lesson for next year."

***

Emery slammed the trunk closed once the parking lot was free of kids. "Are we still doing movie night tonight or do you have other plans?"

She motioned toward Matt and Oliver. Halloween movies after trunk or treat had become our tradition. Emery spent the morning baking an assortment of snacks for it.

"I'm not missing out on movie night and Matt knows that. It's just us sisters tonight."

She scuffed her shoe against the pavement. "I know I forced you into this thing with him, but I'm kind of starting to miss just our time together." It was the first time she had mentioned anything about it. She might give Matt a hard time sometimes, but she had been nothing but welcoming when he was at our place. If he wasn't with us, she was constantly asking if I had plans with him. Just like the night she had bullied me into not coming home, she seemed to always be doing everything she could to force us together. I was starting to think she was trying to get me to hurry up and move out of her house.

My eyes widened. "Why didn't you say something? You've seemed happy to have him hanging out with us."

"I have been."

I tugged her arm. "Come on, I'm ready to get this sister date started." I pointed over my shoulder at Matt. "I'm going to tell him bye and then we'll get going."

Chapter 28

Matt

"Mom, Dad, I'm home," I yelled as I opened the side door. I let out a grunt as I hoisted the heavy tote of Christmas décor up from the garage floor and carried it inside. Shelby followed behind me dragging the storage bag holding the Christmas tree.

"Matt? What are you doing?" Mom looked up from the vegetables she was chopping long enough to see the tote in my arms. She rested the knife on the cutting board and wiped her hands on a dish towel.

"I thought we could help with the Christmas decorations today." I dropped the tote to the floor. I wrapped my mom in a bear hug. Over the summer I had been here almost every day like I was trying to make up for all the time I had missed over the years of living over five hours away from home, but my visits had decreased to weekly and then every other week. Mom had teased me about it only to follow up by telling me she was glad I had started to rediscover a place for myself in Mountain View that didn't involve hanging out with my parents all the time.

"Ask him why today, Mom," Shelby urged as she dropped the tree next to the tote.

Mom squinted her eyes at the calendar on the refrigerator. "Isn't today Halloween? Matt, we can wait until this weekend. Invite your sisters and their families. We haven't had a decorating party in years." Her eyes widened as she spoke, sparkling as she worked through a plan in her mind.

"Ask him what his plans are tomorrow," Shelby prompted again.

I shot her a look to not go there. She had still been picking at me for letting Oliver meet Riley first. The teasing had gotten worse once Oliver filled her in on the details of our trip to the apple festival – the details that didn't involve him or Emery. I tried to get her to agree to the impromptu decorating party tonight without any details of why it needed to be tonight.

I didn't want to tell her how I had been thinking about our childhood Christmas traditions for the past week, how happy I was to participate in them all this week. My mind drifted to having Riley there with me, to the pictures she had sent while helping Emery decorate their house for fall. Would she be that goofy helping me with Christmas? I could see her being the type to hang mismatched ornaments on the tree in a carefree manner, not worrying about making it social media worthy. Like everything with her, it would feel like the fun montage in movies filled with pure joy as we worked.

I wanted the tradition with my family, but I wanted to build a tradition with Riley too. I wanted to see how different it would be with her, how it would be ours. She wasn't ready to be part of my family. I could respect that; give her the space she needed until she was ready. Patience had never been a strength of mine, if I wanted something I wanted it right then, but for her I could be anything. I could redirect my impulses if it meant getting to have her in the end.

My family always started Christmas on November first. Without fail, no matter the day of week, on November 1st Dad would pull out the decorations while us kids helped Mom in the kitchen baking cookies. *A Christmas Story* would play softly in the background, the sound drowned out by blaring Christmas music. It was pure chaos as we all worked, the four of us kids arguing over which pieces of décor we got to place while hyped up on cookies and hot chocolate with mini marshmallows. Mom never told us where to put anything, just told us whoever grabbed it decided where it went that year. As we grew up the collection of ornaments for the tree grew until the tree was hardly visible under the clutter. It was beautiful and loud.

Every year we ended the night with Dad lifting Mom onto his shoulders so she could place the star at the top of the tree. We would all curl up on the couch and start the movie over. The second time around we would drown it out with our discussion of all the things we would do that Christmas season.

To this day I don't think I've ever watched the movie all the way through.

"Mr. Lovesick goober over here wants to spend tomorrow with his not girlfriend starting their own tradition," Shelby's words punched into the nostalgic haze that had filled my mind. The memories crumbled around me the same way they had an hour ago when Shelby told me that they hadn't had a decorating party since I moved away. Our parents put everything out through the month of November on their own.

Both women stared at me, blinking expectantly. My face and ears blazed.

"Girlfriend?" Mom broke the silence.

"Not girlfriend," Shelby clarified.

"We'll have a decorating party on Saturday," Mom declared. "Tell your sisters." She turned back to her cutting board. "Matt, bring your *not* girlfriend."

I glared at Shelby. She smiled, flicked her hair over her shoulder, and turned to the door. I followed her out, the two of us bringing the remaining totes from the garage. I pulled out the themed bakeware, mixing bowls, and measuring scoops to wash up.

"Remember how you used to play your saxophone for the residents?" Mom asked. She transferred the chopped potatoes and carrots to a sheet pan. It took my brain a moment to catch up to what she was asking. When I was first learning to play the residents at the nursing home where she worked as an activity director loved when I would come by, something that had happened by accident one day after school because I needed to practice. Dad worked as a high school history teacher in Fairview, often not getting home until late in the evening. Mom's hours varied through the year so we would spend time there after school until she was able to leave. I wasn't any good to start with, but they acted like I was some child prodigy. It had done a lot for my nonexistent self-confidence.

"Mr. B was bringing students by for concerts throughout the year. Did you know that? They keep asking when the kids are coming to visit."

Mr. B was the teacher whose position I had taken. He was more than just a band teacher for most students. He was a teacher that loved his job, loved the opportunity to help mold the next generation. His classroom was an escape for those that didn't fit in anywhere else. He welcomed everyone, even the students he never taught.

His were the shoes I had to fill.

"I'll see what I can do," I told her.

I should have already thought about that, been making plans for it. Riley kept telling me that I was doing great, that I would find my footing soon. But here we were, a third of the way through the year, and I still felt like I had that first day.

I will never be the teacher that Mr. B was.

Chapter 29

Riley

November

Are you ready to put up Christmas decorations tonight?

Riley

It's November 1st. Emery will kill us if we put them up before Thanksgiving.

November is Christmas time. We can put them up at my apartment. She'll never have to know.

Oh no, you're one of those.

Did you start Christmas music this morning?

You know I did.

> I don't know if this is going to work out.

> No need to be such a Scrooge. Come over tonight and let me show you the light side.

> You going to fill me with some Christmas cheer? *winking emoji*

> Riley Elaine Harrison, are you sending me innuendos while you are supposed to be teaching children?

> Maybe.

> No funny business, only Christmas spirit.

Warm spices flooded my nose when I opened the door of Matt's apartment. He stood over the crockpot on his counter stirring something and dancing to the music playing over the bluetooth speaker on the bar and wearing a checkered Christmas apron. "Thai curry soup," he explained when he looked up to me.

"It smells amazing." I dropped my bag on the table by his door and kicked off my shoes before making my way over to him. "Ready to fill me with some Christmas cheer?"

He laughed and pulled me into his arms. "We have to make the snickerdoodle cookies first and then we'll get started on the decorations." He kissed me and I wrapped my arms around his neck pulling him closer. "Hi, sweetheart."

"Hi. How was your day?"

"I started all my kids on the music for the Christmas concerts today and now I get to see you and decorate for my favorite holiday. It's been a great day."

I smoothed my fingers over the creases of his goofy smile and then pulled him in for another kiss. "I'm happy I get to be part of your great day."

"Every day with you is a great day."

The song playing changed to It's Beginning to Look A Lot Like Christmas and he looped his arms around me swaying me with the music. He moved his mouth lip syncing with the song. My heart swelled watching the happiness on his face.

"You never told me why Christmas is your favorite holiday."

His smile grew until his eyes were barely open. "It's my mom's favorite and growing up she always did everything she could to make it magical for us. The cookies we're going to make tonight were the ones she always made with us before we put up the decorations. My dad told me once that he was a strong believer in saving Christmas for December until he met my mom. He said he would keep the decorations up all year if she wanted because he loved how happy it made her."

"My parents always tried to do all the Christmas things with us, but I could always tell how much it stressed them out. It kind of lost the magic for me once I was old enough to notice." I tucked my head against his shoulder and ran my hands up and down his back.

I pulled away from him and looked over at the stack of totes in the middle of his apartment floor. His fingers brushed my hair back as he gathered it into a messy bun on top of my head. He slid a scrunchie from around his wrist to secure it. He always had a scrunchie ready for me. "Will you let me make it magical for you now?"

"That sounds perfect." I spun around to beam at him. He held out an apron for me to put on before resuming dancing around the kitchen as he pulled out the cookie ingredients. I wanted to be part of this tradition with him every November 1st for the rest of my life.

If he doesn't change his mind.

He sang along to the music as we worked our way through the handwritten recipe. The handwriting on the card was a neater version of his and I wonder which things about him came from which of his parents. Clearly, his passion came from his Mom but his unselfish love came from his Dad. I wondered what being loved by him without me putting roadblocks in his way would feel like.

He held up the mixer attachment once the cookies were in the oven. "Want a taste?" He ran a finger over the paddle and licked the raw dough from his finger.

"Matt, there are raw eggs in that."

He laughed. "It's actually the raw flour that you need to worry about." He offered it to me again. "Almost 30 years of this and I haven't gotten sick yet."

I shook my head. He shrugged and put the paddle in the sink.

We ate our soup standing over the bar while the cookies baked. Matt pointed to different spots in his apartment walking me through the vision he had for the décor. When we finally started going through the totes, I was blown away by the amount of things he had.

"Are you sure this is all going to fit? I think you might have Emery beat for the gold medal in over-decorating."

He pulled a Santa hat down over my head, my bun making it stand straight up. "It might take some creative thinking, but we'll make it work."

The Christmas tree was so tall it touched the ceiling so we couldn't put a topper on it. Every inch of his apartment was covered in Christmas when we finished. I nibbled on another snickerdoodle as I watched Matt scratch the back of his head as he took it all in.

"To be fair, I used to live in a house with way more space for all this. I didn't realize how much stuff I had. I guess it is a lot for this tiny one-bedroom apartment." He turned to where I sat at the bar, still in my apron and hat. He crossed his arms and ran his eyes over me.

"What?" I asked with a mouthful of cookie.

"I could get used to this sight," he answered. He joined me at the bar and picked up a cookie. "Thank you for today. It's been a while since this tradition has felt like this."

I watched him chew while I waited to see if he would share what that meant. I knew he had spent most of the last two Christmas seasons by himself, coming back home to his parents' once school let out for the holiday break, but I didn't know if there was more to it than that. I wondered if his ex had indulged in the tradition with him or if she had given him a hard time.

"Thank you for letting me be a part of it." Sitting there with him beaming at me I knew that I would do everything I could to make sure he had all the magic he wanted for Christmas. I understood what his dad said about his mom. I'd celebrate Christmas all year long for the rest of my life if he wanted. Getting to see that look on his face made me happier than anything else ever did.

I bit into another cookie to keep the words that were on the tip of my tongue back.

Chapter 30

Riley

MATT AND I PULLED the Christmas decorations out of the attic at my house a week later while Emery was out. We hid them in my room and were planning to slowly swap one thing at a time out with the fall decorations over the course of a few days to see how long it would take her to notice.

Matt looked around my room once we brought all the boxes in. "I don't think I've ever been in here," he said.

"What about in September when I started my period and you got here before me? You had my heating pad ready for me. I thought you had come in here for it."

He shook his head. "Emery got it for you. I wasn't coming in here without you telling me I could."

I sat down on my bed and watched him look at the photos hanging on my wall. Most of them are family photos from through the years. A new frame that didn't match the others was front and center filled with a collage of some of my favorite photos of me and Matt. "Well, if it makes you feel better, I don't really care. Growing up with Emery means I don't really have any boundaries when it comes to my personal spaces. She'll probably come in here and find the Christmas stuff before she notices we've swapped anything."

"Just because you aren't used to having boundaries doesn't mean you can't have them," he said. He pointed to the picture of us in the middle of the frame. It was from the morning we had watched the sunset on the porch of the cabin. I still sat in his lap and held my coffee mug up to hide my face from the camera. He whispered in my ear to make me laugh, the edges of his smile barely visible behind my hair. His eyes were wide open and gazing at me in a way that made my knees get weak every time I looked at it. "This is one of my favorites of us," he said.

I reached forward and caught his hand pulling him toward me. "You're allowed to come in here, even when I'm not home if you need to. I guess we just stay in the living room all the time because that's where the tv is."

He braced his arms on either side of me and hovered over me. "It makes sticking to the rules easier when we stay there."

"You've slept in a bed with me multiple times and were a perfect gentleman every time." He looked at me the same way he did in the picture and my whole body felt weak. I knew what he meant. After our weekend trip to Copper Ridge I kept catching myself noticing things about him that I hadn't before, thinking about things with him that I hadn't before. Things like the way his clothes hugged his body, what it would take to see him shirtless again. I would catch myself staring at his long fingers wondering how he would touch me. When I felt his stubble against my face during a kiss, I wondered what it could feel like against the inside of my thighs. When I caught him staring at me a little too long, a hungry look in his eyes, I felt need pulse low in me.

The way he crowded above me made me want to lay back, to pull him down over me. My hands clutched his biceps, and I swallowed hard. It didn't have to be serious; I didn't have to commit to forever with him. All I had to do was tell him I wanted to give us a chance, to open my heart to the possibilities. That's all it would take.

"Matt," I whispered, sliding my hands up over his shoulders.

He rested his forehead against mine. I felt goosebumps rise on his skin as I skated my fingers over his neck until my hands bracketed his face. His arms shook like he was fighting the urge to push me back. His jaw tensed under my palms. The tension between us pressed down on me. I opened my mouth, but the words were stuck in my throat. I dragged my thumb across his lips.

"A man only has so much self-control. I don't want to do anything that makes either of us feel pressured." He pulled back, leaving the space around me feeling too empty without him. The tension in the room dissipated, the pit of my stomach feeling hollow from another moment pushed away because I was still so unsure.

I pointed to the boxes. "So… maybe we should get back to swapping decorations."

Matt stopped at the open basket I kept as my period kit that sat on top of my vanity. I watched as it dawned on him what it was. My period had ended a few days ago, but I had left it out to remind me to restock a couple of things. "Do you need to keep any of this at my apartment? Just in case."

"No, I keep some in my tote bag." I don't add that I won't need more than that as long as we keep the no sleepover rule in effect, a rule we implemented after our weekend at the cabin. We had been spending more time at his apartment the past few days so we could indulge in Christmas fun since my house was still covered in Emery's fall décor. My room was the only part of the house that was decorated my way, always had been. Everything else was up to Emery. It was a fact that normally didn't bother me, but I wanted to let Matt have his extra long Christmas season.

"Okay, well if you change your mind just tell me what you need."
We both knew he would be stocking up on anything he remembered
seeing in that basket without me telling him. He opened the top
decoration box and started digging around. He held up two small
Santa figures. "I'm thinking we swap these for the scarecrows on the
bottom shelf of the tv stand."

***

It took a week for Emery to say something. She had been coming in
late every night and leaving early for work every morning. She spent
most of the time moving around just by the light of her phone, so
she didn't wake me up. She didn't know that I stayed awake waiting
for her to make it home safe. If it weren't for the weird hours she had
been coming and going she would have noticed much sooner. We had
gotten brave and replaced the garland of fall leaves with a Christmas
garland. We were both frustrated that she hadn't noticed yet.

"Riley, what the hell is this?" she said followed by the slam of the
front door. Matt and I were in the kitchen making dinner. We heard
the ladder for the attic fold out. Matt rubbed his hands together and
we moved to the doorway so we could watch her.

She poked her head in the attic and then turned around to us. She
narrowed her eyes and scowled at us. I held back a laugh as she closed
the attic and then went to my room. She came back out holding the
box we had been pulling from. She dropped it at our feet. "It's not
Thanksgiving yet. Put them back." With that she went to her room.

"That was a little underwhelming," Matt said.

"I think you're just not as scared of her as you used to be."

"Nope, still very scared." He pointed to the box. "So, what are we doing?"

"I say we keep it up. Will you take that back to my room?" I plucked a decorative tea towel from the box and hung it on the oven handle.

I heard a door open and thought Matt had made it to my room with the box. I tossed the chopped sweet potatoes and broccoli on a sheet pan with olive oil and seasoning. I could hear low voices in the hallway. I put the sheet pan in the oven, listening to try to make out what was being said before giving up and sticking my head out of the kitchen. Emery stood in her doorway with one arm folded over her chest and the other pointing at Matt. He stood there holding the box with a sheepish look on his face.

"Be nice," I called to Emery.

She raised an eyebrow at me and then turned back to Matt to finish whatever she was saying. I moved back to the kitchen, hiding out of sight as I listened to them.

"Did you know who I was when you made us match?" I heard him ask her. I had been wondering that myself, but there hadn't been a good moment to ask her. I didn't know if I wanted to know. Up until that day at the apple festival I thought Matt and I meeting had been all up to chance, something that was just meant to be. Now knowing that Emery had dated his best friend made me wonder if she had orchestrated things even more than we thought.

"Not at first," Emery answered. I moved back to the counter to resume prepping the food. I didn't need to hear this conversation.

Matt wrapped his arms around my back and rested his chin on my shoulder once he returned to the kitchen. I leaned back into him but kept seasoning the chicken. "What was that about?" I asked.

He kissed my cheek. "Just my weekly talk from Emery about not hurting you."

"What?" I sputtered and turned around. "How long has that been happening?"

"Umm, I think the first one was the moment she first saw me and you ran away. Don't worry, she means well, and she knows there is no way I'm ever going to hurt you."

I studied his eyes for a minute, not sure what I was looking for. He kissed me and spun me back around to finish what I was doing.

Emery

Did you talk to Riley about Thanksgiving?

Matt

No. She was a little freaked out when she saw us talking.

I'm serious, you need to make her let you come. She isn't going to invite you if you don't ask.

You need to let her see how serious you are.

I don't think she's ready.

I'll ask her but I'm not pushing it. If she's not ready, then she's not ready.

She'll never be ready if you don't push it.

I made a promise to your sister. I'm not going to break it just because you think I should.

I've known her for 26 years. I think I know her better than you.

I'm not going to risk pushing her away just to see if you're right.

Chapter 31

Riley

I PASSED EMERY THE pumpkin pie out of the refrigerator to add to the laundry basket she was loading with food. Mom and Emery split the load of cooking, but if Emery had it her way she would be the sole cook. Each time I offered to help this morning she ran me out of the kitchen. I had only been allowed back in to wash dishes. Milo and Jenna offer to take on a few things every year, but Emery refuses to let them. I knew it was because she didn't want to have to go through the process of making sure everything they brought was safe. She had been testing new recipes on Matt and I for weeks, changing small things here and there each time. I was already tired of turkey and pumpkin pie.

"Is Matt on his way? We need to get going." She moved a few containers around in the basket like she was playing a game of Tetris with the food.

I shot her questioning look. "Matt isn't coming." He asked me about it a couple days ago and I told him I still wasn't ready. I kept waiting for him to push the subject a little more after how disappointed he looked, but to my relief he let it go.

I'd been thinking about it since, becoming more disappointed in myself each time. The truth was I didn't know if I really wasn't ready or if I was just too used to being safe. I wanted to meet his family. I bet his mom was the type to pull out all photo albums and tell me the stories that went with every photo. I wanted to hear his sisters tell me what he was really like growing up. I want to feel the love that had molded him into the wonderful man I knew.

"Why not?" She jiggled the basket and then added another towel to the side to help keep everything in place.

"Because he is spending the day with his family." I spoke slowly and knitted my brows. "Why would he be coming?"

I thought back to the day I had caught her lecturing him in the hallway. I knew my sister loved me and that she meant well, but I couldn't shake the discomfort I felt at her trying to interfere in my relationship. The discomfort of her possibly knowing who he was when she matched us on the app.

"Because he's your boyfriend. You guys could have worked it out to go to both families." She gestured for me to move so she could carry the basket out to the car. I opened the front door for her.

"You know he's not my boyfriend, we're still taking things slow. I'm not ready for us to meet each other's family yet."

Emery snorted. "I don't know what taking things slow means to you, but you guys are far from it. You may not be sleeping together or saying you love each other, but you're doing everything else." She paused, waiting for me to open the trunk. She dropped the basket in and then turned to face me with her arms crossed. "Both of you are further gone than most serious relationships at this point." She slammed the trunk for emphasis.

I climbed into the passenger seat and took a few deep breaths to calm the anger that was starting to heat my veins. "Emery, you know I love you, right?" I said as she took her place behind the wheel.

"I love you too, big sis. I'm just worried about you."

"I know you are, but you need to back off. My relationship with Matt is between me and Matt. I really don't need you trying to get involved anymore. Just let us figure this out."

She started the car. "Bring him to Christmas?" She gave me her best puppy dog eyes.

"I don't know, Em. Let's wait and see where the next month takes us." I buckled my seat belt and pulled out my phone to check for messages from Matt.

"Do you want him there?"

I threw my hands up in annoyance. "Of course I want him there. I wanted him here today. Things are just a lot more complicated than you know."

She turned up the radio and backed out of our driveway. A few minutes later she turned to me and said, "the only reason it's complicated is because you're making it complicated."

I turned the radio up more and focused my attention out the window for the drive to our parents' house. Anger burned through me because I knew she was right.

***

I snapped a photo of the finger-painted turkeys Aaron and I were making to send to Matt. Aaron tugged on my sleeve and held his up. "Take a picture of me with mine," he said. I took his picture and flipped it around to show him.

"Okay, you two, time to clean up so we can put the food out," Mom said with her back to us as she bent to pull the turkey out of the oven. Emery moved around her uncovering things.

I closed up the paints and wiped Aaron's hands with a baby wipe. "Go show your mom your turkey," I told him. I cleaned up our art set up, returning it to the basket Mom kept stocked for Aaron. I sent the picture to Matt once everything was put away.

Riley

> Finger Painting with the nephew.

Hot Nerd <3

> I want to fingerpaint. I'm on piggyback ride duty.

He sent a photo of him bent over with two of his nieces clinging to his back. His youngest nephew clung to his leg.

> Save me some of that pecan pie. I haven't stopped thinking about it since last week.

I laughed as I remembered him taking one bite of the pecan pie Emery made last week and declared it the best one he had ever had. I had joked with him that he was just dating me for the perk of Emery's cooking.

***

> Shelby asked Oliver about you. Now everyone won't stop asking about you.

I turned my phone over as Matt's message filled the screen and tried to take a subtle deep breath. Milo furrowed his brow next to me and his eyes flicked between my phone and my eyes. "Why are you always on your phone so much lately?"

"Yeah, Riley, why don't you tell everyone who you're always texting," Emery piped up further down the table.

Dad patted Emery's arm. "Be nice to your sister," he told her. She crossed her arms and sat back in her chair.

I moved my phone from the table to the pocket in my cardigan. "It's no one. Emery just needs to mind her business."

Emery scowled at me and pulled out her phone. A few minutes later my phone started vibrating in my pocket. I ignored it and it started buzzing again, even after Emery put her phone away. I pulled it out of my pocket to see Matt calling. I jumped up and left the dining room to answer.

"Hi," I said.

"Is everything okay? Emery just texted me and said I need to call you." Matt's voice was low like he was hiding from his family too. I could hear them in the background. It sounded like one of the kids was yelling for him.

"I'm fine. Emery is just in an immature mood today. I'll tell you about it later."

"Okay, call me when you get home." I started to pull my phone away from ear when I heard him say, "hey, Riley?"

"Yes, Matt."

"I really missed having you here today." The caution in his voice squeezed my heart. He wanted to love me in any way I would let him, even if it meant me keeping up barriers that hurt him. That hurt us both.

"I missed you too."

I typed a message to Emery saying that we need to talk later. It was time we got everything out in the open between the two of us.

Chapter 32

Matt

THE LIVING ROOM WAS full of smirking faces when I returned from hiding in the bathroom to call Riley. I should have known that Emery was trying to stir shit up when she texted me, but I couldn't fight the flash of panic that went through me. I had to know for myself that's all it was, that Riley was okay. I had missed her voice all day, our morning phone call never felt like enough anymore. In my panic I had dropped my plate to the floor to sprint to the bathroom. Someone had already cleaned it up.

If I had been lucky my family would have assumed it was diarrhea or something. That would have been less embarrassing.

Oliver clapped a hand on my shoulder once I was seated next to him. "Is Riley okay?" he asked in a low voice only I could hear. I nodded at him.

"Emery is just upset that I let her tell me not to come."

He snorted, shifting his plate to one hand to pull his phone out of his pocket. "Emery doesn't have much room to talk," he said. I snuck a glance at his phone to see an open text message thread with Emery. I jerked my eyes away. I had enough to worry about on my own, I didn't need to add whatever was happening to those two to that list.

"You two are both idiots," Ava said from her spot on the floor. Aubrey sat on the couch behind her, Ava's head resting against her legs.

It was already a tight fit for our family since my sisters had married and started having kids of their own. This year the space was even tighter with the Franklin kids here. It was Shelby's idea to invite them to join us. I wished they were able to spend the time with their own parents, but I won't deny the happiness it brought me to have us all together like this, to be surrounded by all the people I loved.

There was just one person missing.

Aubrey leaned across Oliver to pat my leg. "It's all going to work out, Matty. Ava and I danced around each other for years before we opened our eyes."

I rubbed my hand down my face with a groan. Years. I felt like my patience was stretched thin already. I didn't think I had it in me to spend every day with Riley acting like we were something only to deny it whenever the subject came up for years. I promised her I would wait. I promised I wouldn't be like the others.

Loving her was easy. Falling for her happened so fast it felt inevitable. It made waiting for her to get past this wall she built painful. I wanted to be the soft spot for her to land when she was ready to jump. She loved me, I knew she did. She couldn't say it, but she showed it every day. She said it in other words.

It could be enough. It had to be enough for now.

***

Riley

> Emery hid the pecan pie. She won't let me save you any.

> She keeps saying if you want it you have to come get it.

Matt

> Are you saying I can?

I cringed and my skin prickled with anxious sweat as I stared at my phone screen. That was too far. The longer the day lasted the harder it got to be away from her. My dad had turned on *A Christmas Story* and around me everyone was on the cusp of falling asleep, happy in their post dinner food comas. It felt like a sharp contrast to earlier today when the house had been full of us talking over each other. In past years I would have left by now needing to get to Liz's family or to get the drive back home started. I couldn't remember the house ever being this quiet.

The quiet made the ache of missing Riley louder.

> I wish I could tell you yes.

> What's stopping you?

> I haven't stopped thinking about how you should be here all day. Or how I should be there with you.

> I'm scared, Matt.

I've never wanted something this much.

I haven't been able to stop thinking about you all day either.

I want you, sweetheart. I want us.

What if it isn't what we think it's going to be? What if we end up hurting each other?

But what if it is everything we've imagined? What if it's more?

I'm scared.

I've got you.

I slammed my phone down on the armrest of the couch, rubbing the heels of my palms against my eyes. It was progress. She was right there on the edge ready to jump with me, but she couldn't do it. The closer she got to being ready the more frustrating the wait was.

Chapter 33

Riley

E MERY INSISTED ON FINISHING switching out the fall décor for Christmas while we talked. Matt and I swapped about half out already. I gave her the same summarized version of my past relationships that I had only given to my therapist and Matt. I told her about the pressure to love them the way they thought I should before I was ready. She was quiet for a while after I told her while we worked.

"Levi was abusive," she blurted out. I blinked in surprise and tried to reorient myself in the conversation we were having. Levi. The ex-fiancé that I hated.

"I knew there was a reason I didn't like him."

"All of my exes were pretty toxic but he was worse than all the others. He had me so brainwashed I couldn't even think about leaving. I thought he loved me. I loved him so much I kept convincing myself that things weren't that bad, because when things were good, they were wonderful." She threaded hooks through ornaments and passed them to me as she spoke.

"Em, I'm so sorry. I knew something was wrong. I should have tried to help you."

She shook her head. "You couldn't have done anything." She paused and chewed on her lip. "We were trying to get pregnant. That's why I started looking into PCOS. When I got my diagnosis, he left me." She sniffled and swiped at her eyes. "He told me that I was too broken for him. He told me stuff like that all the time. I was too much and needed to learn to act more mature. I made myself so small for him and then he started telling me I was just a shell, and he didn't know what happened to the woman he fell in love with."

I squatted down on the floor next to her and pulled her into a hug. She tried to feed the hook into the ornament she held with shaking hands but kept missing the hole.

"I met Oliver after Levi left. He was amazing, Riley, the total opposite of Levi. I fell hard and fast for him, but I was so scared of getting hurt again. I ended up hurting him and breaking my own heart in the process because I was so scared." She dropped the ornament and twisted her hands together. I held her tighter and pressed her face into my shoulder, swaying her back and forth as she cried. I had never seen Emery cry like this. Even when we were kids, and she would climb into my bed during one of our parents' fights, she would just sit there wide eyed without a tear in sight. I did all the crying for both of us.

"I'm so sorry, honey. I wish you had let me be there for you." I cried into the top of her head.

"Please don't make the mistakes I did. Matt is a good one. Don't let him go just because you're scared," she sobbed into my shoulder.

I held her until she stopped crying and kept holding her as she rested limply against me in silence. Matt was a good one. I didn't doubt that for a second. I just didn't know how to get past the roadblock in my head.

There was still one more thing we needed to address, the one thing that I had been struggling to decide if I wanted to know the answer to. Emery's meddling in my relationship with Matt was worse than it had ever been and I couldn't stop wondering how much she had known during our vacation. Did she push me to meet him because she knew that we would end up running back into each other in our real lives?

I pushed a few ornaments around in the box while I worked through the questions in my head. "Did you know who Matt was that day on the app?" I asked her.

Emery's shoulders slumped. She pushed herself to her feet, her hands still shaking as she moved around the ornaments I'd hung on the tree. "Matt didn't tell you?" She didn't look at me when she spoke. She had to know that I overheard part of their conversation that day. Matt and I told each other everything, of course she would think I already knew how it had ended. "I didn't know when I saw him on the app. Before, when Oliver talked about him, he never showed me recent pictures. I don't know if you've seen pictures of Matt from high school but he looks a lot different now."

He did look a lot different now. In high school he had been lanky with a mouthful of braces and hair long in his eyes like all the other teenage boys we went to school with. It wasn't until after college that he became more recognizable as the person I knew now.

"But?" I prodded. She had told Matt she didn't know at first. That had to mean she had figured it out before the day Oliver came over.

"But I couldn't shake the feeling that he looked familiar. You know how bad I am at remembering faces," she explained with a halfhearted laugh. "When I heard his last name at the district meeting it jogged my memory a little." She tossed an ornament between her hands. "I did a little research during the meeting."

During the meeting she had pushed us together. She could have told me who he was instead of making me think that she was trying to match me up with a stranger. "Why?" I didn't even know what I was asking her.

"I knew anyone that Oliver cared that much about had to be a good person." She shrugged her shoulders and glanced my way, an apologetic look on her face. "The things Oliver told me about him made me think that maybe he would be good for you."

"Why were you so surprised to see Oliver the day of the apple festival?" Out of everything that was the thing that had made the least amount of sense. If she knew who Matt was surely she had to have known that eventually Oliver would be around. "Were you using us to get him back?"

Emery's eyes widened and fresh tears sprang into them. I didn't have it in me to feel sorry for her. She made this mess herself. Emery may act without thinking sometimes, but she was still smart. She said that day at the cabin she thought that me dating again would help break her curse. It all felt like too much of a master mind level plan. "I wasn't using you, I promise. I didn't think Oliver would ever want to see me again, so I thought if it ever came up he would avoid me. I just wanted you to be happy."

I didn't know if I believed her.

Chapter 34

Matt

December

I turned the volume on the Bluetooth speaker playing Christmas music down as I shuffled things around on my kitchen counter. A soft knock on my door caused me to jump, my arm catching on a cold mug of coffee. So that's where I left that this morning. The mug tipped forward, spilling down the front of my sweater and pants. I muttered a few swears under my breath and tugged off the sweater, rushing to toss it in the load of laundry I just started in the washer. I had my pants pushed halfway down my legs when I heard another knock.

"Matt?" Riley's cautious voice asked. I kicked off my pants and tossed them in the washer.

I started toward the door. Why was Riley here? I had to chaperone the dance at Grassy tonight. Did I forget to tell her that? The front door eased open, freezing me in place. I look down at myself and remember that I was in only boxer briefs and socks. I didn't care if she saw me, I wanted her to want to see me naked, but her walking in like this hardly seemed like the right time.

She stammered a few words I couldn't make out as her eyes found me standing there in the middle of my apartment too frozen to move.

Her cheeks turned the same shade of red as her dress and bouquet of roses in her hand, but she didn't look away. Her eyes dropped briefly, sliding over me in a way that made me ache for her to touch me, and then snapped back to meet mine. It felt like a win. A month ago her reaction would have been different. A month ago I would have been terrified this would be the thing that would scare her off.

I took in the way the velvet material hugged her shoulders and chest before flaring out into a softly pleated skirt that stopped at her ankles. "Hi," I croaked out with a smile. I fought the urge to rush for her, to risk pushing things between us and greet her with a kiss as I pressed her against the door. To feel her hands roam over my skin. I forced my legs to carry me backwards toward my bedroom. "I'll be right back."

In my room I rushed to find a change of clothes, slowing when the urge to find a sweater that matched her dress crossed my mind. I found her sitting rigidly on the couch when I came out, the roses laid carefully across her lap.

"Hi," I said again, stopping to stand in front of her. I reached forward, running my forefinger under her chin until she looked up at me. My lips were on hers before she could respond. Her hand gripped my sweater pulling me forward until I had to throw an arm out to catch myself on the back of the couch to keep from falling on top of her. I broke us apart. "What are you doing here?"

"I heard you might need a date for the dance tonight." She lifted the bouquet between us with a shy smile. "Rupert Matthew Fletcher Junior, would you do me the honor of letting me be your date to the Christmas dance?"

She was so beautiful, sitting here in that dress asking me on a date like I wasn't already completely gone for her. I took the flowers from her, pressing a bruising kiss against her mouth to stop myself from telling her how much I loved her. "It would be my honor," I answered.

I looked down at the flowers in my hand. "Wait, what do I do with these? I don't think anyone has ever given me flowers before."

Riley laughed as she stood, her hands gently taking back the bouquet.

"I don't have any flowers for you," I blurted. I ran a hand through my hair undoing all the effort I had put into coaxing it to lay flat a few minutes before her arrival.

"I figured it was time for me to return the gesture." She inched past me until she was no longer caught between the couch and me, spinning toward the kitchen in a motion that sent the skirt of her dress twirling around her legs. She was so beautiful. I caught her hand, pulling her to spin back into me, and watched the dress twirl again. I freed the roses from her hands, tossing them onto the coffee table, and looped her arms around my neck. She pressed against me, making me wish that I hadn't put on clothes. I need her skin against mine. I slid my fingers through the back of her hair and tugged gently until she looked up at me.

Every kiss we've exchanged has been cautious, reserved. It's taken all my self-control to hold back each time, to keep things gentle and unhurried between us. Right then all I could think about was how much I needed her. She was here and invited herself to a work function with me. People would see us together. She doesn't work at the school, there was no excuse for her to be there.

Before now we've kept every interaction at work strictly professional. No one would ever know that we knew each other outside of the few times our paths needed to cross at school.

Tonight, she would be there with me. Holy shit, I felt like I had won the lottery. My Riley on my arm for everyone to see.

My mouth was rough against hers as I lost myself in the scents of her, the feel of her. Her perfume was something with vanilla and cinnamon today. It paired well with the soft scents of her shampoo and body wash. I pulled her tighter against me. Her arms around my neck tightened tugging us even closer.

I couldn't get close enough. Did we have to go to this dance? Was I too old to fake being sick to get out of school? I needed this dress off her.

I broke us apart, bringing my forehead to rest against hers. "You really want to go with me tonight? It's probably going to suck." We were going to be stuck in a stuffy school gym surrounded by preteens, other teachers, and PTA members.

Riley nodded, knocking our heads together.

I pulled back enough to look into her eyes. "You're okay with my coworkers seeing you and knowing that we're...whatever we are?"

"Yeah, I think I am."

I fought the smile threatening to spread across my face. "What are we telling them?" I cringed at the edge of hope in my voice. This was it. It was happening.

"That we're figuring it out," she answered.

My stomach dropped and my heart clenched. We were right there. So fucking close, yet still so far away.

Progress. It was progress. A lot of progress happened in the past few minutes. I smiled brightly at her. "Okay." I patted my pockets with both hands. "Just need to find my wallet and keys." Right, that's what I had been working on before I knocked over the mug.

Riley rushed over to the door, swinging it open and motioning to the keys dangling from the doorknob. That was the second time this week.

***

The principal directed me to a laptop connected to the sound equipment as my assignment for the dance. My only job was to make sure that the playlist of approved songs continued to play for the duration of the dance and that no one tried to change the music. It was a boring assignment, but it gave me plenty of time off in a corner with Riley next to me. Plenty of time to look at her. The kids mostly stood in groups around the gym with only a handful dancing at a time. It brought back a lot of traumatic memories of being that age. Mostly of being terrified to ask a girl to dance and getting turned down the one time I managed to psych myself up.

A few of the students recognized Riley from her years spent as a sub. Watching her with them filled me with pride. She was the teacher I wanted to be, the teacher that Mr. B was. A few asked why she was there. Her favorite response was telling them all that Mr. Fletcher couldn't be trusted with the music choices so she had to help me. I rolled my eyes dramatically each time.

"You know I was just starting to get past the phase where they make fun of me," I said halfway through the night. Riley stood behind my chair and leaned forward to rest her chin on my shoulder.

"I'm trying to make them think you're so cool you would pick better music than what we're allowed to play."

I scoffed. "The bad thing is I'm so uncool that this is the music I would have picked."

She snorted. "Gah, you're such a nerd."

I pushed my glasses up on my nose and tilted my head back, so my lips brushed against the shell of her ear. "Last I heard you were into the hot nerds," I whispered. I thought about the way she looked at me standing in the middle of my apartment in only my underwear earlier this evening, the way she sometimes stared at my hands as she brushed her tongue over her bottom lip. I could feel the heat radiating off her body as she reacted to my words.

She shifted her position to whisper in my ear, "I think I'm just into hot, nerdy Matt."

If we were anywhere else, I would pull her down onto my lap right now. Forget all the rules. I needed to touch her. Have her. Feel her. Fuck waiting on her to decide what this was. I needed her. I cleared my throat, leaning forward and resting my elbows on my knees so my arms covered my lap. I felt a blush climbing my neck and avoided looking back at Riley to check her reaction. Across the gym someone waved at Riley. Her hand dropped to my shoulder, and I looked up to see her give me a quick wink before she walked away.

I think she was trying to kill me.

I watched from my corner as she caught up with the group of teachers around her.

"Mr. Fletcher, is that your girlfriend?" Four of my seventh grade students crowded around the laptop blocking Riley from my line of sight. The one that spoke was one of my more difficult students. He always had a comeback ready in class, always acted like he needed everyone to know he was cool. He reminded me a lot of Oliver at that age. My brain itched with the need to shoo them away so I could see her again.

"Almost," I answered. The sound of my voice was pitiful. I was gone for this woman and couldn't hide it.

"Are you going to dance with her?"

I motioned to the set up around me. "Can't, I have a job to do. Why don't you guys go ask some girls to dance?"

The kid crossed his arms across his chest. "They all just want to dance with their friends," the boy next to him said, looking down at his feet.

"We're nervous," one of the others whispered at the same time.

I remembered all the times this kid had made fun of me in class for being a nerd. "Come on, if someone like me can talk to a girl then you guys should have no problem."

"Prove it."

I waved a nearby chaperone over and asked him to watch the station for a few minutes. Sweat prickled my palms as I walked up behind Riley. I swiped them on my slacks, my ears perking up as I heard their conversation. I slowed my pace as they asked her what was going on between the two of us.

"Riley, come on, that is not the look of a man still figuring things out," one of them said. "The man really does wear his heart on his sleeve," another added. My whole body tingled. I knew I wore my heart on my sleeve, always had. My chest felt tight at the thought of everyone seeing how head over heels I was for Riley while she was still caught in limbo figuring things out.

Riley jolted and then relaxed back against me as I rested my hands on her shoulders. "Hi ladies, sorry to interrupt. I was hoping I could steal Riley for a dance." Riley's ears turned pink as they all wiggled their eyebrows at each other.

"I've got a break for a few minutes. Would you make me the happiest man here and dance with me?" I whispered in her ear. She nodded softly, one hand coming up to cradle mine. I twined our fingers together, pulling her away.

As we swayed in the middle of the gym with an agonizing amount of space between us, I gestured to the group of my students. "Those boys told me they were too nervous to ask the girls to dance. I told them if I could get you to dance with me, they should take the chance."

Her lips lifted in a teasing smile. "So, you're using me to teach some preteens how to talk to girls?"

While, yes, that was what was happening, it wasn't it at all. I could have put up more of a fight with the boys, made them pressure me a little more. The truth was I had been going crazy all night needing her in my arms. I couldn't stop thinking about how that dress would look twirling around her legs while she danced. How it would look pushed up to her waist. "No, I just wanted an excuse to dance with you."

***

Riley insisted on coming up to my apartment when I tried to walk her to her car after we got back. Somehow we ended up here, me on the couch while she stood in front of me twisting the fabric of her dress in her hands. She dipped her head and her hair fell across her face. "Can I tell you a secret?" she asked.

"Always, sweetheart." I wanted all her secrets. I wanted to gather any she would give me and tuck them away somewhere safe for her.

"I haven't been able to stop thinking about earlier all night."

I covered her hands with mine. "What about earlier?" I tugged her hands slightly to pull her closer to me.

She didn't just step closer. Instead she surprised me by lifting her skirt and straddling my lap. Her dress spread out around us on the couch still covering everything I wanted to see. I fought the urge to slide my hands under the puddle of fabric, digging my fingers into the fabric at her waist to hold my hands still. Riley dipped her face closer to mine. "You were naked when I got here. I can't stop thinking about what I wanted to do when I saw you."

Her hands bracketed my face bringing me closer to her. I couldn't help the hum of approval that escaped me when our mouths met. My fingertips dug tighter into the velvet of her dress. I let her control the pace of our kiss, opened up to her when her tongue coaxed my lips to let her in. The smell of her surrounded me. I think this perfume was my new favorite of hers.

Riley's hips rocked against me and my hands couldn't help guiding her. "Did you like what you saw?" I mumbled against her mouth. Her underwear was soaked enough that I could feel the dampness through my pants. She must have really liked what she saw. I couldn't believe she was this wet just from thinking about seeing me for a few seconds.

She nodded making her curls bounce around her face. I peeled one hand from her waist to brush her hair back. My fingers tangled in the strands keeping her close. She rocked one more time and I gritted my teeth to hold back the noises I wanted to make. I took in the sight of her above me flushed with her eyes clenched shut. I liked what I saw too.

This was it. This was the moment when things would change between us.

Best night of my life.

I met the next roll of her hips with a thrust of my own. Her breath came in hot pants against my mouth and soft noises tumbled out of her. My grip in her hair tightened as I took over. I tugged her bottom lip between my teeth. My mouth turned hungry against her, our bodies taking over as we moved against each other. "Can you come like this, sweetheart? Are you going to make yourself come grinding on my lap?" My questions came out as pleas. I should have stopped myself, kept my thoughts in my head. But I couldn't think about how they might scare her away when she felt this good against me. "Do you want me to touch you?"

Jesus Christ, I hoped she said yes. The thought of her riding my hand, of those soft noises she made growing louder almost made me come in my pants. Riley's hands dropped to my shoulders and she pushed herself away breaking the spell. "The rules...we should stop," she said out of breath.

My throat caught as I swallowed. Right, the rules. The one big fucking rule. I was such a dumbass for creating that one. There were other ways we could have established boundaries. "Do you want to stop?" I asked.

She shook her head and then nodded. "This feels so good," she explained rocking against me for emphasis. "But we should slow down."

I wanted to ask more questions, figure out what exactly made her want to stop. But I didn't want her to feel bad, to have to explain herself to me. I've been telling her this whole time I would respect her decisions without pressuring her. I smoothed her hair down while I studied her face. "Yeah, okay, we should slow down."

She adjust her position against me, raising up to put space between us while she still straddled my lap. I whimpered at the loss of contact. "It'll be worth the wait?" I didn't know if she was trying to reassure me or herself. The words came out like a question and a statement at once. Her heavy lidded eyes stared down at me.

"Of course, sweetheart, with you everything is worth the wait."

Chapter 35

Riley

> You have to come to Christmas with our family.

> Riley told me she wants you there.

> You really need to let your sister and I figure out things between the two of us.

> She isn't going to bring it up herself. She's too scared. She needs you to push her out of her comfort zone.

> Please just ask her.

I PICKED UP THE bow we had left over from wrapping gifts and pulled the tab off the sticker. "Hey, Matt, come here." I snuck up behind him in the kitchen loading the dishwasher. Before he could turn around, I reached around his head and stuck the bow in the middle of his forehead.

He turned around with a smirk on his face and chased me back into the living room to tickle me. We collapsed in a heap on top of the wrapping supplies scattered over the floor. I wiggled out from under him trying to catch my breath. He flipped over on his back beside me. I sat up and reached for my phone to take a picture.

"So, how are we doing Christmas?" Matt pulled the bow from his forehead and looked up at me.

"The same way we did Thanksgiving," I said.

He sat up making the wrapping paper under him crinkle. I started moving the wrapped presents under the tree. He caught my arm and pulled me back beside him. "Let's spend it together. We'll split the day however we need to, just tell me we can spend the day together." He tucked my hair behind my ear.

"Matt, you said we wouldn't talk about the future," I said, dipping my head away from him. I reached for a scrap of paper and twisted it between my fingers.

"It's next week, Riley. It's not the future."

"It is the future. What are we going to tell our families when we show up together? What are they going to think?" I pulled my knees up to my chest and focused my eyes on the twinkling lights of the tree. Lately I kept catching myself forgetting how scared I was, felt myself hovering on the edge of admitting to him how much I had fallen for him.

A week ago, I'd walked into his apartment to him standing there in nothing but his underwear. I hadn't felt the urge to panic, to look away. All I wanted was to touch him, to forget all our rules and tackle him to the floor. It felt like a turning point for us. If he had told me we could throw out all the rules I would have gone along with it. I had instigated almost breaking the rules.

I had let his coworkers see us together, let everyone see us dancing together.

The entire time we were at the school I had been so turned on from the image of him flashing across my mind constantly. It was torture to sit there next to him pretending like it didn't happen. We still hadn't talked about.

We were also ignoring how I had straddled his lap after. I could have came that way, grinding on his lap while his fingers clutched desperately at my hips. Those strangled noises he tried to hold back had me imagining what he would sound like not holding back. Then he asked if he could touch me and my brain jolted with a reminder of the rules.

We should talk about it. Maybe we could modify the rules again.

"What do you want to tell them?" he asked. He moved behind me, stretching his legs out on either side of me and wrapping his arms around me. He nuzzled his face into my neck. It was my favorite way for him to hold me.

"I don't know." I wanted to relax back into him, but my body stayed stiff. I forced myself to take a deep breath. Static filled my brain making it hard to hear my thoughts. Meeting his family still felt like a daunting step.

"Riley, please tell me what you're thinking."

This was it. This was the moment that he would tell me he was tired of waiting for me. We had barely made it through five months of whatever this was we were doing. I leaned forward into my knees pulling away from his chest as much as I could. "You said you wouldn't pressure me, that you would wait."

"We can tell them whatever you want." His arms fell away from me, and his hands rubbed his thighs. "You mean a lot to me, and I want to spend Christmas with you. I want you to meet my family." He paused, his fingertips digging into his legs. "I don't want another family dinner where all I can think about is how much I miss you."

I shook my head and buried my face in my knees. I didn't want that either. I belonged next to him. I hated how much just thinking about being apart for Christmas made me miss him when he was right here. "You mean a lot to me too," I managed to say with a shaky voice.

His arms wrapped around me and pulled me back against him. "We don't have to tell them we're anything serious. Please, when I think about Christmas with my family this year I can't stop picturing you there with us."

"It's not that simple." I pulled away so I could turn around to face him. "I don't just bring people to Christmas with my family. If you come with me, they're going to think that we're serious."

His hands reached for me again, but I stayed curled up into myself and shrugged his hands off.

"Would it be a bad thing if they did?" His voice didn't rise, but there was a sharp edge to it. "Tell me that this is still just casual to you."

It wasn't casual at all to me. I was head over heels in love with this man, I had been for a while. I wanted to spend Christmas with him. I wanted to show him off to my family. I want to meet his family and see how I fit with them.

But it all felt like too much.

We had only known each other a few months. I shouldn't love him this much.

I shouldn't feel like he was home, shouldn't miss him so much when we weren't together.

Maybe in a few more months I will be ready to tell him, but right now he was asking for more before I was ready. He wasn't that different from everyone else. He was going to break my heart just like everyone else.

"Riley, please talk to me." His voice was soft again. I looked into his eyes to see tears welling up. My heart dropped to the pit of my stomach. I loved him so much but all I was capable of was hurting him. "Tell me why Emery keeps telling me you want me there but won't tell me you do."

"You said you would give me time," I repeated the words a few times against my knees. My voice shook more each time and tears clouded my vision. I closed my eyes tight enough to hurt. "You need to stop talking to Emery. She's just being nosy and it's driving me crazy."

"I'm just asking for Christmas. Can you give me this one thing? If you're really that uncomfortable with it, you don't have to come. I just really wanted to ask you. Do you really want me there?"

"Are you breaking up with me?" I whispered the words.

"Jesus, Riley, where is that coming from?" He rubbed a hand through his hair. "I can't break up with you if we're not together," he snapped.

I jumped and opened my eyes to see the tears running down his face. He scrubbed a hand over his face and looked over my shoulder. "What does that mean?" I made myself smaller, collapsing into myself as much as I could.

"Shit, I'm sorry, that came out wrong. I'm not breaking up with you. I just really need this one thing. We can tell everyone whatever you want to. Or we don't have to tell them anything at all. Just, please, come with me."

I bit my lip and rubbed my tears with the sleeve of my sweater. "I don't know if I can do that."

"What can you do?" He moved closer but didn't reach for me. "Tell me what you want."

I sat in silence with my sleeve covering my face. Deep breath in. Now out. Deep breath in. Now out. "I'm scared," I finally managed to say.

"What are you scared of?"

"You mean so much to me. I don't want to lose you."

"I'm not going anywhere." His arms wrapped around me from the side.

"You're mad at me," I whispered.

"I'm upset, yes. I just need you to talk to me. You're important to me. I just want all the people that are important to me all together for my favorite holiday."

He was upset because of me. He was crying because of me. I hurt him because I'm scared. I'm scared to leave this limbo he's been letting me keep us in and have everything fall apart once we do. This limbo felt so safe, and I had no idea if leaving it would lead to somewhere else safe.

"I'm sorry," I sobbed out.

"Please, sweetheart, all you have to do is talk to me."

"I don't know how." I tugged the sleeves of my sweater over my thumbs and dug my nails into the palms of my hands. "All I know how to do is be scared." I sobbed again and struggled to catch my breath. "Now you're mad and you're going to leave me just like everyone else." My chest tightened and crushed my lungs. I took rapid, shallow breaths struggling to get enough air.

"Sweetheart, I think you're having a panic attack." He shifted again and moved my arms away from my face, forcing me to look at him. "I'm not going anywhere. Can you breathe with me?" He took an exaggerated breath.

"We're fighting. Fighting always means someone leaves." I couldn't stop sobbing.

"Fighting means we have something we need to figure out. It doesn't mean I'm going anywhere. Are you going anywhere?" He kept taking exaggerated breaths.

I shook my head even though all I wanted to do was run. Every muscle in my body screamed to get up and leave.

We were in my house, I couldn't leave.

"Can you tell me what you need?"

I needed him, but if I told him that and he left anyways it would just hurt even more. Maybe he won't leave today or next week or even next month. Eventually he would.

I shook my head.

"Do you want me to leave so you can have some space?"

"No, please don't go." The words were so quiet I didn't know if he heard me. I shook my head hard. My chest ached.

"Riley, please, seeing you like this is breaking my heart. Tell me what to do."

I was breaking his heart. I was the problem. I had always been the problem. All I did was hurt everyone that loved me.

"Hey, hey, don't go there. I know what you're thinking. I'm still here, I'm not going anywhere." His hands bracketed my head and kept my eyes locked with his.

"I don't want to hurt you," I said.

"I don't want to hurt you either," he rested his forehead against mine and closed his eyes. My hands moved to grip his forearms.

We sat like that until my chest loosened enough for my breath to slow. I squeezed his forearms. "I'm sorry," I said.

"Do you want to pause this and cuddle on the couch while we watch another movie?"

I nodded my head.

He pulled back a little. I could see the serious way his brows knit together. "We're not done talking about it, just pausing."

"Just pausing," I repeated.

I wondered how long that pause would last. I wondered how long it would take me to stop being scared of the best thing in my life. How long he would keep trying before he decided I wasn't capable of the healthy relationship he was pushing for.

Chapter 36

Riley

I'm leaving for the night. Your sister is really upset. I don't know where you are, but you need to come home and take care of her.

Make sure she knows I'm not going anywhere. I'm going to give her some space until she is ready to talk to me, but I'm not going anywhere.

Emery

What did you do to my sister? Is this about Christmas?

I shouldn't have pushed you to push her.

I can't believe I'm such a screw up that I ruined my sister's relationship too.

Matt

> You Harrison women really need to stop saying stuff like that about yourselves.

> She's going to be mad at you too. Please don't let her push you away.

Emery exploded through the front door within minutes of Matt leaving. Her hair was a disaster with the small clips on each side barely holding on. Her cardigan was on inside out and her skirt twisted. She threw her arms around me whacking me in the side with her purse and pushing the rolls of wrapping paper I held into my face.

"Oh my god, Emery, what are you doing?" I leaned back to avoid having the cardboard tubes shoved into my nose.

She dropped her arms and slung her purse onto the coffee table. "I'm sorry. I'm such an idiot." Her hands waved around in the air as words rushed out of her. "You told me to stop meddling, but I can't help myself. Watching you two dance around each other like this is driving me insane."

The tape in my hand fell to the ground. "Matt told you?"

She bit her lip and nodded as she bent over to dig through her purse. "Go ahead and say whatever you need to say to me, I deserve it." She whipped around to shove her phone at me. "Here you can read our messages. Matt told me to stop. None of this is his fault."

I dropped the armful of stuff I held, pressing a hand against her phone to force it back toward her. "Emery, I don't need to read your messages with him."

She caught my hand and slapped her phone against my palm. "Yes, you do. You need to see what he says about you. Ri, he loves you so much and all he wants is for you to be happy. He texted me to come home and make sure you were okay tonight."

I crossed my arms across my chest and furrowed my brows at Emery, taking in her disheveled appearance. There was a hickey blooming on her throat and beard burn across her collarbone barely visible because of her tattoos. "So, you stuck your nose in my business until you caused a fight between the two of us and then rushed home while you're in the middle of a hookup to do what?" My face was hot, my chest tight, and I could feel my blood pounding in my ears. I pointed a finger at her with my arms still crossed tight. "I don't need you trying to get in the middle of things any more than you already are."

"I know that. Okay? I know that." She dropped her shoulders. "Tell me what you need. Tell me how to fix this."

I took a deep breath and let it out slowly, focusing on the feel of the air moving through me. "I need to figure out how to stop being so scared."

Emery planted her hands on my shoulders and steered me to the couch. She tossed a blanket over my lap and disappeared into my room, returning with my journal and a pen. She laid them on my lap just as the phone in my hand buzzed. I forgot it was hers and glanced at the screen. A text message from Oliver lit up the screen.

Emery yanked it from my hand. "Riley, you're not ever going to stop being scared if all you think about is how scared you are. You have to face it. Rip the band aid off and see what happens. The longer you leave it on the harder it's going to be."

"Is the hickey from Oliver?" If she was going to keep meddling in my life, then as far as I was concerned, I had every right to do the same.

"We're not talking about that right now." She pulled her cardigan up around her neck and tapped the journal in my lap.

"I think we should absolutely talk about it right now." I picked up the pen. "Matt told me you hurt him pretty bad last time."

"Nothing is going on between me and Oliver." She spun on her heel and marched to her bedroom.

"Is that where you keep disappearing to?" I yelled after her. She was never home anymore and never told me where she was going. I pulled my phone from my pocket and laid it on my lap next to the journal. I spent a few minutes tapping the pen against the cover of the journal while I stared at the dark screen of my phone. It felt like hours had passed when it lit up with a message from Matt, but it had only been a few minutes.

Hot Nerd <3

> Hi, sweetheart, I made it home. Get some sleep, okay? I promise I'm still not going anywhere.

I could feel the unwritten I love you. I could hear him saying it as I opened my journal and poured my heart out.

Chapter 37

Matt

R ILEY DIDN'T TEXT ME back. I stared at my phone in my hands, my forehead resting against my apartment door holding my breath waiting for a response. She thought I was going to call everything off just because of a fight. She looked so scared I almost couldn't bring myself to leave. I should go back. I should stay there until she knows that we're going to be okay.

"Dude, what the hell?" Oliver ran down the hallway of our apartment building. He pulled the keys from my hand and unlocked the door. "Alright, let's get you inside."

All I could do was stare at my phone.

I told her I wasn't going. I almost typed the words I was dying to say.

Fuck it.

I typed another message into the box.

I love you, sweetheart. I love you and I'm not letting you go over one fight.

I stared at it, my fingering over the button to send it. Then my phone was gone, and I was staring at my empty hand.

"Not doing that. Nope, no way. I did that once and it made everything worse."

I ran my hands through my hair. Oliver steered me toward the couch, shoving me hard onto the cushions. Cushions that smelled like Riley.

"Alright, let's start from the beginning. Tell me what happened." He shuffled around in my kitchen, opening and closing cabinets to pull out baking supplies. I didn't know he could bake.

"It was about Christmas. I just want her to meet everyone. I'm so sick of this are we or aren't we. Why can't she just admit that things between us are serious?" I slumped forward to rest my elbows on my knees and dropped my head into my hands. "I want to marry her, Oliver." Something clattered in the kitchen and then a crash of something shattering on the floor. I didn't care enough to look.

"Did you break up?" he asked in a tense voice.

I huffed out a breath. "No, but she thinks we're going to all because of one fight."

"Did you tell her you love her and want to marry her?"

I choked on a laugh to hold back the pain swelling in my chest. "No, but I want to."

"Okay, no, you're going to be patient. Let her say it first."

I nodded my head against my hands. I knew that. That's what I had been waiting for. She had too much history with people barreling forward without checking to see if she was behind them. The only way she was going to feel safe was if I let her lead the way.

"But what do I do?" I sat up and looked behind me toward the kitchen. Oliver had his phone out tapping rapidly on the screen. He rubbed his other hand over his beard and then laid his phone screen side down on the counter.

"Emery said she's upset at all of us right now." He rubbed the back of his neck and fought back a smile. There had been more to that message than just talking about Riley. My stomach twisted at the thought of them being happy while things were a mess between Riley and me. I'd been worried about him for months and now that he was finally happy I didn't like it. What was wrong with me?

"She kept saying she was scared. She really thinks I would leave her." It felt like arrows burying into my chest to say the words to him. I thought I was showing her that we were going to be okay. I thought she trusted me.

I thought I was her safe place.

"Don't say that. You and I both know it has nothing to do with you. She has a lot that she's working through. Tonight you're going to give her some space."

"And in the morning? I call her every morning. I can't remember what it's like to start my day without hearing her voice." I didn't care if I sounded ridiculous. Starting my morning talking to her was a routine I couldn't let go of. The only thing that would be better would be waking up to her next to me in bed.

That's the direction we were headed in. I thought we were so close to being there. So much had changed in the past couple of weeks but here we were taking a million steps back.

I had a ring in my drawer.

For the second time in my life, I had a ring in my drawer taunting me while the woman I loved couldn't commit.

"I'm such an idiot," I groaned. Something hit the back of my head, bouncing off and then landing on the floor behind me. I turned to see a bag of mini marshmallows on the floor. They were peppermint flavored. Riley picked them out at the grocery store last week for hot chocolate.

"This isn't a repeat of things with Liz. You guys have known each other - what five months? That's hardly anything. It's just your first fight."

"But what if it is? How does this keep happening to me?"

I rubbed my hands through my hair again. I was getting too worked up about this.

I need to be patient with her. I need to let her work this out on her own. We weren't going to get past this if I kept pushing her before she was ready.

Chapter 38

Riley

I WOKE UP TO my phone ringing before my alarm went off, that first photo I took of Matt lighting up the screen. I smiled softly as I looked at the photo before the memories of last night rushed into me, carving a pit into my stomach. My chest tightened as I swiped to answer.

"Good morning, beautiful," he said in his low morning voice. He sounded different this morning, the usual brightness in his voice was gone. That was my fault. All my fault.

"Good morning, handsome," I answered. My response was robotic, the same way I greeted him each morning, but it was taking all my self-control to keep the emotion out of my voice.

"Are you okay?" he asked.

I nodded and then shook my head. "I don't know. I, uh, think I still need time to process everything," I finally answered him. I braced myself for his response.

"I know, sweetheart. I'm here when you're ready, okay? Just tell me when. We're going to figure this out." He paused. "It was just a fight, that's all. All couples fight, even my parents and they're practically couple goals." It was hard to tell if he was trying to convince me, or if he was trying to convince himself.

I tried to laugh but it came out mixed with tears. "You said we weren't a couple."

He sighed then muttered something under his breath that I couldn't make out. "That was a stupid thing to say, and I've been regretting it all night. I'm sorry, I shouldn't have snapped like that. I know we haven't put a label on this, but in my mind, we've been a couple this whole time."

I threw an arm over my eyes. "It's my fault we haven't put a label on things."

His side of the line went quiet for a while. I lay there listening to his breathing while he worked through his own thoughts. I could picture the creases in the corners of his mouth as he bit the inside of his bottom lip the way he always did when he was trying to focus. He probably had one hand tugging at his hair.

"I'll come over after school today and we can talk," he finally said.

"I have a therapist appointment today and then I promised my sister-in-law I would babysit while she does last minute Christmas shopping." I paused and tried to push the picture of his face out of my mind. "I think we should both take some time today to just think about things."

You should take some time to change your mind and get out while you can, I wanted to say to him.

"Okay, yeah, we can do that."

We said our goodbyes. Hot tears flowed down my face as I went through my morning routine. I was going to really need that therapy appointment today.

Chapter 39

Matt

MY PHONE DROPPED HEAVILY on top of Oliver's tool cart, the case causing it to bounce and send sockets rolling around. There was probably a fresh crack on the screen of my phone. One socket ricocheted off a rachet, tumbling over the edge and hitting the concrete with a loud ping, rolling over to the next bay.

"Whoa, what's going on?" Drew asked as he caught the socket with the side of his boot. "If you've got some anger to get out, I have a brake rotor I could use some help knocking loose."

I shoved my hands in my pockets, glaring at my phone. It had been quiet all day. A few times I thought I felt it vibrate during class, the sensation causing my heart to skip a beat each time. Later I would check only to find that I didn't have any new notifications. She needed space, I could respect that. I really could.

I just missed her.

I missed her silly updates of how her day was going.

I missed her random thoughts of plans for us.

I missed her telling me she couldn't wait to see me after work.

I had a nagging feeling she wasn't asking for space for herself to process things. She had said she thought we both needed time to think about things. Did she think I was going to change my mind? Was this her starting to push me away to make me change my mind?

I rolled up the sleeves of my shirt. "Tell me what to do," I said to Drew. Working at the shop had been my first job as a teenager. Pop said everyone should know how to do basic maintenance on their own car. The summer that Oliver, Ava, and I all worked here was one of my favorites. There was a time after my breakup with Liz that I had considered giving up my teaching job and moving back here to work at the shop while I waited for a position to open. I had been doing the maintenance on my own car at that point, and while I was rusty about a lot of things I knew it wouldn't take any time for me to relearn things.

Oliver told me he'd kick my ass if I did that. It didn't matter how much the shop needed help; he was not going to let me give up everything I had worked so hard for.

Oliver lifted his head up from the engine he was bent over. "You're not working in your school clothes." He waved an arm over to the break and locker area. "Go change."

"Is there anything my size in there?" Oliver was shorter than me with a stockier build. Drew was closer to the same height but thinner. Wade was both taller and thinner. There was no way any of their clothes were going to fit me.

"Your old coveralls might still be in there," he said. Yeah, my old coveralls from the awkward teenage years that had lasted all the way up until my early twenties. I had been about Drew's size back then and the pairs of coveralls had been two sizes too big since they were extras. Pop had been adamant that the job was just a stepping stone and thought if he ordered me my own uniform I'd think it was more permanent.

I pointed at my phone on the tool cart. "Do something with this. I can't keep looking at it."

My old locker still had my name on it, the label yellowed and faded over the years. Oliver had made a lot of changes in the past year to the shop, but the employee area felt like stepping back in time. There were still lockers for Pop and Oliver's dad. The only people who ever worked here were family so there wasn't a need to keep swapping out the names for new employees.

My backpack fell out when I opened the door, just like always. The backpack I shoved in there after the last day of class senior year. It was unzipped, loose pages and textbooks hitting the ground around my feet. I guess that's where the books I thought I lost were this whole time. That day had also been the last day that Pop let me work, telling me that I needed to spend the summer having fun before I went off to college. "You've got plenty of time to work ahead of you. It's time to enjoy being young and irresponsible right now," he said to Oliver and me both. The two of them had fought about it all summer.

There was a wadded-up pair of clean coveralls shoved in the back. I shoved everything else back in, slamming the door closed before another avalanche could start. I pulled the coveralls over my school clothes wishing I had brought a change of clothes with me. I usually packed a change for after work but I had skipped that today, a re-minder to myself that I couldn't go to see Riley. Memories of being seventeen washed over me.

"The gang's back together," I announced back out in the shop. I motioned to my clothes, "told y'all I'd grow into them eventually." Oliver grunted out a laugh.

"Why are you here instead of with Riley?" he asked.

"We're taking some space away from each other today."

Drew winced and held out a mallet. He gestured to the rotor that was stuck and showed me where to hit it.

"I told you to stop being clingy," Oliver barked. He stopped what he was doing to watch us. I slammed the mallet against the rotor. The impact sent shockwaves up my arm that made me feel more agitated. A hand gripped my forearm, pulling my arm back from taking another swing. "You're going to hurt yourself doing that." I couldn't tell if he meant how I was hitting the rotor or how clingy I was.

I couldn't help it. Up until yesterday Riley had made me believe she liked when I was clingy.

I don't think I want you to ever stop touching me.

I think you've ruined me for all future first dates.

I like how clingy you are.

I've never wanted something this much.

I think I'm just into hot, nerdy Matt.

Sometimes she was just as clingy as I was. She always came up with reasons why I couldn't leave just yet at the end of the day, always reaching for me if we weren't touching, always leaning into my touch. She broke all our rules more than I did.

"At least he's smart enough to not let the woman he loves get away," Drew said. I almost gave myself whiplash turning my head to look at him in shock. Drew didn't say things like that. He pushed the wheel he held onto the front of the car.

"Kid, I'm not taking relationship advice from someone that's never had one." Oliver turned his back to Drew, missing the way his ears and face turned blazing red. Drew was five years younger than us, and as far as we knew a late bloomer when it came to everything including dating. I'd never even heard him express interest in anyone, not that we were close enough for him to feel comfortable telling me those kinds of things. His hands shook as he put the lug nuts on the wheel.

"Maybe you should take it easy on him," I reminded Oliver. "What if we hang out like old times tonight?" I asked Drew. Like really old times when Drew and Wade were young enough to beg to hang out with Oliver and I. Wow, we were getting old. "We could have a Mario Kart night."

Chapter 40

Riley

I CHECKED MY PHONE every chance I could throughout the day at work. There were never any new notifications from him. I knew he was doing what I asked him to do, but I missed him so much. We hadn't gone this long with talking since he came back into my life in August.

I'm doing the right thing for me, I kept telling myself.

I typed and deleted several messages as the day went on. I wanted to tell him that I loved him. I needed to know he was okay. I needed to fix this.

Nothing I had done was wrong. I had made the decisions that I needed to in order to protect myself, to give myself time to trust him. I knew that. He knew that. I still should have reacted differently last night. I could have handled myself better and still stuck to my boundaries. That was the thing I regretted.

"Thank you so much for watching him," Jenna said as she watched her son run toward my kitchen. She reached for her purse and started to stand from the couch.

"You know I love hanging out with him." I watched as Aaron turned the apron I'd laid out for him around in his hands. "Can I ask you a question?"

She settled back onto the couch. "Of course." Concern washed over her face reminding me that we had never really been close.

"How did you know Milo was the one?"

Her eyes sparkled, and her mouth lifted in a soft smile. "How much has Milo told you about us?" She brushed a strand of blonde hair out of her face and adjusted her knit beanie to keep it back.

"Not much really. He called me one day not long after you two met to tell me about this amazing woman he had met and that you had a kid. He wanted to do whatever it would take to win you over."

Jenna laughed and twisted her wedding band. "Yeah, I think he was all in from day one."

"But you weren't?"

She shook her head and looked in the kitchen where Aaron sat at the table digging through the box of cookie cutters. "My ex-husband and I got married straight out of high school. We were too young and neither of us knew how to have a healthy relationship. We tried for years to make it work. We thought having a kid would fix all our problems but not long after I found out I was pregnant things just went from bad to worse. He wasn't a bad guy; we just weren't right together." She kept her eyes fixed on her son the whole time she spoke, her love for him written all over her face.

I reached over and squeezed her hand.

"We finally decided we would be happier divorced when Aaron was just a few months old. Back then it felt my whole world was falling apart, but now I'm glad we had enough clarity to call it quits. I couldn't imagine having my baby grow up in that toxic environment." Her voice shook. "After a year of living in my childhood bedroom trying to get back on my feet, my parents decided to convert their basement into an apartment for us. My brother owns a construction company, so my parents asked him to help with the remodel."

"Milo works for your brother," I said. I knew that part.

She nodded. "Any time he was at the house we would always end up talking. I don't remember how it happened but sometimes he would be the only one there working, and I would find myself helping. Being around him felt easy. I was the single mom of a toddler, and I was so focused on raising him I forgot how to be myself. Being around your brother reminded me that I was more than just a mom."

"Were you scared?" I asked.

"I was terrified. I had already made a mistake with who I chose to have a child with. Even though everything with Milo felt so easy, and he was great with Aaron, I was so scared to let him fully into our lives. What if I made a mistake in choosing him and I put Aaron and I back into another toxic situation?" She squeezed my hand. "Once the renovation was done Milo just kept showing up for me. He let me have my space, but he was always there showing me love any way I would let him."

She took a shaky breath and focused on Aaron. "For Aaron's third birthday my parents went all out. They rented one of those blow-up bounce houses. Technically Aaron was a little young to even be in one of those, but we made sure he was only in there by himself, and I was right there watching. He had been to other birthday parties for kids in my family before and was always upset that he was too little to jump with them. He was in the bounce house when he saw my parents bringing out his cake. I was sitting at the entrance and opened the flap to let him out thinking he would go straight for my arms. He got so excited he jumped straight out, flying past me and landing on the ground."

"He broke his arm," I said, remembering not long after that Milo brought Jenna and Aaron to my parents' house for a cookout for the first time. Aaron's little arm had been in a rainbow cast.

"Milo scooped him right up and took us to the hospital. I was panicking the whole time and felt like such a horrible mom, but he stayed calm and took care of us. Seeing him step so easily into a father role in that emergency made me realize how much he was a perfect fit for our little family."

"Were you still scared?" I asked.

She laughed. "Oh yeah, but I was more scared of missing my chance." She stood and went over to Aaron, wrapping her arms around him and planting a kiss on the top of his wild hair. "Riley, is there someone...." Her words trailed off.

I nodded and joined her and Aaron. He stayed focused on picking the best cookie cutters.

"I know I haven't been part of the family for long, so I haven't been around for all your past relationships, but Milo has told me about them. Whoever this new someone is, I can tell that they make you happy." She ran her fingers through her son's hair trying to smooth it out.

I thought back to the one time I had brought my ex around the family after Jenna joined us. It hadn't been long before we broke up. Looking back, I could see he had been trying to distance himself from me and I had been on edge waiting for the other shoe to drop.

"I really think he's different," I said. "But I always think that." I shrugged and picked Aaron's apron up from where he had dropped it on the floor. "I'm scared I'm wrong about him like I've been wrong about all the others."

Jenna opened her arms to me and motioned for me to step closer. "I think you should give him a chance. Even if you turn out to be wrong about him, at least then you'll know. You can't let a hypothetical heartbreak keep you from a chance of happiness." She wrapped her arms around me and squeezed tight.

"My therapist told me the same thing," I said into her shoulder.

"Then maybe you should listen to us."

"All the others always seemed like they were more worried about how I could make them happy," I said as I squeezed her back.

"What about him?"

Matt was always happiest when he was making the others around him happy. He loved everyone and everything around him with boundless energy. He wore his heart on his sleeve from the moment we first met, never leaving room for doubt. "He cares more about making me happy." I sniffled as I felt tears start to burn my eyes. He didn't just care about making me happy. He has gone out of his way to ensure I felt safe, felt seen every step of our relationship. Matt had been loving me in a way that was so soft it made falling for him not feel like falling at all. More importantly, this whole time he hadn't been just showing me how he felt, he had been showing me that I deserved his love even when I struggled to reciprocate. "He makes me feel like I deserve to be happy."

***

Aaron and I finished rolling out the sugar cookie dough and were picking out cookie cutters when the front door slammed open. I jumped, the cookie cutter in my hand clattering onto the table. Aaron looked up at me with wide eyes, freezing with a snowflake in one hand and a snowman in the other.

"Where's my favorite nephew?" Emery called from the doorway. Aaron relaxed as a smile brightened his face. Emery draped her jacket over the arm of the couch, ignoring the coat rack right behind her. "I know you two aren't making cookies without me." She tiptoed up behind his chair, catching him by surprise and tickling his ribs. "Did you forget to invite me, buddy?" Aaron giggled as he twisted in her grip.

"I thought you had plans," I said. I pressed a round cutter into the dough, focusing all my attention on twisting it for a clean cut and avoiding Emery's eyes. She had been home less and less this month, always refusing to tell me where she was going. The tension between us had been growing exponentially. I felt like I barely knew her anymore. Last night's argument between us may have been over her constant meddling, but there was something underlying we hadn't touched yet.

"Being here with the two of you was more important." The corners of her mouth twitched. She pushed up the sleeves of her sweater on her way to the pantry to pull out an apron. Her fingers stumbled over the ties.

"You don't have to be here if you don't want to." I struggled to keep my voice low and smooth, not wanting to fight in front of Aaron. I looked back to where he knelt in the chair next to me. He pressing the snowman shape into the dough, not paying attention to us.

"I know I messed up, Riley. I'm sorry and I won't do it again. Will you forgive me already?"

I shifted my attention to helping Aaron transfer the snowman to the baking sheet. "I want to decorate it," he said, trying to grab it from me. His tongue wiggled the loose front tooth that looked like it was barely hanging on.

"We have to bake it first," I reminded him. He nodded and then started cutting out another cookie. "Why won't you tell me what you've been up to?" I asked Emery as she moved to his other side.

She spun a Christmas tree cutter around her fingers. "I don't want to jinx it," she answered after a long pause. A frustrated huff escaped me before I could remind myself to be calm. She always expected me to tell her everything but couldn't return the favor. I could keep prodding until she told me something, or until she got mad enough to leave. That had never been something I could do, even when just once I wanted to give her a taste of her own medicine.

"I can watch Aaron if you want to go see Matt." She looked at me over his head, blinking at me like she was doing me a favor.

My heart raced and Matt's tear covered face filled my mind. My body tingled with a craving for his touch. It hadn't even been twenty-four hours since he left after our fight, yet it felt like forever. A whole day of not talking to him, not seeing him, not feeling him. I missed him so badly it hurt.

Could I just show up after telling him I needed space? The space was for both of us, to give us both time to think about everything we had said. I couldn't just take away the space we both agreed we needed, no matter how much I ached to fix this.

I had to give him the time to change his mind.

Emery went to bed as soon as Milo came by to pick up Aaron. My body buzzed with excess energy. I scrubbed the house clean, wrapped Matt's Christmas presents, and baked another batch of cookies. At midnight I checked my phone to see a voice message from Matt. It was like he knew I needed to hear his voice.

"Goodnight, sweetheart," was all he said. No pressure to talk to him, pressure to not take the space I told him I needed. Just a reminder that he was there and thinking about me.

I loved him. I wanted the first time I told him to be a big deal.

He deserved a big deal.

Chapter 41

Riley

I JUMPED OUT OF bed as soon as I heard Emery leave for the morning and pulled my overnight duffle bag out of my closet. I threw things in it without paying attention as I tossed plans around in my brain. I had nodded off for maybe an hour at one point during the night, jumping awake with the pages of my journal stuck to my face and pen marks on my sheets, but I was buzzing with energy. The only part of the plan that I could decide on was that I should have an overnight bag with me.

I needed to be with him tonight. I needed to wake up with him in the morning.

If he would let me. If he would have me.

I held on to hope that he would.

I tried to push away the thoughts of doubts as I emptied the bag and tried to pay attention as I repacked it.

It took several tries.

My phone rang as I packed my lunch for the day, and I smiled as I saw that Matt was calling me for our morning call. "Good morning, handsome," I answered before he could speak.

"Good morning, beautiful. You sound chipper this morning."

My face already hurt from smiling. This was going to be a long half day. "I'm coming over after work. We need to talk." My words were rushed. It was hard to get a deep breath with how excited I felt.

Matt's voice was cautious when he spoke. "Are we going to talk about Wednesday?"

"Yes, we're going to talk about it. We really need to talk about it."

I love you.

I love you.

I'm going to tell you I love you today.

"Okay. I'll see you after school." His voice was calm without a hint of emotion. I couldn't even hear a smile in his voice.

I looked at the bag I had packed and left next to the front door. Was I making a mistake? Was it about to happen again? Did he take the space I gave him yesterday and decide that none of this was worth it?

I pushed the thought away. This was it; I was going to do this. Whatever happened would happen. If it blew up in my face, then it blew up in my face.

I couldn't go another day without telling him I loved him.

If he changed his mind and broke my heart, that was on him. It wasn't a reflection of me. I repeated it like a mantra as I struggled through the short school day.

***

Matt

I had never been more thankful for the half-day before Christmas break in my life, not even when I was in school. I couldn't even begin to think about working today. Attendance and then turn on *A Christmas Carol* – that was the extent of my abilities as a teacher today.

I turned Riley's words over in my head on repeat until I had convinced myself that she had sounded freaked out, like she was hiding something. She was coming over to my place. She didn't ask me to come see her.

Was she planning for a quick escape?

Was she going to decide that this was all too hard and run away?

We need to talk.

We need to talk.

The words twisted in my stomach, in my heart. Famous last words before everything went downhill.

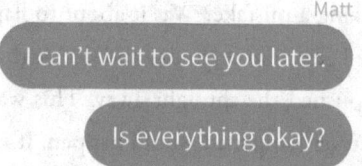

Matt

I can't wait to see you later.

Is everything okay?

Stop being clingy, I reminded myself. Every moment that went by without a response was agony. At least after today I would have my answer. Either this was going somewhere, or it wasn't.

I'd live in the place of limbo we'd been in these past few months forever if it meant getting to keep her in my life. *I don't need more*, I lied to myself. I can be happy here if it means keeping her.

Chapter 42

Riley

I KNOCKED ON THE door and walked in without waiting for him to open it. Matt froze on the other side just a step away with a hand reaching forward to open it. He must have just gotten home. He was still in the Christmas sweater he must have worn to school and his teaching bag was on the kitchen island. His hair stuck up like he had been running his hands through it. My fingers ached to rake through it.

He backed up a few steps to give me room to enter. Any other day he would have taken my bag from me and then wrapped me in his arms. Today his arms hung by his side. My body tingled with the need to have his hands on me.

"Hi," I said out of breath. My heart swelled as I took him in and pushed a smile to my face.

"Riley, what's wrong? You've had me worried all day." He stood frozen in that spot.

I closed the door behind me and dropped my tote bag and duffle bag by my feet. "Why are you worried?"

"Last time we saw each other we argued and then we didn't talk yesterday. This morning you said we needed to talk and then nothing else for the rest of the day. Then you bust in here like you ran the whole way."

My smile dropped as I remembered his messages asking if everything was okay close to the early dismissal time. I had been so wrapped up in getting through work so I could get to him I forgot to respond. My heart raced. I had already screwed this up.

"I know. I'm sorry. I just need some time to think. I'm ready to un-pause." I sucked in a breath. I clenched my hands by my side and forced myself to maintain eye contact. "I don't want to keep doing whatever it is we're doing." I held up a hand to stop him from speaking.

"No, fuck, that was the wrong way to start this." I let out a frustrated grunt and tried again. "I spent all night trying to think of a way to tell you this. I was going to try to make it special, romantic. But the truth is, I suck at all that and all I could think about was getting here as fast as I could." I dragged a hand over my face. "God, I'm so bad at this. I'm just trying to say, I'm tired of acting like this isn't something serious, of avoiding talking about the future. I want to wake up next to you every morning and not to a phone call. I want to meet your family and introduce you to the rest of mine. I want the big scary things and the small moments. I love you and I'm so tired of denying it. I trust you. I want to call you mine and to hear you say I get to keep you." I pressed my back against the door and stared at him.

He ran a hand through his hair and took half a step toward me. "Riley."

I looked down at the floor and tapped one foot against the other. "I'm sorry I didn't make it romantic. I know you like that kind of stuff and that's what you would have done for me. I just couldn't keep it in anymore."

He stopped a step away from me and stood still watching me. His mouth pulled tight, and his eyes were wide, one hand in his hair and the other by his side in a fist.

"Please say something. I feel like I'm going to throw up right now," I whispered.

"What changed? Why now?" His voice was unsteady, like he wasn't sure if he was allowed to ask.

"I told my sister-in-law about you last night because all I've been able to think about since Wednesday is how much it hurts to see you upset just because I can't get through my own shit. Because we are together, we have been this whole time just like you said yesterday morning, but I was too scared to say it. You've done nothing but show me that you're all in and I keep comparing you to people you're not. I thought I was protecting myself by denying how I felt, but I was just hurting us both. I can't keep hurting us anymore. I love you and I need you to know." My face was a mess of tears and snot and makeup. I didn't care. "We deserve happiness. You're the only person that's ever shown me that I deserve happiness."

He smiled and closed the distance between us. The sight of those slightly too big front teeth had never made me happier. His hands cupped my face, and his body pressed me into the door. His mouth hovered over mine long enough for my heart to skip a beat before finally covering mine. This was different from how he normally kissed me. His mouth against mine was always sweet and gentle, because that's how he was with me. This time his mouth was rough and hungry, more like the night of the Christmas dance. I wrapped my hands in his sweater and pulled him closer. Our teeth and tongues clashed as we made up for all the time we spent holding back.

"Matt," I said into his mouth.

"Yes, sweetheart?" He broke away just a little. "Is this okay?"

"Yes, it's perfect. It's just, I need...". I let my words drop off as I searched for the right one. "I don't want to pressure you or anything, but I really need you to talk to me. Are we okay?"

His body stayed firmly pressed against mine, but he pulled his head back enough for me to see his full face. "I love you too, Riley. Is that what you need to hear?" His thumb stroked over my bottom lip. "I know you already know it."

"I love you," I said again. "I'm sorry it took me so long."

He kissed me again. "It just took you a little while to say the words, but you've been telling me in other ways for a long time."

"Have I?"

"You have." He kissed me again. Again. Again. Again.

"How?" I asked as we broke for air.

"Riley, I've been thinking about this moment for a long time now. Will you let me focus?"

"I just need to know," I said.

He moved his mouth to my ear. "The way you texted me so much your sister had to put you in time out. The way your face lit up when you saw me at the district meeting."

"Right before I ran away from you," I interrupted him.

"The way you touch me like you'll never get enough. The way you trust me with things you've never told anyone else. When you hype me up whenever I doubt myself. The way you get excited about every little moment of time we're able to spend together and refer to even the smallest things as a date. You love me so softly in all the little ways all the time."

"Okay, okay," I said. I tried to turn my head to catch his mouth with mine.

"There's more, so much more. Can I keep going?" His mouth followed my ear denying my mouth.

"Later. I need your mouth," I said.

He caught my ear lobe in his mouth, sucking and biting. "My mouth is right here," he said around it.

"I need it back over here." I tried again to turn my face toward him.

"Details, sweetheart, I'm going to need more details. There are a lot of places I've been dying to put my mouth."

A wave of heat washed over me and settled between my thighs as I struggled to think. He felt so good pressing into me like this. We felt so good pressed against each other.

"Kiss me. Please, kiss me."

He trailed kisses down my throat. "I am kissing you."

I wiggled against him and reached for his head to pull him back to my mouth. In a flash he had both my hands pinned above me against the door.

"Use your words." His eyes were back on mine. "Where do you want my mouth?"

"Kiss me," I said again.

"Where?"

I swallowed and tried to lean toward him. He leaned just out of my reach and smirked. "On my mouth." I swallowed again and took in the man in front of me. My sweet, sunshine Matt was gone and replaced by someone with dark eyes full of want. "Everywhere," I whispered.

"That's what I'm trying to do. You keep stopping me."

A nervous giggle bubbled out of my mouth. Matt released my hands from the door and moved them to bracket his face. The long stubble on his cheeks dug into my palms. "I'm sorry," I said. "I'm really nervous and excited."

"Why are you nervous? It's me, you don't have to be nervous with me."

"I can't believe this is real." I planted kisses all over this face. "Are you really mine?"

He nuzzled his cheek against my hand. "I've been yours."

"Do I get to keep you?"

"You can keep me forever if you'll have me."

I cried harder. "I want that."

His thumbs brushed my face before he pulled me into a hug. "Happy tears?"

I nodded my head against his shoulder. Happy tears. Relieved tears. Thankful tears. "I don't know if you've noticed but I'm kind of a crier." I laughed and wiped the tears with the back of my hand. "Matt?"

"Yes, beautiful?"

"When you propose I want it to be as big and romantic as you want to make it, okay? No holding back."

He pulled back to tilt my face up to his. "I love you so much." The gorgeous smile that always set my heart aflutter appeared again. "How long do I have to wait? I would be down for proposing right now."

"I have other plans for right now." I kissed his smile. "Any time after tonight is fine with me." I wiggled out of his arms and bent down for my duffle bag.

"Riley, I need you back up here."

I stood up and held up the plastic bag I had retrieved. "I wasn't sure if you would have condoms here or not. We didn't really get that far whenever we talked about things so I thought I would come prepared just in case."

Matt lifted his eyebrows and took the bag from my hand.

"I mean, if you want to. We don't have to, if you don't want to."

He pulled my body flush against his again. "Does it feel like I don't want to?" he asked as he pressed his hips against mine, letting me feel how hard he was against his pants.

"Funny business is approved?" I rocked my hips against his drawing a gasp from him.

"Funny business is very much needed," he answered.

Another wave of heat washed over me as I pressed harder against him enjoying the feel of his hard length against me. My fingers went to the hem of his sweater. "Clothes. Off. Now."

He untangled my hands from his clothes and pulled me toward his bedroom. "Someone is impatient," he laughed.

"I've never wanted someone as much as I want you, Matt. I haven't been able to stop thinking about it," I said. I waited for embarrassment to take over, but it never came. All my past relationships had just happened to me, but with Matt I got to choose. I got to choose to want him. I got to choose how I loved him. I got to choose what I told him and when. It was impossible to feel embarrassed when I knew he wanted me just as much, that he was choosing me too. I tugged on his hand until he turned around, and I could capture his mouth with mine again. There had always been a measure of control over our kissing, both of us always toeing the line of the boundaries we had set but never crossing them and stopping ourselves when we almost did. That control was gone. I liked the way he kissed without control. "I don't think I'll ever get enough of kissing you like this."

My back slammed into the wall next to his bedroom. "Me either." His mouth moved against mine alternating between soft tender and hard hungry kisses. We poured love and want into each other with our mouths and hands. "I need to tell you something," he said against my mouth.

"Later, you can tell me later." I needed him against me, his skin touching mine, right now. It was all I could think about, his body all I could feel. I wasn't capable of hearing any other confessions.

My fingers worked on his belt while his hand slid under my sweater and dug into the waistband of my leggings. "Clothes, please," I begged.

He pulled away and moved me from the wall to push me through the bedroom door. His hands went to work on his belt, his eyes heavy as he watched me. I tugged my own clothes off and moved to sit on the edge of the bed. I moved my arms to cover my stomach and pushed up my breasts without even thinking.

"Jesus, Riley, I wanted to do that." His sweater fell to the floor, followed by his belt and pants. He stood there in his undershirt and boxer briefs, eyes behind his glasses roaming over me. He was gorgeous. It was the same thing I had thought when I walked in on him the day of the dance. "Move your arms."

I moved my arms at his command and relished the way he looked at me like he had found his new favorite thing until I couldn't handle him not touching me. "You were taking too long." I reached for him, needing him back against me. "Stop looking at me like that."

He moved in front of me, his hands pressed into my shoulders urging me to lay back. "You are so fucking sexy, I can't stop looking at you." His mouth followed his hands down my shoulders and then over each arm, over the tops of my breasts, over the soft roundness of my stomach and every stretch mark. Goosebumps covered my skin everywhere he touched. One hand ghosted back up my body to settle on one breast, thumb circling the fabric of my bra right over my nipple. My hands tugged at the bottom of his undershirt dragging it up, needing his skin against mine.

He leaned back to pull the shirt over his head revealing that swirl of music notes that I had dreamed of touching again. I pushed myself up and reached back for the clasp of my bra. His hand covered mine. "Are you going to let me take my time with you?" His crooked glasses teetered precariously on his nose.

"We have the rest of our lives for that." My free hand reached for his glasses, fingers grasping the frame lightly at one temple to tug them off.

Matt's hand cupped around mine, pulling my fingers to his mouth to press a kiss against each finger tip as he shook his head. "Those stay on. I'm not missing a single detail of you." He rested my hand on his shoulder so he could resume his task of learning every inch of me even slower than before. Slow enough to remind me of that first night when he made the comment about making me beg. I tilted my hips up to rub against him. His eyes flicked up to meet mine and a wicked grin stretched across his lips as he lifted his hips away from mine.

"Now you're just being mean," I groaned.

"I have every intention of being nice, you just need to be patient." He pressed his mouth against my collarbone. "It's been a while. If you keep doing that it's going to be over way too soon." His mouth trailed over to my other collarbone. "You said you wanted my mouth everywhere." His free hand skated between my spread legs teasing me with his fingers against my inner thigh. He hadn't even touched me, and I was already soaked.

"Touch me before I lose my – oh." I moaned as his fingers brushed over my clit above the fabric of my underwear. I lifted my hips wanting more. "More," I begged. He circled faster, groaning as I pressed myself against his hand.

He lifted himself up and looked down at where his hand touched me. Just when I was going to tell him I needed more, needed his skin against mine, his hand stopped moving. An embarrassing whimper escaped from me. His pupils were so blown out I could barely see a ring of blue when his eyes met mine. "Do you want my mouth here," he asked, tapping a finger against me.

God, yes. I wanted that so badly. "Please."

His hand disappeared and he tugged my underwear down my legs, then he moved each of my legs over his shoulders, his hands gripping my hips to pin me in place. His eyes held mine and he swiped his tongue in a slow lick that made my hips arch up. I was going to come faster and harder than I ever had. His mouth closed over my clit as he pushed his fingers inside me. He worked until my thighs clenched around his head and shook from the pleasure building in me. The one hand on my hip to pin me down fought a losing battle. I dug my hands in his hair, my fingernails scrapped against his scalp, and he moaned against me. I don't know who was moaning louder, him or me. My body tensed and bucked against him as waves of orgasm exploded through me, my mouth falling open with moans and whimpers. I closed my eyes and tried to catch my breath.

He rested his head against the inside of one of my thighs, eyes full of adoration and crooked glasses smudged. He wore the same wide grin I always thought of as cute. Right now with his head between my legs and his wet fingers pressed against my hip that grin was the hottest thing I'd ever seen. "Worth the wait?" he asked.

"Mmm, I haven't decided yet," I mumbled with a soft smile.

"Now who is being mean?"

I reached for him, tugging him back up to me for a kiss. His skin against mine was heaven. I've never been able to get enough of his touch before and even now I felt like I never would. "Will you please shut up and get inside me already?"

He groaned and reached for the condoms. I tugged the waistband of his boxer briefs down while he opened the box and stroked him. His breath shuttered and his fingers fumbled with the wrapper while his eyes watched my hand work, noises tumbling from his mouth. Once the condom was freed, he gently moved my hand so he could roll it on. Both of us scrambled to push his underwear down his legs.

"Matt?" I ran my hands over his back as he settled over me.

"Yes, sweetheart?"

"I love you." Telling him for the first time was like a dam bursting and now I couldn't stop myself from telling him over and over. I had been biting the words back for so long I felt like I had to make up for all the missed opportunities.

"I love you too," he whispered in my ear as he finally filled me and then stilled. It may have been the most still he'd ever been around me. His forehead dropped to rest against mine. "You feel so good, Riley."

My muscles clenched around him urging him to move. "It'd feel even better if you move."

His body tensed over mine and another groan shuddered out of him. "Please stop." Muttered curse flowed out of him when I clenched again. "Riley, please, if you keep doing that I'm going to embarrass myself."

"It's just me, Matt. There's nothing to be embarrassed about."

Then we were a blur of skin against skin, lips on lips, and slow strokes. He sped up and thrusted into me harder when I dug my nails into his back. His fingers circled my clit while he muttered half formed words mingled with moans and pants against my mouth begging me to come around him.

"Please," he begged with every word punctuated by a thrust, "Let. Me. Feel."

Hearing the way his voice broke before he could finish his thought sent me over the edge with his name on my lips. I loved the noises he made, that he didn't hold back.

One of his hands reached back to bring my hands away from his back. He laced our fingers together and pressed my hands into the mattress. Then he followed me over the edge.

He dropped his face to my neck while he caught his breath. "Worth the wait," he muttered with a shallow laugh.

Chapter 43

Matt

RILEY WAS ON MY couch in nothing but an oversized hoodie and a pair of thermal socks she stole from me with a Christmas blanket spread over her lap. It was taking all my self-control not to strip everything off her and throw her back in my bed. We had taken the best nap of my life after we had sex. I had woken up with her head on my chest and her naked body wrapped around mine. Then her stomach growled and she admitted she'd been so nervous all day she had barely eaten anything. I stirred the pot of beef and sweet potato stew on the stove top wishing it would warm up faster. The stew was from a batch we made and froze a couple weeks ago, and I had pulled it straight from the freezer after our nap.

I was too far away from her.

Riley's arms wrapped around my waist from behind. It's like she had sensed how much I needed her touching me again. "We still need to decide what we're doing for Christmas," she said. She pressed a kiss against the bare skin of my shoulder.

"Well, based on today's new developments I'm going to say it sounds like we'll be splitting the day between my family and yours. Any certain time we need to be at your parents' house?" I turned around in her arms until I could pull her against me. She's always fit against me perfectly, but now was even better without the wall she had been holding up between us.

"Jenna's family always celebrates on Christmas Eve so we all usually just get to my parents' house sometime in the morning and stay all day. We open gifts once everyone is there and have brunch. Then we settle in to watch *Polar Express* while we build gingerbread houses."

Her family kept things simple compared to my family. There were less of them than us but I was willing to bet it would be just as loud. Riley focused a lot on the negative memories she had from growing up, sometimes it made me dislike her parents for all the ways they planted the seeds that would later grow into her insecurities and doubts around relationships. Then she would tell me about how things were now, how much her parents had grown, and I couldn't wait to meet them.

I smiled and twisted one of her curls around my finger. "I think I love your family already."

Her eyes focused on my finger and her whole body blushed. "They're going to love you," she said.

I tilted her face up to kiss her. Our lips were swollen and a little chapped from the amount of kissing that had happened over the past few hours, but I couldn't get enough of her mouth on mine. The passionate way she kissed me back told me the feeling was mutual.

"What about your family?" She pulled away from me to open the cabinet. Her in my kitchen – our kitchen - doing something as simple as pulling bowls out of the cabinet was perfect. She was perfect.

"It's an all-day affair too. Everyone sort of comes and goes. My two older sisters split the day between us and their in-laws, so they usually show up around dinner time. Shelby and I get there around lunch and stay until after dinner. Oliver and his siblings will probably swing by whenever they can. My mom likes to do a huge spread, so we usually help with all the cooking while we sing along to Christmas music. Then we do presents and games if we can all focus long enough." I laughed. We never got through the stage of explaining the instructions for games before everything devolved into utter chaos. Everyone shouting over each other to re-explain parts or ask questions while the kids interrupted for help opening toys.

Riley bit her bottom lip and tried to process how we could juggle the two. "So, we'll start with my family?" she asked. "We still have a couple of days. Maybe I can ask them if we can start a little earlier. I don't know if we'll be able to leave in time to get to your parents by noon but maybe close to that? I don't want to keep you away from helping your mom."

I caught her mouth with mine again and smiled against her lips. "That sounds perfect. What if I tell my parents we'll be there around two? We won't have to rush with your family, but we'll still have time to help my mom." I pulled her tighter against me and deepened the kiss. The stew started to bubble at the same time her stomach growled again.

She pulled away laughing. "I'm sorry I freaked out the other day. I really am excited about getting to spend Christmas with you."

I moved the pot off the stove eye with one hand while the other arm stayed wrapped around Riley's waist. I spun her so her back was pressed against the counter top. "At least we got our first fight out of the way." I lifted her left hand and kissed her ring finger. It was still bare for now, but I was going to change that as soon as possible. "Now, there are other things we need to discuss."

Not only did she say she wants me forever, but she also said she wanted that forever to start soon. I could propose whenever and however I wanted. I didn't have big plans, and hadn't let myself get that far ahead of things, even if I did let myself get far enough ahead to have a ring already. The how or when didn't feel important, just that she said yes.

She was going to say yes.

She looked at her finger, watched as my thumb swiped over the spot where the ring would sit. "Introducing you to my family as my boyfriend doesn't feel like enough," she said. Her eyes lifted to mine, hesitation flashing across them. "Is it too soon for us to be more than that?"

I shook my head. "I don't care if it's too soon or not." She could have said all this in June after our first date and it wouldn't have been too soon. I knew it then, and every day since I knew even more that she's the one. We could get married tomorrow, skip the engagement altogether, and it wouldn't feel like soon enough. "Were you serious that I could propose any time after today? We can wait if you want. I'm okay with just being together right now knowing that you want to marry me in the future."

"Whenever you want to and however you want to. My only request is a simple ring, nothing expensive. Or, you don't even have to get a ring. I'm going to say yes, no matter what."

My hands drifted to her thighs, edging up the hem of the hoodie until I gripped the bare skin of her soft hips. "You're getting a ring," I told her. I pictured the dainty white gold ring with a small solitaire diamond that I had hidden in my nightstand. I needed to find a better hiding spot. "It's going to look so perfect on you."

Her eyes studied mine as her mouth formed a soft O. "You said you were ready to propose earlier. Do you already have a ring?" She didn't even try to sound surprised that I might already have a ring for her.

"I'm not answering that question. You can talk to your sister about that." Emery had started sending me links for rings in September. The night of our first kiss while Riley had been in the shower all I could think about was the future with her. Up until that moment I had refused to look at any of the links Emery sent. That ring was the second one. Seeing it had felt like a piece clicking into place, so I ordered it right then. Riley walked out of the bathroom right as I finished checkout, no idea how close to catching me in the act she had been.

Riley cupped my cheek, and I leaned against her hand. "Have you and my sister been conspiring?" she asked.

Her hand moved from my cheek up to rake her fingers through my hair. Her touch was pure bliss. My hands tightened on her hips. I could lift her onto the counter and take her right here. Push this hoodie up and sink into her. Riley licked her lips. I forced myself to pull my hands away from her, reaching behind her for the bowls.

"You need to eat," I told her. I filled the bowls with soup and motioned for her to go back to the couch. She leaned back, her elbows resting on the counter behind her.

"Do you remember the first day of school, when you came over to cook." She paused and waited for me to nod. "After I put the flowers on the table, you grabbed my wrist and pulled me toward you."

I groaned and looked up at the ceiling. "You still want to know what I was thinking."

Riley nodded.

"I was thinking about how I want to bring you home flowers every day for the rest of my life." I sat the bowls down on the stove top. "I was picturing you in a kitchen that was ours." I moved to pin her against the counter, hands resting next to her elbows to cage her in. "I also was thinking about bending you over that table and pushing up your dress." I planted a kiss on the corner of her mouth. The dress she had been wearing that day was the same silhouette as most of the ones she wore – fitted up top and then flared at the waist and hips. All I could think about was how soft she was under the flare of that fabric, how she would feel under my hands.

"I like the sound of that." She pressed her hips against mine. She couldn't get enough of me either. Fuck, it was so sexy when she told me what she wanted. Not too long ago she'd been nervous about letting me see her in a swimsuit. Now she was in my – our – kitchen begging to be bent over and fucked from behind. I slid one hand under the hoodie.

"Do you remember when we went swimming at that waterfall?" she asked.

I brushed my thumb over the bouquet of flowers on her ribs. I'll never forget that day. "I wanted to break all our rules that day."

"Me too."

She planted kisses to the trail of music notes at the top of my arm and followed them over my shoulder. "I dreamed about doing this that night."

My thumb moved higher, brushing against the soft skin on the underside of her breast. "I almost lost my mind when you told me you were self-conscious. Then you took that tank top off and I think my brain short circuited."

"I was so scared to let you see me."

"Are you still scared?" I bunched the fabric of the hoodie up in my hands and started to pull it up.

She shook her head and lifted her arms. "I seem to recall getting frustrated because you were taking too long to take my clothes off earlier." She had. I wanted to take my time, unwrap her like a present, but she was so damn impatient.

I pulled the hoodie over her head and tossed it toward the couch. "New rule. When you're here, no clothes allowed."

"I'll think about it."

She squealed as I threw her over my shoulder. "No negotiations on this one, it's a rule." I dropped her onto the couch.

She hooked a finger into the waistband of my pajama bottoms and popped it against my hip. "Only one of us is breaking that rule."

"I wouldn't have to if I could trust you to stop getting distracted." I dodged her hands reaching out for me and stepped back toward the counter for our soup. "Dinner first. I'll bend you over something later."

Her nose wrinkled. "It's so weird seeing this side of you," she said.

"What side is that, sweetheart?"

"You being all bossy. You're normally so sweet and stuff." I wanted to point out that the Riley I was used to would never be spread out naked on my couch and not even bothering to cover up. "I don't hate it," she added with a shy smile.

Chapter 44

Riley

I WOKE UP SURROUNDED by Matt. I had learned from our past sleepovers that he was clingy in his sleep, but this morning he held me like he thought I might run away. Both his arms were around me and his legs were tangled in mine. I squeezed his arms tighter around me and wiggled even closer to him. Waking up with Matt was always something I loved, but waking up with naked Matt was even better.

"Good morning, girlfriend," he said as he nuzzled into the space between my neck and shoulder. The arm over me started gliding up and down my body.

"Good morning, boyfriend," I said. It felt so good to say. I wiggled again. I couldn't get enough of the way his skin felt against mine. The noise he made into my neck sent flutters through me. "Is this real?"

He shifted so I lay on my back, and he lay on his side propped up on one elbow looking down at me. "It better be." He kissed me slowly, the way he did the first morning I stayed over. His free hand wandered over my body, fingers tapping against my skin to whatever song was in his head. "Call me that again."

"Mmmm, call you what, Rupert?"

He groaned and moved his hand up to cup my face as he kissed me slower. He pressed himself against my hip. He pulled away from my mouth to drag his thumb over my bottom lip. "Do you need a hint?" He dragged his thumb down my jaw, then my neck, then down down down. He stopped right above where I wanted him.

I rolled onto my side and locked my leg around his hip. He moved with me, flipping us so I was on top of him. His hands squeezed my hips and then slid around to cup my ass.

"Still waiting on that hint." I moved my hips ever so slightly against him. I tapped my chin like I was thinking hard. I bent down to his ear and whispered, "boyfriend."

He turned his head to kiss me hard, one hand skating up my body to hold my neck.

"If you react like that to being called boyfriend, I can't wait to see how you react the first time I call you husband."

He kissed me harder and flipped me back onto my back and I erupted in a fit of surprised giggles. "You're going to kill me," he said before pinning me to the mattress and showing me how much better waking up together was than a phone call.

***

Despite how many times I repacked my bag I did not remember all the essentials, or enough essentials as Matt declared. He insisted on driving me back home to pack more clothes and anything I needed for at least a few days. When we pulled up to the house Emery's car was gone, but there was a truck I didn't recognize parked in my normal spot. Matt's hand on my thigh squeezed so tightly I yelped in surprise.

"Riley! I'm so sorry," he shouted as he yanked his hand away. He slammed the car in park and turned to face me, his hand fluttering over my thigh. "Are you okay? Oh my god, I didn't mean to squeeze that hard. Does it hurt?"

Laughter tumbled out of me at his concern. I reached for his face and kissed away the concern pulling at his mouth. "Matt, I'm fine. You just surprised me," I said through my laughter.

"Are you sure?" His eyes studied mine.

I smiled and brushed his temples with my thumbs. "I promise." The concern still in his eyes made my heart swell. I'll never understand what I did to deserve someone so sweet. "Do you want to tell me why you squeezed me so hard?"

"That's Oliver's truck" He pointed. "Why is it here and where is Emery?"

I shrugged and unbuckled my seatbelt as I turned to look at the empty grey Chevy. The windows were frosted over so it had been there for a little while. "Let's go inside and see what we can find out."

Inside the house we found some of Emery's clothing scattered over the couch. The kitchen was a disaster, almost every mixing bowl and measuring cup we owned was dirty. There was dough on top of the stove in a covered bowl rising. Dry ingredients covered the counter with her recipe notebook spread open beside them.

Matt took a picture. "Next time Emery says she 'cleans as she goes' and 'isn't that messy' I'm showing her this." He opened the refrigerator door, no doubt looking to see what baked goods she had stashed in there.

I looked at the recipe that she had opened and then over the laid-out ingredients. "She must have realized she was missing something and went to the store."

Matt and I looked at each other, the same question on both of our faces. Without a word he called Oliver and put his phone on speaker.

"Hey, man, what's up?" Oliver answered.

"Nothing much, just wanted to see what you're up to today. I was thinking we could hang out later," Matt told him. He rubbed the back of his head and looked at me with pleading eyes. I slapped my hand over my mouth to hold back giggles.

"You aren't spending the day with Riley today?"

"Yeah, I'm at her house right now, but I thought we could do something later. It's been a while since we hung out." More rubbing the back of his head. He was so cute when he was nervous.

"I just saw you Wednesday night and Thursday."

What? I locked eyes with Matt and dropped the hand I held over my mouth. "Hey, Oliver, do you know where my sister is?"

There was fumbling on the line and what sounded like someone trying to fake static before the call dropped. I raised a brow at Matt as he slid his phone into his pocket.

"So, Wednesday night and Thursday?"

"I was a little freaked out, okay? I thought I had pushed you too hard and that you were going to decide I had blown my chance. Oliver came over for moral support." He rubbed a hand down the side of his face. "I'm so damn clingy that Thursday I was going crazy not being able to talk to you, so I went to the shop."

I held my hands out for him to take. He did so cautiously, looking at me with wide eyes and his mouth turned down. "Is that why you thought I was coming over yesterday?"

He nodded. I squeezed his hands and gave them a couple of tugs until he pulled me into him. "I know I kept telling you everything was going to be okay, but I was so scared I had lost you."

I moved his hands to my waist and then wrapped my arms around his neck, swaying us in a small dance. "I thought you were going to decide I wasn't worth the wait. I was so scared when I showed up with the stupid overnight bag yesterday that you were going to send me away." I brushed a finger over the corners of his mouth until they relaxed. "I'm not going anywhere. I'm yours and you're stuck with me."

"I'm sorry I pushed you so hard and I'm sorry for whatever I did you make you think that I would change my mind about you. You've been worth the wait. Even if you had kept me waiting for longer, you would still be worth it." He squeezed me tighter against him. "You're stuck with me too."

We swayed in the kitchen for a few minutes until he started twirling and dipping me, kissing me every time our lips were close. Just when I thought about suggesting he bend me over the kitchen table like he had thought about back in August we heard a car pull up. We could hear Emery and Oliver arguing outside the front door. Matt grinned, waggled his eyebrows, and sprinted to the front door. He swung it open catching the two of them off guard. Emery held two large reusable grocery bags.

"Emery, you have a lot of explaining to do," I said with my arms crossed.

She rolled her eyes and turned toward Oliver. "Thanks, now I'm in trouble."

Oliver shoved his hands in his pockets and tried to hide a smile behind a scowl. "Someone has to be around to clean the kitchen after you."

I covered my mouth. Matt spun on his heels and gripped my elbows, keeping his back to the two idiots standing in the doorway so they couldn't see how hard he fought to hold back a laugh. I shot Matt a look to say we should just get my stuff and leave. As much as I wanted to be nosey about what my sister was up to, I was way more interested in getting back to Matt's apartment. He gave me a silent nod and steered me to my room.

Chapter 45

Matt

I BRUSHED RILEY'S HAIR off her face, and she wrinkled her nose. She was in the center of the bed spread out like a starfish; her hair halfway escaped from the bun she twisted it into last night. I don't know why she even bothers trying to tie it up. There had to be a better way.

"Riley, it's time to wake up." I whispered against her lips. She reached for me to pull me back into bed, her eyes stayed closed. I smoothed more of her hair back. "Come on, my love, wake up." I brushed a kiss on each of her eyelids until she opened them.

"Why aren't you still in bed?" she mumbled squinting at me. I smiled softly. I knew Riley wasn't a morning person, and had experienced it on a few occasions now. Maybe one day it would be one of those things that bothered me about her, but for now her snuggled up in my bed and trying to pull me back in was cute. She reached up to run a finger over my bottom lip. Her fingers moved up to the damp hair hanging down over my forehead "You showered without me? How long have you been up?"

We said I was the clingy one, but Riley was the one that hadn't been able to be away from me long enough to shower. It was like she was obsessed with me or something.

I couldn't get enough.

"A little while. Wake up, I want to open our presents together before we need to get ready." I pulled the blankets back and goosebumps raised on her bare skin as she shivered. I sat on the side of the bed and pulled her up into a sitting position, rubbing away the goosebumps. I held up a sweatshirt and encouraged her to lift her arms.

"We could open them in bed." She let me tug the sweatshirt down over her. "Why are you dressing me? I can do that." She squinted at her phone. "Matt, it's so early."

It was 7 am but the way she said it sounded like I was waking her up at 4 am. I wanted time with her this morning before we had to rush off to be with our families. I was excited for everyone to meet her, for how packed our day was going to be, but having her all to myself the past few days made me a little selfish for our time together.

I wrapped a thick knit blanket around her shoulders and pulled the covers the rest of the way off her. "Come on." I tugged each of her feet onto my lap so I could slip on her favorite thick knit socks. She was constantly stealing them from me, and had been since the weekend at the cabin. I'll happily spend the rest of my life buying pair after pair for her to steal.

She rubbed her eyes and then reached for my face. "Merry Christmas, boyfriend." She kissed me slowly.

"Merry Christmas, girlfriend. Now get your cute butt in here and open all your presents." I looped one arm behind her and the other under her knees, standing up with her cradled against me.

"You better not have gone overboard."

"First of all, do you even know me? Second, you don't have room to talk. I saw how many gifts you added under the tree last night with my name." We had agreed on a limit of gifts, a limit that I swiftly ignored. She thought she was being sneaky last night, adding another gift whenever I wasn't looking while separating out gifts going to each of our families.

I lowered her onto the couch, tucked another blanket over her lap, and handed her the mug of coffee I had ready for her. "You need to let me spoil you for once," she told me. Then she shrugged and added, "they're all small."

"You spoil me all the time. Small gifts are the best." Small gifts were always my favorite, little things that a person saw and immediately thought of you. I couldn't remember ever receiving a gift accompanied by the words, "sorry it's small," that wasn't one of the most thoughtful things I'd ever been given.

Riley sipped her coffee as I sorted out our gifts, making a pile next to her on the couch and then another on the opposite side. I pointed to mine and then to hers a few times to make a point. Mine was larger by two.

"You still went over the limit," she argued.

"One is technically for me too." I did go over the limit, and she had another gift buried in the box full that we were taking to her family. I placed a box in her lap. "Are we taking turns or just opening all at once?"

"You're going to open all of yours first while I drink some coffee." She took an exaggerated sniff of the mug. Her favorite flavor for this time of year was maple and cinnamon. I had been making it every morning since she told me.

Riley's first gift to me was a braided leather bracelet with a large metal clasp. She motioned for me to look at the back of the clasp to see the date of our first date and the coordinates of the café. I traced my fingers over the metal, beaming.

"We're on the same page," I said. I moved the smallest box from Riley's pile onto her lap. "Go ahead and open that one."

She held up her coffee and shook her head. "Keep going."

I pouted for a moment before I fastened the bracelet on my right wrist with my watch and picked up my next gift. I hated the feeling of anything on my left wrist growing up because of the way it felt against the desk at school when I wrote. The habit stuck with me.

The next gift was a coupon book for different dates. They varied from things like cooking, dance, and art classes to an assortment of at home dates. There were a total of thirty different. I couldn't help the goofy smile on my face as I flipped through them. Each one had been hand drawn. She must have been working on this for a while.

The next two were T-shirts with cheesy music jokes on them, followed by a few other items that she said made her think of me. My favorite was a bumper sticker that said "don't follow me. I'm lost too."

When I picked up the final gift Riley focused on her coffee, avoiding looking at me. Inside was a leather portfolio filled with handwritten letters. I opened the cover to the first one.

> I started this as a form of journaling, a way to write out how I felt about you when I wasn't ready to tell you. The first one was after our first date, an apology as well as a way for me to write down everything positive and negative those few days leading up had made me feel. It was supposed to be a one-time thing, but once you came back into my life in August I started writing more. It's probably weird and you don't have to read them if you don't want to. I wanted to give you the chance to see all the things I've been struggling to tell you.

I flipped through the pages, my eyes catching words and phrases here and there.

Love at first sight.

You were always meant to be someone important to me.

The moment I knew.

She was still staring at her coffee when I closed the book. I moved it aside and squatted on the floor in front of her. I gently pulled the mug from her hands, moving it behind me to the coffee table. I brushed the hair off her face and waited for her to look at me.

"I wrote those without ever intending to give them to you," she spoke slowly as she tried to explain without panicking. "But then I thought maybe it would be nice to let you read all the things I've been wanting to tell you but wasn't ready to at the time." Even after everything she was still bracing herself for me to get scared.

I dipped my head until I could meet her eyes. "You keep saying you're not good at romance, but then you go and do things like this."

She lifted her face, and I adjusted my position so I could keep our eyes locked together. "It's not weird?" she asked.

I shook my head and kissed her. "I love you." I sat back and tapped the gift in her lap. "Now open yours." None of the gifts I got her could compare to everything she had given me, but they would put a smile on her face.

The first was a small silver locket necklace with the same engraving as my bracelet on the outside and our favorite photo together inside. She laughed as I fastened it around her neck, running her fingers over the metal. "Great minds think alike."

The gift for both of us was the same dress she wore when I first kissed her but in light blue, my favorite color for her to wear. "As much as I like the black one, I wanted you to have it in a color that was more you."

The largest box held four different sized matching flower vases. "So you have somewhere for all those flowers I keep buying." They were supposed to be for her house with Emery, a little something to put around that was all hers. Now that she was moving in, she needed them even more. We had been back and forth to her house picking up more things for her to bring here every day. The apartment was getting cluttered while we moved my things around to make room for hers. All my drinking glasses were full of flowers.

I should buy another set. Or two. Or three.

My personal favorite was a hoodie with a picture of me making a kissy face printed on it. Riley laughed so hard she couldn't breathe and the only sounds coming out of her were wheezes. "I might wear this to meet your family today," she said, sending herself into another fit of laughter.

"As excited as I am to see you wearing that, you know the dress code is Christmas pajamas." I tried to maintain a straight face as I spoke but erupted into laughter. She pulled off her sweatshirt and tugged on the hoodie.

Was it normal for me to feel this happy seeing her wear something with my face on it?

"What if I wear it over the blue dress?"

I pinned her to the couch and tickled her until we were both wheezing from laughter.

I can't believe I get to marry her. I can't believe I ever thought someone else could be the one.

Chapter 46

Riley

MATT WRAPPED HIS ARMS around me from behind and rested his head on my shoulder. I leaned back into him, meeting his eyes in the mirror while applying my mascara. "We need a bathroom with more counter space," he said looking down at all the makeup and hair products I had scattered over the tiny bathroom vanity.

"Sorry, once I get done and put it away it won't take up that much space."

His forehead creased as his eyes returned to mine in the mirror. "That's not what I mean. I love seeing all your stuff taking over all our counter space. I just want more space for you to take over."

Our counter space.

I reached for my perfume, but Matt took it from my hand. "Wait." He bent and pulled something from the cabinet under the sink. "Wear this today."

I looked at the bottle. It was from my favorite brand, but one of the scents I hadn't picked up yet. I had been thinking about it for a while but kept telling myself I would wait until I used up at least one of the perfumes I owned.

I turned around and planted a kiss on his mouth. "How did you know?" I asked him.

"A helpful tip from Emery." Everyday I found out about more "helpful hints" Emery had been dropping. He took the bottle from my hand and sprayed it on one of my wrists, then brought my other wrist over to dab them together the way he had watched me apply my perfume for the last few days. "I know you probably have something else you always wear for Christmas, but I thought you might want some new scent memories this year."

"Careful, that makes it sound like you're up to something."

"Sweetheart, it's Christmas, of course I'm up to something. It's my favorite day to be up to something."

"I guess I made the right call with the waterproof mascara today."

He raised his eyebrows. "Are you planning to cry today?"

"You're meeting my family for the first time and it's Christmas. My dad is going to cry at some point today, which means I'm going to cry at some point today."

He smiled and turned me back toward the mirror. I watched as he moved his mouth to my ear and whispered, "happy tears only today. Okay?"

I nodded and leaned back into him, smiling at the reflection of us in matching pajamas. We looked good together. I sniffed the inside of my wrist as I took a mental picture of this moment. He trailed kisses from my ear down my neck, eyes locked on mine in the mirror. "I can't believe you're mine," I said as I watched him.

He hummed against my throat. "I love when you call me yours."

Our counter space, the words he had said vibrated in my head. "Matt?"

"Yes, sweetheart?" he said against my skin.

"You called it our counter space."

"Yes, because it is."

I turned around and lifted his face so I could see it. "Is it? We never talked about me moving in."

His brows knitted together in confusion. "I thought we had already made it clear you were moving in. Isn't that why we've spent the past few days bringing your stuff here? We need to get around to getting the rest of it soon."

My heart pounded and I blinked rapidly as my head spun.

"If you want to move in, that is. I should have asked. I just got so excited, I guess, and didn't even think about it. You said you wanted to wake up every morning with me." He was right, I did say that. Every time caught myself thinking about Christmas break ending and going back to my house with Emery I dreaded it more. It had been just a few days but I didn't think I would ever be able to sleep without Matt in the bed next to me again.

I nodded so hard I felt like I might give myself whiplash. "Yes, I want to move in with you"

Matt gripped my hands in his and pulled me out of the bathroom.

"Where are we going?" I asked. "We need to leave in a few minutes."

"I'm taking you to our bed."

"Matt, we're going to be late and you're going to ruin my hair." It was still a little damp from washing it this morning, but the curls already looked promising for a good hair day.

"I guess you're just going to have to ride me. I won't touch your hair."

Chapter 47

Riley

WE WERE LATE. WHEN we pulled up to my parents' house there were six faces watching us from the front window. Matt gave me a nervous smile. "Are you sure you're ready for this?" he asked me.

"I've never been more sure of anything," I told him. "Are you sure you're ready for this?" I pointed at the faces filling the window. "If you walk in there, that's it, you're stuck with me forever."

"I've never been more sure of anything. I wish you would stop acting like you aren't already stuck with me." He lifted my left hand to his lips and kissed my ring finger. The finger that I hoped would have a ring on it soon. He had dropped so many hints this morning I couldn't stop myself from hoping.

Please let that be the something he was up to.

After another silent exchange and nods from both of us Matt got out of the car, insisting that I stay put and let him open my door. "I can't have your family thinking I don't have any manners," he said.

"You've met my sister. Do you really think that doesn't come from somewhere? You probably have more manners than all of us combined."

The front door flew open, and Aaron came running out. "They're sending the kid for reconnaissance," I said to Matt.

"I guess it's a good thing I have plenty of experience being the best uncle in the history of forever." He winked at me and then turned toward Aaron. Matt dropped into a squat and held his arms out to welcome my nephew in for a hug. I couldn't wait to get to his parents' house so I could see him with his nieces and nephews.

Matt and Aaron talked in hushed whispers as I opened the trunk to pull out the basket of Christmas gifts. Matt started to stand, "Sweetheart, let me get those." Aaron pulled on his hand and redirected his attention.

Milo appeared by my side and took the basket. "Looks like he has Aaron's approval," he said. We watched Aaron pull Matt by the hand toward the house to my waiting family. The kid was pointing at each person and telling Matt who they were. "Jenna told me about him the other night."

I looked down at my feet and scuffed the toe of my boot against the ground. "I didn't know I could feel like this about someone, Milo. How do you handle feeling like this all the time?"

Milo looked at his stepson and wife. His eyes clouded with tears. "You never forget how lucky you are to have it." He poked me in the side with his elbow. "I'm glad you're happy, Ri. I'm also mad that you've kept it a secret from all of us."

"I can't believe Emery didn't tell y'all." I followed my brother into the house.

The sight of Matt exchanging hugs with my parents while Aaron clutched his hand brought tears to my eyes. He turned to look over his shoulder with a smile at me that dropped as his eyes locked on mine. He looked down at Aaron. "Hey, bud, I think your aunt Riley needs a hug." Then Aaron and Matt were both wrapping their arms around me. "Happy tears?" Matt whispered in my ear.

I nodded and dabbed at my eyes with the backs of my hands. Matt studied my face and then planted kisses over my face.

"Eww, Matt, really? There's a kid here." Emery yelled.

I laughed against Matt.

"Oh my god, Emery, just let them be happy," Milo shot back.

Over breakfast Matt and I filled everyone in on how we had met over the summer and then had been surprised to see each other at the district meeting. We left out most of the parts about all my hesitation, except for when we wanted to give Emery a hard time about all the meddling she insisted on doing.

Over the past few days I kept imagining how it would feel to have him here with us. It was truly better than anything I had imagined. I hadn't realized how relieved I would feel to have their approval of him. Just like always, Matt never stopped touching me. A hand hold there, a thigh squeeze there, the occasional knock of his knee against mine. It felt like we had been doing this for years.

He insisted on helping my dad and Milo clean up the kitchen when we finished eating. My mother insisted that he was a guest and didn't need to help, but he shrugged and said he was used to helping clean up after Emery.

"I'll remember that next time I have a kitchen full of baked goods you want to raid," Emery said with an eyeroll.

***

Aaron wanted to hand out everyone's gifts and asked Matt to help him. I had been Aaron's favorite since he joined the family, and it was clear that Matt would replace me after today. I wouldn't have it any other way.

Matt squatted down in front of me and placed a small box with a card on top in my lap. This must have been why he kept insisting on handling all the gifts when we loaded up the car to leave this morning and when we got here. He must have slipped into the mix while I wasn't watching.

Around us everyone opened their gifts after Aaron announced that was all of them. We were never a family that made everyone go around taking their turn to open their gifts. Milo had a small basket of bags sitting at his feet that he wasn't passing out. I smiled as I watched everyone.

Matt reached up and stroked my cheek drawing my attention back to him. "Open the card first," he said in a low voice just for me. He ignored the pile at his side and focused only on me. The fingers of his left hand tapped patterns on my knee.

I tried to open the envelope with careful hands, but it ripped in a jagged line. I pulled out the card with shaking hands unfolding the paper inside. It was creased like it had been folded and unfolded a few times, the ink smudged with fingerprints close to the edges in a few places.

Hi Sweetheart,

I had a big speech that I wanted to give you, but I also really wanted those words to be just for us. I'm resorting to this card instead so I can still do this in front of your family like I wanted.

You're asleep in our bed beside me right now and I'm trying to write this without waking you up. You are so beautiful and fit so perfectly here. I could have you in bed next to me every night for the rest of my life and I would still feel so lucky to have you here. Thank you for letting me call you mine.

I think I've been in love with you since that first date in June. It feels like so long ago already even if it has only been a few months. I fall in love with you a little more than I thought possible every day. I can't believe I get to love you.

Letting you take your time has been torture, but it was all worth it. Even if things had turned out differently, it would have been worth it just for the time I've been lucky enough to have you in my life.

I have so many dreams for our future together, but I'm trying to stop and take in all these little moments on the journey there. Learning about you has been the best thing I've ever had the privilege of doing. Falling in love with you has been my best decision. Getting to be loved by you has been the greatest gift I've ever been given.

I've been holding onto this ring since the night of our first kiss. I had thought for a while that you might be it for me, but that first kiss was the moment I knew without a doubt I had found my wife. Riley, sweetheart, look up at me. I have something I need to ask you.

The words ended there, and I noticed wet spots where tears had already slid from my face onto the paper. I looked up to see Matt kneeling on one knee. The box was gone from my lap and opened in his hands. Everything was blurred by my tears, but I could see the love in his eyes clearly.

"Yes!" I yelled before he could say anything.

He laughed and his special smile for me lit up his whole face. "You have to let me ask first."

I fanned my face with the letter and the tears came harder. The noise of everyone else had quietened. It was just me and Matt. I bit my lip to try and hold back.

"Riley Harrison, will you –"

"Yes!" It slipped out and then I was on the floor next to him wrapping my arms around him. He pulled back to slide the ring onto my finger and kissed the tears from my face.

"Either all of you are crying or I'm crying so hard this time it looks like everyone else is," my dad said.

I laughed into Matt's mouth as he kissed me. I parted from him to look around the room. Milo pulled out a tissue box and was passing out tissues to everyone.

"We're all a bunch of big babies," Emery said as she dabbed at her eyes. She pointed at me, "I told you. I better get to be the maid of honor. I already have my speech written."

I wrapped my sister into a bear hug and swayed her from side to side. "Of course! This is kind of all your fault."

Milo cleared his throat, and we all turned our attention to him. "Might as well do this while the tissues are already out." He held up the basket of mini gift bags. "I don't want to ruin your announcement, but Jenna kind of had something we need to tell everyone."

There was more squealing and crying as we all pulled the little ultrasound photos from the bags.

"Best Christmas ever!" Dad yelled. He held out his arms and then we were all gathering into a big group hug. We all broke apart and passed around the tissue box. "What about you Emery, any news?" he asked.

She fell back on the couch and shook her head. "I think I'm going to get a cat. Or maybe a dog. Maybe both."

Chapter 48

Matt

I couldn't stop smiling as I held Riley's hand, running my thumb over her ring finger while I drove us to my parents' house. The muscles in my face twitched from how hard I smiled.

"I'll come back out for the gifts later," I told her as I jumped out of the car and ran over to open her door. I could hear the music inside from the driveway. Her hand gripped mine as I led her inside at an almost run.

"Mom, Dad, I'm home!" I announced shouting over the music.

Riley's eyes widened as she took the decorations that covered the kitchen. It put my apartment to shame. Mom and Shelby had their backs to us peeling potatoes at the counter. Dad had the oven open sliding pans into it. All three were belting out "All I want for Christmas is You."

I reached for the speaker on the table and turned the volume down. "Mom, Dad, I'm home!" I tried again. I lifted Riley's left hand showing off the ring. "And I have someone for all of you to meet."

"You must be Riley," My dad said, turning around first.

Shelby had us in a bear hug before I could register that she had moved from her spot at the counter. "Matt has not shut up about you for months. I can't believe you're actually here." It had been hard for me to open up and share about Riley, but once I did I couldn't turn it off. She was all I wanted to talk about to anyone that would listen. Shelby pulled back to look at us. I'm sure Riley was thinking the same thing everyone did when they first met Shelby.

"Wow, you and Matt are –"

"Please, please hold that thought. Getting told I look identical to my brother is not really a compliment," Shelby interrupted her.

"Hi, it's nice to meet you too. Shelby, right?" Riley corrected herself.

"That's me. Don't tell Madison and Grace, but I'm Matt's favorite sister."

I reached over and patted her head. "Everyone already knows that, Shelby." I reached for Riley's hand again and held it up. "Is no one going to say anything?" This was a big deal, right? They should be more excited about this.

Shelby rolled her eyes and pulled us both into another hug. Mom and Dad smushed us in from each side talking so fast I couldn't understand a word they were saying. All I cared about was that my fiancée was right here with me.

Fiancée.

The world felt so right. She said yes. This was real.

Months ago I swiped right on this beautiful woman and had the best date of my life thinking I would never see her again. Now she was beside me with my ring on her finger meeting my parents.

I pulled Riley to the walk-in pantry and grabbed two aprons off the hook. "Thank you," I said, pressing a kiss against the top of her head.

"For what?" She reached for the ties around her waist. I knocked her hands away softly, pulling her against me and reaching behind her to tie them.

"Everything."

I twirled her around to the soft music flowing in from the kitchen for a few moments, ignoring the instructions Mom was already shouting at us. "Better than I imagined," I said against her lips as I kissed her one more time before letting her go.

Epilogue

Riley

June

I TWISTED MY ENGAGEMENT ring around my finger as Emery walked around me touching up the way my dress lay, looking around me and out at the mountains from the back porch of the cabin. "It doesn't have to be perfect," I told her. "Hurry up, I want to see him already." It had been three hours since we woke up and went our separate ways to get ready. I wanted to get ready together, to not spend a moment of our day apart. He insisted on separating to get ready so he could have the surprise of seeing me.

She stepped back and rolled her eyes but smiled at me. "Okay, okay. I'm going to go get him now."

The photographer stepped away from where she stood near the door and moved to the other side of the cabin porch. I took a deep breath and smoothed my hands over the flowy fabric of my dress. It was a simple white dress with a silhouette similar to the coral dress I wore a year ago today and a short train. I try not to touch the curls that Emery worked so hard on, making sure they fell just right over my shoulders.

Matt walked through the door with a hand over his eyes, Emery behind him guiding him gently by his shoulders. She guided him to stand in front of me and backpedaled into the cabin. I took another deep breath as I reached for his hand.

He was smiling before he even opened his eyes. He opened them slowly as I moved his hand to cup my cheek. We stood there, taking each other in silence with goofy grins spread across both our faces. His eyes filled with tears that felt like a fist around my heart.

"Hi," I said, finally breaking the silence. "Happy tears?"

He nodded and rubbed his hands over my shoulders and arms. His fingers paused to toy with the straps of the dress before resuming their paths.

"Matt, say something," I pleaded.

"You are so beautiful," his voice cracked when he finally spoke. "I can't believe this is real."

"Me too." The tears I had been trying to hold back spilled over.

"Can I kiss you now or do we have to wait?" He leaned toward me, lifting my chin with his thumb and forefinger. If he didn't kiss me I might lose my mind.

"I think we get to make those rules, it's our wedding after all."

Our ceremony flew by. I was so focused on the man in front of me I couldn't remember a single other detail. We opted to keep the day simple, inviting our families to share the largest cabin we could find for vacation this year. Matt and I rented a smaller one nearby so we could have our privacy tonight. We let our moms and Emery do whatever they wanted with the food. All I cared about was that Matt had whatever he wanted today.

The day felt like a dream; we had to keep squeezing each other's hands to reassure ourselves.

The reception at the big cabin our families were renting together felt never ending. Matt and Emery forced me to stop and eat at some point. Just like during our first date, Matt's hand never left mine.

***

Matt pulled me into our little cabin, the same one we had stayed in during our trip in October and locked the door behind him. He leaned against the door and let his eyes roam over me. His shirt was half untucked from me tugging at it on our short drive here from the big cabin, his tie loose around his neck.

"Why are you looking at me like that?" I asked him. I reached for him and pulled him against me.

He tucked my hair behind my ears and locked his eyes with mine. "I'm just taking in the moment."

I fisted his shirt in my hands and pulled him closer. "I need to tell you something really important."

His smile dropped and concern filled his eyes. "Is everything okay?"

I laughed and kissed his mouth until he was smiling against mine. "Hi, husband."

His eyes darkened as they roamed over my face, his thumbing brushing against my bottom lip. "New rule, you're not allowed to call me anything other than husband."

"What if I just call you mine?"

"Only if I get to keep you." He smiled and turned me to back me against the door.

"Only if you plan to keep me forever."

He hovered his mouth over mine as he pressed his body against mine. His fingers twisted in the straps of my dress as butterflies swarmed my stomach. I tried to lift my lips to meet his, but he pulled away, keeping the distance there as he dragged his left hand down my arm until he could intertwine our fingers. He lifted our hands up so I could see the rings on my finger and twisted them to show me the ring on his. "It's a good thing that's exactly what I plan to do, wife."

His lips met mine. The buzz of anxiety that had been in the back of my mind all day went silent. A year ago today my heart met his and told me I was home. Today, I knew home was here to stay.

Acknowledgements

O H MY GOSH, I can't believe I finally made it to this point.

There are so many people I need to thank for their help in the creation of this book as well as all the people that have been part of my journey to get here.

First of all, thank you reader for giving my book a chance. It truly means the world to me that you've taken the time to read my work.

Thank you to all the librarians and teachers that have fueled my love for books through the years. The librarians at the North Georgia library system as well as all the school librarians I've had the pleasure of knowing all kept the voracious bookworm in me well fed growing up. Librarians and teachers were also the first to nurture my love for writing. Thank you for always being so eager to feed my hunger for books and for being my first cheerleaders for my writing. Also, thanks for always letting me read in class.

Thank you to the friends from school that were always enthusiastic in supporting my writing, even when it sucked. You all gave me the confidence to one day take the step of finally putting my work out there for the world. The support in the past few months from all of you, many of whom I haven't spoken to in years, while I prepared for this release has not gone unnoticed.

Thank you to Lyssa at Booked Forever Shop for bringing Riley and Matt to life. I'm still so in love with this cover and can't wait to see what you do for my future books.

Thank you to author Nikki Hailee for beta reading. Your comments and enthusiasm were a true help on the days I struggled to give Matt and Riley the story they deserved.

THE BIGGEST FUCKING THANK YOU TO MY SISTER! I know we haven't always been close but repairing our relationship over the past year has been one of the best decisions ever. Thank you for always being my number one cheerleader even when I didn't know it. Thank you for picking me up so many times through the process of this book. I can't believe you let me ramble so much about people I made up in my head and loved them as much as I do.

Lastly, my wonderful amazingly sweet husband. I had to save the best for last. Even after a decade together I still can't believe that I get to love you and be loved by you. Thank you for being the safe space I never thought I would have. Thank you for not even batting an eye when I said I wanted to try making my dreams a reality. Thank you for the endless support and comfort on the days I felt discouraged. Thank you for listening to me talk about made up people and offering advice when I needed it. Ready to do it all again?

About the Author

Ellie Harper Smith grew up with her nose always stuck in a book as a way to both escape and process the world around her. As a strong believer that everyone deserves a happy ending Ellie writes romance books featuring characters with neurodivergence, chronic health conditions, and mental health struggles. Ellie's books are set in a small town in the foothills of the north Georgia mountains inspired by the area she lives in.

Turn the page for sneak peek at Emery and Oliver's story.

Love Me Endlessly

Coming Fall 2025

Chapter 1

Now- Emery

I stood in the kitchen adding topping off my dairy free pumpkin spice lattes with pumpkin pie seasoning. I had spent years perfecting this recipe after having my heart broken as a teenager over not being able to partake in the most popular drink of my favorite season. Story of my life, growing up with food allergies, had always been a life of feeling left out and learning to create alternatives.

The front door opened, and voices filled the living room. "Em, hurry up, they're here."

They?

I poked my head around and my breathe caught when I saw the man with freshly cut dark hair just long enough on top to show a slight curl and a short neatly trimmed beard standing behind my sister's boyfriend – well not boyfriend according to her. His hands were shoved in the pockets of his jeans as he took in all the fall décor that covered the room. It looked like the fall section of Home Goods had thrown up in our living room, just the way I liked it. He wore a dark green button down open over a white t-shirt, the sleeves were bunched around the top of his wrists from his pockets. *That outfit always looked better when he rolled those sleeves up.* The silver chain around his neck that disappeared under the collar of his shirt was new.

"Riley, can you come help me for a second?" I said with a forced smile.

My sister placed the flowers she was holding in the vase she had prepared on the coffee table before joining me in the kitchen. Matt was always bringing her flowers, way more than necessary, so she always had a vase ready for them now-a-days. I gestured to the three lattes in paper to-go cups decorated with fall leaves. Those cups had brought me so much joy when I saw them at the store last week, but right now looking at them made my stomach burn. "I only made three," I told her. "You didn't tell me that someone else was coming with us."

"Oh yeah, I thought we could make this a double date. I know you probably get tired of third wheeling with us all the time. Just make another one."

I sighed and started the espresso machine while I prepped another cup with my homemade pumpkin sauce. "That's not the point."

She twisted the bottom button of the cropped corduroy shirt I told her to wear over her navy plaid dress. "I thought it was time for us to play matchmaker for you." The natural down turn of her lips was exaggerated by her worry and her cool brown eyes were wide. The wild curls that framed her face fell over her eyes.

Our features were nearly identical, some people thought we were twins, and I wondered if the look on my face was the same. We didn't look as much alike now as we used to since I constantly changed my hair style, and we styled our makeup differently. We weren't total opposites when it came to our styles, never had been, but there were enough differences. Our mannerisms on the other hand, have been and will always be identical.

I rolled my eyes, knowing she was thinking about what I had said to her during the summer while pushing her to use dating apps. I needed help, we both knew it, but I wasn't ready yet.

I had been testing the waters, but she didn't know that. There were a lot of things my sister didn't know about my dating history, even if she was my best friend. The most important thing she didn't know was that the man standing in our living room wasn't a stranger.

The man that stood in our living room was the only man that had ever been good to me.

I poured oat milk into the milk steamer.

Riley looked into the living room and then back at me. "Just play along. If you don't like him, that's fine. Just be nice, okay? He's a friend of Matt's."

I schooled my face into a neutral expression of flashes of memories washed over me. I had known Matt looked familiar when I had shown him to Riley on the dating app back in June, but I thought he just had one of those faces. After hearing his full name at the district meeting all the stories I'd heard about him came rushing back to me. I had been even more sure then that he would be perfect for my sister.

I just never expected Oliver's path would cross with mine again because of them.

I finished the latte with unsteady hands and then handed two to my sister, who was standing there with a guilty look on her face. I picked up the other two and made my way to where the guys stood in front of the tv stand. Matt's friend pressed the button on the front of the musical haunted house figure. He jumped back in surprise as lights flashed and it started to play creepy music overlayed with monster noises.

Matt shook his head at him, "I told you not to touch anything."

"Matt, aren't you going to introduce us?" I asked, coming up behind them.

Both men turned to face me. His friend's eyes widened, but I gave him a quick shake of my head. His eyes dipped and fixed on the deep purple corduroy mini skirt I wore over semi-sheer black tights with a cropped light weight cream sweater that slouched off on shoulder showing off my tattoos there. I wondered if he was thinking about how much he used to like this skirt. I watched his eyes move lower and take in the new tattoos covering my legs that were just barely visible through the tights. I had been slowly covering myself in them since before we met, but in the last year I had started to run out of blank skin.

Matt was looking behind me at Riley and didn't seem to notice the movement. "Yeah, um, Emery, this Oliver. Oliver, this is Riley's sister Emery," he said with a quick wave of his hand between us.

Oliver stuck out a hand ready to shake on our faux introduction but noticed my full hands. He transitioned to a small wave. "Hi, Matt's told me a lot about you," he said.

I rolled my eyes and then glanced at Matt. "Don't listen to anything he says. I promise I'm not as bad as he probably told you." I was probably worse than anything Matt had said about me, and Oliver knew it.

I started to offer a cup to him, but stopped, remembering the question I always ask every new person. My sister may be distracted, but I still couldn't risk her noticing. "Any food allergies?" I asked him. Most people never consider checking for allergies before offering anyone food, but for me it was a given. It was a courtesy I wish more people would give me.

He paused, stunned by my question. We both knew that I knew the answer. I motioned with one of the cups over my shoulder at Matt and Riley. "Please," I mouthed at him.

I studied his thick dark brows and deep brown eyes while I waited for his answer. Those eyes had haunted my memories for two years.

"No food allergies," he finally responded. His voice came out steady and clear, his accent controlled the way it always was when he was trying to stay calm. The bastard was using his customer service voice on me.

I passed him a latte. "It's dairy free. If you don't like it, I don't want to hear it." He'd had this drink before; hell, he had helped me perfect it. Again, it was a statement meant more for the others in the room. I reached for my keys and a large crossbody bag hanging on the hook by the door. I normally preferred a smaller bag, one just big enough for my wallet and EpiPen case but today required a bag large enough to hold emergency snacks.

"I'm driving," I told them all. I pointed at Matt before adding, "I'm not going to be in a wreck on my favorite day of the year because you're too busy eye fucking my sister."

Riley flicked her eyes to me for a silent check in. She knew I had to drive so I wouldn't get car sick, or at least that's what I always told her. I tried to avoid Oliver's eyes. He knew the truth that I had never found the courage to tell my sister.

Matt threw an arm around Riley, "That's fine. We could use some time in the back seat being chauffeured around."

I made a gagging noise as I walked through the front door.

***

Oliver and I sat at the picnic table. I watched Riley and Matt walked toward the line for lunch until they were swallowed up by the crowd. He folded his hands on the tabletop. His hands were rough with calluses, scars, small cuts in various stages, and a spot that looked like a burn.

"Still not wearing gloves when you work on cars?" I asked him.

"I didn't know it was you until you walked out of the kitchen," he blurted out. He scrubbed a hand over his beard and then moved it to rub the back of his head. "I know Emery isn't a common name, but he didn't really tell me enough details to make me certain it was you. You've moved since before."

I wondered if he'd had any suspicions when he saw Riley.

I reached for the small pendant on my necklace and slid it back and forth over the chain. "I didn't know anything about this until you guys showed up." I looked up to his eyes and searched for any sign of what he was thinking.

He drummed his hands on the table and glanced back to where Matt and Riley had wondered off to find a food truck for lunch. "So, your sister doesn't know about me?"

I looked down at my lap as I shook my head. "She doesn't know a lot about any of my past relationships." His hand crept into my field of vision, and he rubbed his thumb over the back of my hand. My skin prickled at the touch. My head shot up as I narrowed my eyes at him. "Would you just go ahead and get this over with?"

"Get what over with?"

"Yell at me, tell me you hate me. Whatever it is you need to say to me." I pulled my hand away from him, crossing my arms over my chest.

He snorted. "Em, I'm not going to yell at you."

Of course he wasn't going to, he never did. Even when I deserved it. Even when I was so scared I ruined everything because I was tired of waiting for the other shoe to drop.

In the sea of abuse and toxicity that had been my past, Oliver was the only bright spot. The one I didn't deserve.

"But what I did to you was -"

"Very shitty," he finished for me.

"I'm trying to get better," I told him. It was too little, too late. I knew that. My therapist knew that. Hurting Oliver Franklin would always be at the top of my list of mistakes.

"Your sister makes Matt happier than I've ever seen him," Oliver said pulling me from my thoughts.

"He does the same for her."

"He told me that he thinks she's the one." He bounced his knee against mine. "He's my best friend, so I imagine that we're going to keep crossing paths."

I shook my head. "No, I can find a way to make sure you don't have to see me anymore."

"Look, you hurt me, and I understand why you did it, but it still hurt. All I'm saying, is I can play nice if you can."

Play nice, I can do that. It's the least I can do.

He worked his jaw and rubbed the thumb of his right hand over the burn on the back of his left. There were lines on his forehead and between his eyebrows that weren't there two years ago, the type of lines that come from carrying extra stress and worry. He had always been so serious, so focused, now he looked like the years had taken their toll.

"How are Granny and Pop?" I asked.

His hand went to the chain around his neck tucked under his shirt and then he pulled it away quickly. "I don't want to talk about them."

I looked back down at my hands on the table. Ollie had never shied away from talking about things when I asked, even the hard things he didn't like talking about.

"I like your hair like this," he said.

I looked up at him and smiled softly as I tucked the highlighted front pieces of my short shaggy bob behind my ears. I had gone through several different styles in the short time we knew each other, and a few more after. I had decided to go back to my natural ash brown last year but added highlights over the summer. I don't think he had ever seen it this close to natural. "You always said that no matter what I did to it."

For a moment his face softened, and his mouth lifted in a smile. It was like we had slipped back into the past. "You look beautiful no matter what." Just like that he was the man that cheered me on every time I start scrolling through hair inspiration because I was bored and wanted a change. He was the man that handed me a pair of clippers the day that I got frustrated and said I was going to just shave it all off and told me I would look badass with a buzz cut.

Then his jaw tensed, and his brows knitted together as he cleared his throat. "You look happier now."

I shrugged my shoulders. I was happier. In the two years since I last saw him, I had been putting in the work. I was in a place where I felt like I was starting to figure things out. After all that work, I still felt like there was a piece missing.

A piece that was now sitting next to me.

I swallowed back the "I missed you" that threatened to slip from my lips.